Praise for earlier Cram myste

"A fun read with humour throughout…"
Crime Thriller Hound

"An excellent novel, full of twists and turns, plenty of action scenes, crackling dialogue - and a great sense of fun."
Fully Booked 2016

"A highly enjoyable and well-crafted read, with a host of engaging characters."
Mrs Peabody Investigates

"An amiable romp through the shady back streets of 1960s Brighton."
Simon Brett

"A highly entertaining, involving mystery, narrated in a charming voice, with winning characters. Highly recommended."
In Search of the Classic Mystery Novel

"A romp of a read! Very funny and very British."
The Book Trail

"Superbly crafted and breezy as a stroll along the pier, this Brighton-based murder mystery is a delight."
Peter Lovesey

"It read like a breath of fresh air and I can't wait for the next one."
Little Bookness Lane

"By the end of page one, I knew I liked Colin Crampton and

author Peter Bartram's breezy writing style."
Over My Dead Body

"A little reminiscent of [Raymond] Chandler."
Bookwitch

"A rather fun and well-written cozy mystery set in 1960s Brighton."
Northern Crime

"The story is a real whodunit in the classic mould."
M J Trow

"A fast-paced mystery, superbly plotted, and kept me guessing right until the end."
Don't Tell Me the Moon Is Shining

"Very highly recommended."
Midwest Book Review

"One night I stayed up until nearly 2.00am thinking 'I'll just read one more chapter'. This is a huge recommendation from me."
Life of a Nerdish Mum

The Mother's Day Mystery
A Crampton of the Chronicle adventure

The Mother's Day Mystery

A Crampton of the Chronicle adventure

Peter Bartram

Deadline Murder Series Book 2

THE BARTRAM PARTNERSHIP

First published by The Bartram Partnership, 2018

ISBN: 9781729289037

For contact details see website:
www.colincrampton.com

Text copyright: Peter Bartram 2018
Cover copyright: Barney Skinner 2018

All characters and events in this book, other than those clearly in the public domain, are entirely fictitious and any resemblance to any persons living or dead is purely coincidental.

All rights reserved. Except for brief quotations in critical articles or reviews, no part of this book may be reproduced in any manner without prior written permission from the publishers.
The rights of Peter Bartram as author have been asserted in accordance with the Copyright, Designs and Patents Act 1988.

Book layout and cover design: Barney Skinner

Also by Peter Bartram

Crampton of the Chronicle Mystery novels
Headline Murder
Stop Press Murder
Front Page Murder

Deadline Murder Series novels
The Tango School Mystery
The Mother's Day Mystery

Novella
Murder in Capital Letters

Morning, Noon & Night Trilogy
Murder in the Morning Edition
Murder in the Afternoon Extra
Murder in the Night Final
The Morning, Noon and Night Omnibus Edition
(All four Morning, Noon & Night books are also available as audiobooks)

Short stories
Murder from the Newsdesk

Chapter 1

England. Four days before Mother's Day, 1965.

Shirley Goldsmith jabbed me in the ribs and said: "I knew you'd blow it."

Shirl was delivering her verdict on a lecture I'd just given to the Workers' Educational Association. My subject: the ethics of the press.

I said: "I thought it went rather well. I'm even thinking of changing my byline to Colin Crampton, crime correspondent *and* orator."

Shirl snickered. "Forget it. Your whole talk went tits up as soon as you told that joke about the archbishop."

My girlfriend Shirley is from Australia. She speaks her mind. As a critic she's as sharp as the coral in the Great Barrier Reef.

It was a few minutes after the meeting had ended. We were walking back to my car down a narrow street in Steyning, a picture-book village of flint walls and narrow lanes. We passed a tiny thatched cottage with lattice windows and a weathered oak door.

Ahead was a small green shadowed by beech trees. It was a gloomy place with the smell of evil about it. It was where villagers used to burn witches before they found a more humane way to keep them out of mischief. These days, they make them join the Women's Institute.

"This place is creepy," Shirl said.

She reached for my hand. I took it and gave a reassuring squeeze.

But Shirl was right. Heavy clouds cast the street into twilight. Yellow beams from a single street lamp glimmered through a mist. It was as though the evening was drawing a veil over my speech.

Too bad.

It hadn't been my idea in the first place. The workers had invited Frank Figgis, my news editor at the *Evening Chronicle*, to address them. But at the last moment, Figgis decided he had more pressing business. Like cutting his toenails. Or counting his paperclips. Or picking his nose.

He'd drafted me in as his replacement.

I'd tried to winkle out of it, but Figgis pointed out I hadn't exactly been overworked these past few weeks.

I tried to explain that I only reported on murders - I didn't commit them. And if there weren't any, there was nothing I could do about it. But Figgis was insistent. If I couldn't produce the front-page splash he wanted, I'd have to develop a new line as a public speaker.

So that's how I'd come to be standing before a group of bored faces telling them about the time an English archbishop visited New York.

I said: "That archbishop story wasn't a joke. It was true."

Shirley rolled her eyes. "Who says?"

"Frank Figgis. He told me about it when I joined the paper."

"What for?"

"He was making the point that, like George Washington, journalists can never tell a lie."

"Now that is a joke."

"But, according to Figgis, we can invent the truth."

"Now you're just playing with words," Shirley said.

"Not at all. The archbishop story demonstrates the difference. That's why Figgis told it to me."

"It never happened."

"I'll admit that it might be apocryphal."

"A poke re… what? A poke in the eye more like. To the poor saps in the audience who had to listen to you rambling on. I was sitting up the back. Their shoulders all tensed when you delivered the punch-line. Especially that big cobber with the bulbous nose and tonsure of curly white hair."

"How was I to know he was the suffragan bishop of Horsham and had been mates with the same archbish as the one in the story?"

"Perhaps the obvious clue that he was wearing his collar back to front."

"We orators don't notice things like that when we're in full flow."

We turned a corner into a narrow alleyway paved with ancient granite flagstones. Walls made out of old Sussex flints towered over us. Our footsteps echoed as we hurried along. The first lazy fat raindrops had started to fall. We pulled our coats more tightly around ourselves and walked faster.

Shirley said: "Just supposing that story was true, could it really have been as recently as the nineteen-fifties before an Archbishop of Canterbury visited the United States for the first time?"

"So Figgis claims. About ten years ago. These days, this country is changing fast. But back in the 'fifties America was years ahead of Britain in its attitudes. There was none of this deference to so-called betters and forelock tugging which you still get here sometimes."

"Including among newspaper reporters?" Shirley asked.

"Especially among some reporters," I said. "Present company excepted. The days when a reporter would open his notebook and respectfully ask a VIP like an archbishop whether he had any thoughts to share with the nation are disappearing now in Britain. But they'd vanished years ago in the United States."

"So the old Archbishop was in for a shock when his plane touched down in New York," Shirley said.

"Like he'd just stepped into an elevator and pressed the button for Hell rather than Heaven by mistake. Back in Blighty, the journos would've been penned behind a red rope. But in New York, the reporters surged in a gang round the aeroplane's steps.

When the Archbishop came down them he was surrounded by hacks screaming questions at him."

"They all wanted a good quote they could use in tomorrow's paper?" Shirley said.

"Yes. They wanted to get his take on social trends in America. So before he'd even put his foot on the ground, he had a reporter from the *New York Times* yelling in his face, 'Hey, your reverence, what do you think about this rock and roll that's driving our kids crazy?' What was the old boy supposed to say? Usually, he'd be asked what hymns he was planning for Sunday's service. He just shrugged his shoulders and mumbled, 'Oh, I don't know... does it really have that effect?'"

"Seems fair enough," Shirley said. "He was giving the reporter guy the brush off."

"But there are dangers in that. Next the *Herald Tribune* hack screamed at him, 'Mr Canterbury, what do you think about the violence in all these TV cop shows like *Dragnet*?' I mean, he'd never heard of the show. He shook his head and mumbled, 'Oh dear, is it really that bad?'"

"And, as you told it during the lecture, that's when he should've walked to his waiting limo," Shirley said.

"Not easy when you're surrounded by pushy journos. Especially like the one from the *Daily News*. It's the Big Apple's scandal sheet. His question was, 'Archie, baby, what do you think about all these new striptease clubs opening in New York? And, by now, the poor archbish thought he'd entered one of Dante's circles of Hell. Probably the ninth one. I think it's treachery. All he could think to say to the question was, 'Oh dear, are there many?'"

"Fair answer," Shirley said. "Admitted he knew nothing about it."

I said: "The Archbishop finally pushed his way through the melee of reporters and climbed exhausted into his Rolls Royce relieved it was over. But it wasn't. Even though some of the reporters thought they'd wasted their time. They hadn't got anything out of him. The guys from the *New York Times* and the *Herald Tribune* reckoned they'd come away without a story. But the hack from the *Daily News* knew he had something. Not by telling a lie, but by inventing the truth."

"And that's when you had the suffragan bishop turning as pink as a pig in a pulpit," Shirley said.

"The following morning, the *Daily News* began its story: *England's Archbishop of Canterbury flew into Idlewild Airport last night and immediately asked, 'Are there many strip clubs in New York?'*"

"And you call that honest reporting?" Shirley asked.

"No, I call that accurate and misleading reporting."

"It can't be accurate and misleading at the same time."

"The Archbishop did ask whether there were many strip clubs in the city - which makes it accurate. But the story leaves out the context of the question - which makes it misleading."

"Would you scam your readers like that?"

"Not under my byline. But ordinary people play the same trick in conversation all the time. Perhaps they want to bamboozle someone or get their own way on the basis of shaky facts. All I'm saying is: if you're going to invent the truth, invent all of it."

"Sounds like a shonky argument to me," Shirley said.

We stepped out of the alley into a small car park lit by a single lamp. The rain was now falling steadily.

My MGB was parked under a horse chestnut tree. The tree's branches creaked in the rising wind like they were in pain. Not far off, a fox barked and a cat yowled. The lamp flickered, then died.

Shirley grabbed my arm. "Let's get out of this place," she said. "It spooks me. It's like one of those places where you meet a killer in the shadows and then trip over his victim's corpse."

I put my arm around her shoulder and squeezed gently.

"Don't worry," I said. "The place looks sinister in the dusk, but Steyning is a harmless village. You'll never find a murder here."

Chapter 2

Shirley leaned forward and stared out of the rain-streaked windscreen.

"Jeez, Colin, where are you taking me?" she asked.

We were in my MGB heading out of Steyning the dangerous way - on a narrow track which climbed over the South Downs range of hills. Ahead, the road became steeper. The engine note rose as I changed down from third to second gear. High banks overgrown with bushes and nettles closed in on either side. The track was slick with muddy water. If we met a car coming the other way, there'd be a stand-off. Whoever blinked first would have to back up hundreds of yards to a passing place.

I'd rather reverse around Piccadilly Circus in blindfolds.

But after my talk my throat was dry. I needed a drink - and was taking the shortest route I knew.

I said: "There's a great little pub called the Marquess of Granby in the village of Sompting on the other side of the hills. We can get some supper there."

"Sounds great. But is this road the only way? It sure is lonely."

"It's called the Bostal," I said. "It's a Sussex word for a narrow track leading up a hill. This one heads over the Downs to the coast. And you're right - not much traffic ever comes this way. Especially at night. Or in weather like this."

Pounding rain ran in rivulets across the windscreen. The wipers struggled to clear the water.

I said: "The loneliness of this road made it popular with smugglers not so many years ago."

Shirley swivelled in her seat and stared open-eyed at me. "You mean the real ones with black patches over their eyes and spotted handkerchiefs tied round their necks?"

"And parrots on their shoulders screaming, 'Pieces of eight'. No, not like the smugglers from fiction. Not even like Rudyard

Kipling's smugglers. You remember the poem: 'Five and twenty ponies trotting through the dark, Brandy for the parson, baccy for the clerk…' These were real smugglers who were in it for profit. Big money. And woe betide anyone who stood in their way. Even in my granddad's time there was a gun battle up here between smugglers and customs men. Two smugglers were shot dead."

"You wouldn't get them fighting it out on a night like this," Shirley said.

The engine note fell as we reached the summit of the hill. I changed up a gear and we picked up speed. To our left, the hills fell away in a steep escarpment. The blackness of the night was broken by pinpricks of light on the horizon. They flickered dimly through the rain.

I pointed. "Brighton."

I depressed the accelerator and the MGB surged forward. The tyres fizzed as they cut through spray from the road.

"Stop," Shirley yelled. "Stop, now!"

"What the…?"

I stamped down on the brake. The tyres squealed on the wet road. The MGB's rear-end fishtailed. The headlights wavered. The engine cut as we shuddered to a halt. So what? A perfectly executed emergency stop in my book. And I'd defy any driving instructor to disagree.

I turned to Shirley, but she'd already wound down her window and was staring at something back along the road.

"What is it?" I said.

"There's something lying on the verge."

"A person?"

"I don't think so."

"It's probably a dead fox," I grumbled. "Road kill. But we'd better check."

I grabbed my torch from the glove compartment and we climbed out of the car. The wind blew needles of rain into our faces. We hunched our shoulders like a couple of old ditch diggers. We scrunched up our eyes and stared into the darkness.

I said: "There is something there. Looks like a lump by the side of the road."

I shone my torch, but it just made the raindrops sparkle like falling diamonds.

We slithered towards the lump. Our feet splashed through puddles and squelched on mud. We skidded to a halt on the wet grass at the side of the road.

The lump turned out to be a bicycle.

It lay abandoned by the roadside. I shone my torch downwards. It had been a smart bike, too. A bike it's owner would have taken pride in. A Norman 7I - the I stood for Invincible - made by the British Cycle Corporation. But it wasn't an invincible bike now. The back wheel was broken. The spokes splayed out like a busted rake. Some were bent, others had snapped. The rear tyre was shredded. One brake cable had severed. Red glass from the rear light lay broken on the road. The handlebars were twisted.

I said. "Looks like this cycle was hit from the rear by something. Probably a car. And going at speed."

"Is it recent?" Shirley asked.

"Hard to say," I said. "But the biggest question is what happened to the person riding it? There's no sign of blood, but that could've been washed off by the rain. Let's take a look around."

Shirley wandered a few steps onto the grass verge.

"Be careful," I called after her. "The escarpment falls away sharply and there's no fence."

But, as usual, she'd ignored me. She'd vanished into the blackness of the night. I waved the torch around a bit, but I might as well have been lighting matches down a coalmine.

I called out: "Shirley." But my cry was carried away on the wind. By now, the rain had seeped under my shirt collar and was running down my back.

"Shirley," I called.

No reply.

I strained my ears and listened for a sound. The wind sobbed in the trees. But there was no crash, no scream as a body hurtled through undergrowth to the foot of the escarpment.

The rain down my back had reached my underpants. Nothing about this was going to end well.

I yelled again: "Shirley!" My voice sounded shrill, or perhaps it was just the way the wind distorted it.

Silence.

And then…

"Over here," Shirley shouted.

I sighed with relief and ran towards her voice. Didn't care whether I was near the escarpment's edge. Couldn't be bothered the rain had now soaked the seat of my trousers. I was just so relieved to hear her voice.

My torch waved wildly around. I played the beam on Shirley's face. And knew at once there was trouble. Her eyebrows were drawn down and her lips were compressed with tension. She pointed at the ground.

I swung the torch down.

A crumpled body lay face down in the long grass. It was tall, more than six feet, I guessed. It was dressed in a long gabardine raincoat and a sou'wester. I knelt down, reached under the sou'wester for the neck and felt for a pulse. None.

I looked at Shirley. "Dead," I said.

I handed Shirley the torch. "Give me some light while I do what I've got to do," I said.

I took hold of the figure's shoulder and rolled the body over.

Shirley gasped. "My God! It's a boy."

We looked at the face of a teenager.

"No older than seventeen or eighteen," I said.

"A young man," Shirley said. "And he'll never be an older one now."

"Shine the torch on his face."

Shirley shifted round and a pale circle of yellow light illuminated his head like a halo.

"He'd never look like an angel," Shirley said.

She was right. The lad had a pudgy face with a little too much fat around the jaws. He had a thatch of brown hair which I guessed was normally curly. Now it was plastered by rain to his head. He had a narrow mouth with lips that were open as though he wanted to cry out. His brown eyes were close together. They bulged in unblinking surprise as eyes often do in sudden death. As though they're saying: "This can't be happening to me."

I leant forward and gently closed his lids.

"Let's see if we can find out who he is," I said.

I reached inside the pockets of the raincoat. Empty. I undid three of the raincoat's buttons. Underneath, the lad was wearing a blue blazer with an elaborate badge on the breast pocket. A lion on its hind legs which looked like it was dancing the hokey-cokey. I think heraldic buffs call it a lion rampant.

I said: "This is part of a school uniform. I think he must be a pupil at Steyning Grammar School."

"But who is he?"

I reached into one of the blazer pockets. Pulled out three toffees and nine pence in loose change. I reached round to the other pocket. I felt a bit like a body snatcher rifling a corpse. I put my hand inside the pocket. Took out a thick card with rounded edges.

Shirley shone the torch on it.

There was a single name typewritten in capitals on one side: SPENCER HOOKE.

I turned the card over. The typist had written: "Hollow Bottom Barn, 7.30 tonight. Don't be late."

Shirley said: "Do you think he was meeting a Sheila for nooky?"

"Seems likely," I said. "Steyning Grammar is a boys' school

with boarders. A teenager with raging hormones. No female company on the premises. And long lonely nights in the dorm with only his cricket bat to cuddle. But where he was heading is only the second question."

"The first being how he was killed?"

"Yes." I glanced at my watch. Eight-twenty. "If Spencer was heading for an assignation, he could've passed this point an hour ago."

"Looks like he's been killed by a hit-and-run driver," Shirley said. "Probably couldn't see his bike in this weather."

I looked from our position by Spencer's body to the road and back again.

"If he was hit and left for dead by a car, how come he's over here?" I said. "He must be at least twenty yards from his bike."

I took the torch from Shirley and shone it on the ground.

"Look, the grass has been flattened just here - and over here," I said. "It looks as though the body has been dragged from the roadside."

"If he'd been injured he could have crawled this way before he died," Shirley said.

"Why crawl away from the place where you're most likely to be found?"

"The lad was confused. Probably delirious. Didn't know what he was doing."

"I don't think so. If he was crawling, the marks on the grass would be different. The grass would only be flattened where he'd rested his hands and knees. This grass is flattened in a long swathe. Means he had to have been dragged."

"By the driver of the car who hit him?"

"Who else?"

"Guess the guy hoped to hide the body while he got as far away as possible. What a bludger!"

"That's the best that can be said of him," I said. "If it was a man."

"A woman wouldn't drive away from an accident like this."

I said: "You may be right. We don't know. But, just now, we've got two things to do."

"I guess the first is to call the police," Shirley said.

I shifted uncomfortably as my wet trousers stuck to my legs.

"And the second is get out of these clothes," I said.

I turned away from Spencer's body and looked towards the road. It snaked away across the ridge like a black ribbon in the night. A schoolboy had died on a lonely hill in the rain. Perhaps it was a hit-and-run accident. But, to my mind, there were too many unanswered questions.

I couldn't get a line of Kipling's Smuggler's Song out of my mind.

"Them that asks no questions isn't told a lie."

But I had plenty of questions to ask. And, I suspected, plenty of lies to hear.

Chapter 3

"With a hit-and-run, you've got no chance."

Detective Inspector Bernard Holdsworth leaned back in his chair with a smug grin as though he relished the thought.

"You mean the victim has no chance of avoiding the collision?" I asked.

"No, I was saying there's not a ghost of a hope of nabbing the culprit."

It was the morning after the accident. We were in Shoreham-by-sea police station. Holdsworth had reluctantly agreed to see me to answer questions.

He was a burly man with a large head. He had puffy cheeks and a jowly chin. He had tired eyes with heavy lids. His brown hair was fashioned in an elaborate comb-over which failed to hide the fact that he'd soon be bald. He was wearing a dark blue suit in some kind of serge material. The jacket was at least a size too small. His large stomach bulged against the buttons like a suet pudding bursting from its boiling bag.

He said: "The trouble with you journalists is that you're always trying to make something out of nothing."

I said: "Spencer Hooke wasn't nothing. He was a pupil at Steyning Grammar School. Do you know anything else about him?"

"We've been in touch with the headmaster. He was a boarder at the school. Eighteen years old. Parents both dead, apparently. Nearest relative a distant uncle, coffee planter in Kenya. We haven't had chance to contact him yet, but the school is passing on the hard word."

"Did he have any particular friends at the school?" I asked.

"We haven't been able to get into that yet. We know he was studying for his A-level exams. Apparently, he hoped to go to Cambridge University to read chemistry. And he was a member of the bell-ringers at the local church."

"For whom the bell tolls," I said. "Now it will toll for a young lad on a bicycle who was knocked down by a car and ended up dead."

"Chances are in weather like last night's the motorist didn't even realise."

"That's ridiculous. I saw the bike. The back-end was shattered. It must have left damage on the car. Scratches, dents, perhaps worse."

"Maybe. But where does that leave us? We can't search for a car with unspecified damage to it. You can be sure the driver will arrange to have that repaired pronto."

"So ask around the garages," I said.

"Not as simple as you believe. If the driver thinks the damage will raise awkward questions, he'll hide the car. Or he'll cover the existing damage by staging a fake accident - like driving into his gatepost. Anything that will give him a legitimate reason for presenting the car for repair at a garage."

I frowned and made a note in my finest Pitman's.

I said: "What about witnesses?"

Holdsworth shrugged. "Up on the Bostal in that filthy weather? We'd have more luck finding Alfie Hinds hiding out in the station canteen."

I sniffed. I'm rather good at a sniff which makes clear I've just treated an idea with contempt. I'd already decided Holdsworth was the kind of copper who wouldn't recognise Houdini Hinds, the legendary prison escapee, if the man served him his afternoon tea wearing prison fatigues.

I said: "Don't dismiss the idea of witnesses. They wouldn't have to see the accident. Perhaps someone in Steyning noticed a car being driven erratically."

"I don't have the manpower to start an enquiry like that."

"There could've been a passenger in the car. Why not put out an appeal? Offer a reward for information received? If there were a passenger, perhaps he or she would come forward."

"Not after the car failed to stop. Any passenger should've reported the accident immediately. If someone turned up now, we'd have some awkward questions to ask."

"So what now?" I asked.

"We finish the paperwork and file a report. Another unsolved hit-and-run. Too many of them I'm afraid."

"What if it wasn't a hit-and-run? Suppose it was murder?"

Holdsworth leant back in his chair and laughed. A deep rumble like an empty barrel rolling down a hill.

"Weird way to murder someone. The killer would have to know that Hooke was cycling along the road at that time."

"What about the note in Hooke's pocket - the meeting in the barn?"

"No date on the note. It could have been an old one referring to a previous meeting. Besides, there's no certainty a driver could kill a cyclist by knocking him off a bike."

"But I saw clear signs that the body had been dragged to the edge of the escarpment."

Holdsworth shook his head. "That could be anything."

"But it could mean the driver stopped the car after he'd hit Hooke. Perhaps he realised he wasn't dead and finished the job off."

"How?"

"I don't know. But if Hooke was already unconscious it wouldn't have been difficult to smother him. Then if he pushed the body over the escarpment into the thick undergrowth below - and followed it with the bicycle - it wouldn't be found for weeks."

"There's no evidence to support that."

"Isn't there?" I said. "What about the flattened grass?"

Holdsworth tried to emulate my contemptuous sniff. It sounded like a broken foghorn.

He said: "The grass could've been flattened earlier by a tractor or something driving over it. Besides, if they planned to push the body down the escarpment, why didn't they do it?"

"I expect the killer saw the lights of a car approaching. He'd have to leave the job unfinished and drive off quickly."

"Did you see another car on the road?"

"No, but we didn't come along until at least an hour later."

Holdsworth clapped his hands together, like he'd just proved his point.

"There you are," he said. "No witnesses. Isn't that what I said a few minutes ago? Besides, I have too many other bases to watch. We have to police Shoreham harbour. Ships coming and going all the time. But hardly anything happens in Shoreham harbour that I don't get to hear about."

Holdsworth picked up a file and opened it. His sign the meeting had ended.

An hour later, I was in the newsroom at the *Evening Chronicle* fuming at Holdsworth's complacency.

It was late morning and the deadline for the midday edition had passed. For a moment, typewriters had fallen silent. Telephones rang less insistently. Knots of journos hung about the room and swapped stories or whispered secrets in corners. Phil Bailey leant back in his chair and lit one of his Dutch cheroots. Susan Wheatcroft bustled back from the tea room carrying a plate with two large Chelsea buns.

Sally Martin, who edited the woman's page, ambled over to me. She brushed some loose papers to one side on my desk and perched on the edge.

"Figgis was looking for you this morning," she said.

"No doubt to congratulate me on making a successful speech last night - and landing a front-page story on the way home."

"He had a look on his face like he'd just swallowed a fag-end."

"So I should head off somewhere safe? Like South America. At least until he's cooled down."

"Just a friendly warning."

Sally slid off my desk and strolled over to the Press Association newswire.

I leant forward in my captain's chair. I pulled my Remington typewriter towards me and rolled copy-paper into the carriage. I typed the catchline Crampton/Hooke…1 and then sat back in my chair. It should have been a straightforward one-shot story. Boy hit by car and dies. A tragedy and a life summed up in three hundred words before I typed the word "ends".

No, I just couldn't see it like that. Holdsworth's complacent attitude had unsettled me. Was there any crime that he'd take seriously? I accepted that it wouldn't be easy to trace the driver of the car. But that didn't mean he shouldn't try. The story I wrote now shouldn't be the end of the matter. It should be the beginning. This may have been an accident, but the fact the driver hadn't stopped made it an offence. And the fact a boy had died made it a serious crime in my book.

And I couldn't get out of my mind the idea there was more to it. Holdsworth had dismissed my idea that the body had been dragged to the edge of the escarpment. But I'd seen the trail of flattened grass in the torchlight. And if I was going to give this story the front-page treatment and uncover the truth, I'd need Figgis's backing.

But, if Sally was right, Figgis was in a bad mood.

I stood up, crossed the newsroom and headed for Figgis's office.

I knocked on his door.

From inside the room, a voice which sounded like a sergeant major with laryngitis bellowed: "What?"

I opened the door, stuck my head round the side and said: "Actually, that should always be 'who?'"

Figgis looked up from some galley proofs he was reading. He removed a Woodbine that was hanging like a miniature censer from his bottom lip and glared at me.

I said: "As an inanimate object will never knock on your door, the query should never be 'what?'."

He said: "In your case, it's usually why?"

"I'm glad you see it that way," I said.

I stepped into the room, crossed to his desk, and sat down in the guest chair without waiting to be invited.

Figgis stubbed out his ciggie and said: "Before we go into that, I want an answer to the question "How?"

"How what?"

"How you managed to rile the suffragan bishop of Horsham at the Workers' Educational Meeting last night."

"I was giving a lecture on the ethics of the press. The lecture you'd been booked to give."

"*Ahem.*" Figgis flushed, a sign I'd embarrassed him. "I had pressing business elsewhere."

"The Coach and Horses?"

"Never mind about where. The bishop complained you told a story about the Archbishop of Canterbury making visits to New York strip clubs."

"No, only getting into hot water by giving an inept answer to a daft question. Anyway, why was the bishop calling you? I'd have thought he'd have taken his complaint direct to His Holiness."

Gerald Pope was the paper's editor. He was an upper-class twerp who'd got the job because he talked posh. He spent most of his time hobnobbing with the county set on the pretext he was making important contacts. But His Holiness wouldn't recognise a useful contact if it plugged itself into a power circuit and gave him an electric shock.

Figgis fiddled with the galley proofs on his desk. "I like to keep complaints away from Pope. I arranged for the switchboard to route all calls about the lecture meeting to me."

That had my attention. It was the first time I'd heard Figgis claim he wanted more calls. Especially more complaints. When the switchboard put them through, he'd normally treat the telephonists to a mouthful of fruity language. There had to be a reason and I thought I knew what it was. But for the moment I decided I'd keep that in reserve.

I said: "You've heard about the death of the young lad up on the Bostal road near Steyning last night."

Figgis nodded. "Hit-and-run, I hear. We'll take one column on an inside page and leave it at that. Perhaps a follow-up par about the funeral, but that's it."

I said: "I think it may be more than a hit-and-run."

Figgis shot me a sharp glance. He reached for his fags, shook one out of the packet and lit up.

"Another of your theories?"

"Perhaps, but they've often been right in the past."

"Tell me the tale."

So I told Figgis why I thought the killing could have been a murder.

I said: "The cop investigating the case is a guy called Bernard Holdsworth. He just wants to clear his in-tray and close the file. I need some time to investigate more."

Figgis sucked on his Woodbine and stroked his chin.

He said: "Leave it. It's going nowhere. There'll be other stories."

"I haven't got other stories at the moment. I've got this one - and I want to take it further."

"My decision is final," Figgis said. He picked up his galley proofs to show the meeting had ended.

I said: "I thought I might give His Holiness a briefing on my lecture. Just in case he speaks to anyone else and gets the wrong idea about my archbishop story."

Figgis dropped the galleys. Sat up straighter. Gave me a flinty look.

"You steer clear of His Holiness on that."

"Why?"

"He doesn't want to be bothered about your blundering debut as a public speaker."

"That's not the only reason, is it?" I said.

"What do you mean?"

"You know perfectly well. That's why you're reaching for another fag. Pope ordered you to make the speech, didn't he? He doesn't know you passed the poisoned chalice on to me."

"Look, there are policy issues here you don't understand…"

"Like who should deliver speeches?" I said.

"Yes."

"And what stories we should cover?"

Figgis sat back in his chair and folded his arms in a petulant gesture. He knew when he was beaten.

"Very well. Take two days to look into the hit-and-run. No more. And I assume we'll hear no more about contacting Pope about suffragan bishops."

I stood up and headed for the door.

"Not from me," I said.

I reached for the handle and opened the door. Turned back to Figgis.

"By the way, the bishop may have complained about my story - but he laughed."

I stepped swiftly through the door and closed it behind me.

Chapter 4

I suppose I should have skipped back across the newsroom like a spring lamb.

It's not every day that someone shafts Figgis. Crack open the champagne! I'd blackmailed him into giving me time to develop the story.

Trouble was, I wasn't sure how to do it. (Developing the story, that is, not skipping like a lamb.)

I wasn't even sure I was right. Although I'd come down on Holdsworth like an Alpine avalanche, the hard evidence for murder was thin.

It rested on the fact I thought Hooke had been dragged to the edge of the Bostal escarpment rather than crawled there in his dying moments.

I slumped back in my captain's chair and stared at my Remington. But it didn't provoke any bright ideas.

I had two days to make the story stand up. There was no way Figgis would grant an extension. Right now, he'd be sat in his office fuming that I'd outwitted him. He'd scheme what to do if I came back with a fresh demand. He'd dream up a crafty wheeze to put himself in a good light with Pope should the truth about the lecture come out.

Worse, if I didn't make the story stand up, my reputation would take a hit. No more front-page bylines. No more generous expense account. I might even have to pay for my own lunch.

What made the job more difficult was the fact the Shoreham cops were handling the case. If it had been my old mate Detective Inspector Ted Wilson at Brighton Police Station, he'd have quietly briefed me on his progress (not much) over a couple of whiskies. But I didn't think Holdsworth would come across with anything useful for a large scotch - or even a bottle. Besides, he'd made it clear that, as far as he was concerned, the case was closed. Short of the killer driver putting his own hand up, there'd be no further investigation.

So I was on my own.

But not entirely.

I stood up and headed for the morgue, the room where the paper's archive of press cuttings was housed.

When I walked into the morgue, Henrietta Houndstooth, who ran the place, was at her desk stuffing a large bunch of daffodils into a vase.

Her assistants, Mabel, Elsie and Freda, crowded round. The three were known around the paper as the Clipping Cousins, which was only half right. Yes, they clipped the newspapers and filed the cuttings. No, they weren't related.

At the moment, they were arguing the toss about the best way to display the daffs.

I strolled up to them and said: "Daffodils. Couldn't be a better choice as I'm 'in vacant or in pensive mood'."

Mabel adjusted a painful ruck in her surgical stocking and said: "What's he talking about?"

Elsie scratched the hairy wart on the side of her chin and said: "I think it's something to do with that Lake District poet who 'wandered lonely as a cloud'."

Freda lifted a leg to ease her flatulence and said: "He can't have been that lonely then. When my old man and I went to the Lake District the only thing we saw were clouds - and the rain they brought with them. Even the clouds had clouds."

Henrietta said: "That's no way to speak of William Wordsworth, one of our greatest men of letters. Mr Crampton was referring to the poem about 'a host of golden daffodils'."

"Except you've got the daffodils and I've got the pensive mood," I said. "I was hoping you could help me with that."

Henrietta put the vase of daffodils on a shelf. The Cousins drifted back to the large table they shared in the middle of the room. They started to bicker about clouds.

Henrietta and I crossed back to her desk.

"You're in a pensive mood because of that hit-and-run," Henrietta said. "Did finding the body upset you?"

I perched on the edge of her desk. "It's never a pleasant experience. But I've seen dead bodies before - and ones in worse condition than Spencer Hooke. There wasn't much sign of blood. I expect the post-mortem will show massive internal injuries."

"And you want to know whether we have any cuttings on him in the morgue?"

"He was an eighteen-year-old schoolboy so it's unlikely. But I would like to know more about his school, Steyning Grammar."

"Let's take a look," Henrietta said.

To one side of her desk an archway led into a cavernous room. It was packed with floor-to-ceiling filing cabinets arranged in aisles. Fluorescent lights hung from the ceiling but the place had a claustrophobic feel. Every time I walked in there, it felt like being shut up in a pharaoh's pyramid.

But I forced this thought from my mind and followed Henrietta deeper into the maze of corridors. Her shoes click-clacked on the cracked linoleum. We reached the S corridor. Henrietta stopped and yanked open a cabinet drawer. She rifled through the files, let out a little yelp of delight, and pulled a mouldering brown folder from the cabinet.

She handed it to me. "Looks like we've been keeping this one for a long time," she said.

Henrietta was right.

Back at my desk, I opened the folder and flipped through the cuttings. There were about fifty, some yellowing with age. Some so brittle, the edges flaked off. The oldest dated from the nineteen-thirties, the most recent only a few days old. Well, there'd be another addition soon when pupil Hooke's story was filed.

I sat at my desk, with the machine-gun rattle of typewriters building towards the next deadline, and read the file.

Steyning Grammar School, I learnt, had been founded way back in 1614, two years before Shakespeare died, by an old bloke called William Holland. He'd been born in Steyning, but later moved to a city to the west called Chichester where he'd made his money. In those days, I guess, his cash would have been in crowns and groats. The cuttings never explained why he wanted to splash his cash to set up a school. Perhaps it was some kind of seventeenth century status symbol. Today he'd be more likely to fork out for a villa on the *Côte d'Azur*.

In one of the cuttings from the 'thirties, there was a picture of the school. It was a handsome Jacobean pile built out of narrow ochre bricks. There were fat time-blackened oak beams supporting the place. There were latticed windows high up on the walls. There was a wrought iron gate in front of the main entrance.

Apparently, Holland had set up the place for the "promotion of godliness and sound learning". I had an uneasy suspicion I wasn't going to find much of either in this story.

Some of the post-war cuttings described how the school had expanded its pupil rolls. A lot of the students were boarders who slept in dormitories. I thought back to those Billy Bunter stories I used to read as a kid. Tuck boxes and midnight feasts in the dorms. Perhaps it was like that at Steyning.

A three-year-old cutting told me that the school had modernised some of its classrooms. There'd been a new art room and a chemistry laboratory. There was a picture of the lab with a smiling young man wearing black gown and mortar board. The caption identified him as Owen Griffiths, chemistry master.

Holdsworth had told me that Hooke had been studying for his chemistry A-level and hoped to read the subject at Cambridge. In which case, Griffiths - the proud master of the new lab - could know Hooke better than others.

Perhaps if I approached him right, he'd talk. I tried to remember what I'd learnt about chemistry. There were acids and there were alkalis. And if you mixed them together they neutralised one another. That didn't sound like something that would grab anyone's attention.

But there were also Bunsen burners and test tubes and if you heated up the right mixture of stuff it would change colour. Or it would bubble and give off a pong like a hippo's fart. Or, if you were really lucky, it might explode.

That sounded altogether more promising.

Finding the chemistry lab at Steyning Grammar School later that afternoon proved surprisingly easy.

I just had to follow my nose.

Chemistry labs everywhere radiate a stink which loiters somewhere between a gas works and a swimming bath. A scrap of chemistry knowledge had come back to me. Sulphur and chlorine. Both guaranteed to assault the nostrils.

I took a lung-full of the last half-decent air I expected to breathe for some time, opened the lab door, and stepped inside. The place was furnished with rows of those laboratory benches you see in films about mad scientists. The benches were strewn with abandoned equipment. There were beakers and flasks and pipettes. There were crucibles and tests tubes and spatulas. There were funnels and droppers and tongs.

It looked like the mad scientists had just held a party.

But among the abandoned kit, there were dark brown bottles with glass stoppers labelled "Poison".

On the drive from Brighton, I'd decided I'd hang around until school was out. I'd pounce on the lab a few minutes after the bell for the end of school had rung. I reckoned that, with a subject like chemistry, there'd be some clearing up to do and Owen Griffiths would still be in the place.

And there he was.

But not clearing up.

He was sitting behind a bench at the far end of the room. He was attaching a long glass tube to one of those conical flasks with a spout sticking out of the side. They look like a teapot without a handle. The flask was resting on a tripod with an unlit Bunsen burner beneath. There was a rack of test tubes containing different coloured powders by the side.

Griffiths was wearing goggles and bright yellow latex gloves. He was dressed in regulation chemistry lab white coat. It was stained with chemical spills. There were brown splodges that looked like a mud splatter. There were bright yellow patches that looked like an oriental disease. There was a swathe of purple and scarlet spots that looked like a psychedelic dream.

He didn't look much like a mad scientist. In the films I'd seen they usually had swivelling eyes, wild hair, and a nervous tic in their cheek.

Griffiths looked like Mr Normal. At least, Mr Fairly Normal. Actually, if I were a woman - Shirley, for example - I might classify him as Mr Fairly Good-Looking Normal.

He was about my height (six foot one inch), about my weight (11 stone, 4 pounds, I tell no lie), and about my age (30, if you must know). He had light brown hair cut short and combed with a side parting. He had one of those Roman noses that women seem to find sexy. He had a tiny dimple on his chin they'd probably call "cute". He had a generous mouth with soft lips, all the more to whisper sweet nothings in your ear, *ma petite*.

But I was getting carried away. He probably wasn't such a big hit with the ladies, after all. He wouldn't be Shirley's type. He probably lacked my *joie de vivre*.

He looked up as I walked across the laboratory and pushed the goggles up on his forehead. He frowned. (Looked like I was right about the *joie de vivre*.)

He said: "You look too old to be a pupil and too young to be a parent."

I said: "That's me. Neither one thing nor the other."

I strode up to him and held out my hand. He peeled off the latex gloves, took my hand, and shook it reluctantly.

He shot a sideways glance at the equipment he'd been assembling, reached for a cloth, and draped it over the flask and Bunsen burner.

He gave a little nervous laugh and said: "Just a little surprise I'm preparing for the sixth form tomorrow."

I said: "I'm sorry you'll be a boy down."

Griffiths let out a sigh. "Spencer Hooke. What a tragedy. Such a promising life lost so young."

"He was one of the stars of the chemistry class, I believe?"

"Yes, destined for Cambridge. He'd have excelled there, in my opinion. The whole school has been in shock today."

Griffiths sat down on a stool behind the bench. He removed the goggles from his forehead. Shot me a suspicious look from the corner of his eyes. For a teacher who'd lost a star pupil, he seemed very composed. But tragedy takes people in different ways, I decided.

"Why are you here?" he asked in a brisk tone. "Did you have a connection with Hooke?"

"One that I'd have preferred not to have. I found his body."

"You're that newspaperman."

"Colin Crampton, *Evening Chronicle*."

Griffiths stood up, grabbed a cloth, and began to wipe some green stuff off the top of the bench. He rubbed away with the energy of a man who'd rather be doing anything than talking to a newspaper reporter.

I said: "We've all got jobs to do, but I hope you understand that mine doesn't usually involve finding dead bodies."

Griffiths stopped rubbing and tossed the cloth aside. He sat down again on the stool.

He said: "This has affected us all."

"I just wanted to learn more about the boy I found," I said

lamely. "About the boy I wish I'd been able to save."

This time, Griffiths nodded thoughtfully. "I think I understand," he said. "For some time I've wished I'd known him better myself."

"I thought he was a star student."

"Certainly, a brilliant one. But there were…" Griffiths's voice trailed off. He glanced at the rack of test tubes with the coloured powders. Pushed them under the cloth he'd draped over his apparatus.

"Sometimes brilliant people can seem difficult to we mere mortals," I said.

Griffiths managed a thin grin. "That's one way of putting it. Spencer kept things to himself - often trivial things that didn't seem to matter."

"Such as?"

"When I set the boys an analysis test - where they have to determine the chemical nature of a substance - I ask them to keep notes on the tests that were negative as well as positive. Spencer used to destroy the negative results and only present the positive. I told him this wasn't good laboratory practice, but he argued that the only thing that mattered was getting the right result."

"And did he?"

"Always. And generally well ahead of anyone else in the class. But I didn't like the secretive streak in him. Another time, I found that he'd sneaked into the lab after school hours to do a series of experiments on the reaction of different metal compounds to acid. I found out and asked him why he'd been doing it. He said he thought it would help his Cambridge entrance exams. I told him he didn't have to do that in secrecy - I'd be happy for him to use the lab for extra work, but he just nodded at me and stalked off."

I thought about that for a moment and asked: "Was he the same with other teachers - perhaps also with other students?"

"I don't think Spencer was liked around the school. It wasn't just that he was secretive. He was also aloof. He didn't seem to join in with the other students when they were organising a football game or playing cricket. Don't get me wrong. People treated him with respect - most of the students knew he was cleverer than they were. But they didn't like him."

"He was a loner?" I asked.

"Yes, I suppose a loner. But one who had a purpose in life. It's just that nobody could work out what it was. I tried to get him interested in activities outside the school. I'm a member of the bell-ringing team at the local church. I persuaded my fellow team members to let him join."

"And did he take to them?"

"I think so, but even after a few weeks some of the relationships seemed strained. That's really all I'm willing to say about Spencer Hooke."

"Did you like him?"

"I wouldn't wish him dead," Griffiths said.

"I suppose you were at the school last night?" I asked.

Griffiths shot me a suspicious look. "Actually, I was at a meeting of the Sussex Chemical Society." He rummaged on his desk and handed me a small card. "Here's their calendar of events."

I cast my eye down it. There'd been a meeting in Horsham yesterday evening. Something about polymer chemistry. The kind of thing that makes my brain shut down.

I made a mental note of the telephone number on the card and handed it back to Griffiths.

I said: "Quite a drive to Horsham for an evening meeting."

"I took the train. My car is in for a service and its annual MoT check this week. Now, if there's nothing more…"

He stood up and shuffled along behind the bench towards the door.

I said: "One last question: have you any idea why Hooke was

cycling along the Bostal road last night - especially as it was pouring with rain?"

Griffiths shook his head. "That's another mystery. Boys are supposed to get a pass from their housemaster if they want to go out in the evening. There's also a rule about not riding a cycle after dark. Spencer seems to have broken both those rules. But I suppose that doesn't matter now."

"He had a message in his pocket. Something about meeting at the usual place at 7.30pm. Any idea what that meant?"

"This is an all-boys school. It wouldn't be the first time a lad here had fancied a bit of female company."

He moved towards the door with a confident stride like he was cock-of-the-walk.

"And now I need to lock up the lab," he said.

I extended my hand and Griffiths shook it.

"Hope our little chat has been of help," he said.

"It has. Good to see the inside of a chemistry lab again - first time since school days."

"Were you good at chemistry?" Griffiths asked.

"Absolutely hopeless. I thought the periodic table was something you only sat at occasionally."

For the first time, Griffiths smiled. His eyes lit up. If I were a suspicious person, I'd have thought he was delighted at my chemical ignorance.

I left Griffiths taking off his white coat and made my way back through the school.

I'd reached the stairs which led out of the old Jacobean building when a dark shadow in the corner moved.

The shadow lightened as it detached itself from the dark of the ancient wood panelling.

It stepped alongside me and said: "I'm Sneath."

I looked down at a little goblin of a boy, barely five feet tall, with a broad face, big ears and pink cheeks. He had a tangled mop of fair hair and a grin that revealed a row of gapped teeth.

I said: "Who?"

He said: "Sneath of the remove."

"The remove? That's the class before the sixth form."

"That's right," Sneath said. He had a voice that was trying to break. It wasn't the treble of the boy. It wasn't the fine tenor - or perhaps basso profundo - of the man. Sneath's hadn't decided what it was going to be. At the moment, it sounded a bit like a 78rpm record playing at the wrong speed.

"If you're in the remove, Sneath, that would make you about fifteen," I said.

"Yes, but I will be sixteen one day."

"A fine ambition. What can I do for you, Sneath?"

"Ask not what your school can do for you but what you can do for your school," the little tyke drawled.

"You're not the late and much-missed John F Kennedy so get to the point, Sneath. I'm busy."

"Not too busy to hear this. I know stuff about Spencer Hooke that you don't."

That had my attention. "What kind of stuff?"

"Stuff that Stinker Griffiths didn't tell you."

"How do you know what Mr Griffiths told me?"

"I was next door in the physics lab. There's a ventilation grill in the wall between the two. If you stand on the workbench and press your ear up to it, you can hear what they're saying in the chemistry lab."

"That's the latest research in physics, is it? Albert Einstein would be proud of you. But let's get to the point. What do you know about Spencer Hooke that I don't?"

Sneath stuffed his hands in his pockets. Shifted from one foot to the other.

"I'd like to visit the tuck shop," he said.

"Don't let me stop you."

"I can't because I've spent my pocket money this week."

"So what's this information going to cost me? A couple of gobstoppers? A bag of toffees? A string of liquorice?"

"We could go to the tuck shop and see. They might have buns."

"Buns?"

Sneath nodded. "Cream buns."

"I've never before paid for a tip-off with buns," I said.

Chapter 5

The tuck shop was on the other side of the street from the school.

It was a quaint little eighteenth century cottage built out of Sussex flint. It had a small display window to the left of a duck-or-grouse door. The door would have been installed in those far-off days when if you were six feet tall people thought you were a giant. There was moss growing on the roof and a brown iron stain on the wall by the drainpipe. There was a window box with some peonies in bud. It was the kind of place where you'd expect to find an old spinster still knitting woollen socks for the lover who never made it home from the First World War trenches.

The window had a display of the shop's goodies. There were big brown buns and biscuits with pink icing. There were tarts filled with jam like congealed blood. There were dusty jars filled with toffees and gobstoppers and cough drops.

Sneath hurried up to the window and pressed his nose against it.

He turned to me grinning. "They've got two cream buns left and I'm having both of them - and some liquorice toffees."

He shoved open the door and rushed inside.

I followed him, wondering whether Sneath was scamming me for his tuck or whether he really had hard information to trade about Spencer Hooke.

I stepped into a small room with a wooden counter topped with a glass-fronted case. To the side of the case was a set of balance scales with its weight tokens. Behind the counter were shelves loaded with jars of sweets. There were chocolate drops and sherbet lemons and liquorice allsorts. There were humbugs and fruit gums. There was barley sugar which glowed yellow like it was radioactive.

The air was loaded with a sickly scent like it had been

sprinkled with sugar dust. If you breathed in deeply, you felt you were dancing.

To the right of the shelves, a heavy velvet curtain covered a doorway. A hand with long fingers and red-painted nails reached around the curtain and pulled it to one side. And I immediately realised I'd been wrong about the spinster with the knitting.

The young woman who stepped through the door could have walked right out of a French film. One of those naughty ones they showed at the Continentale cinema in Brighton's Kemp Town. She'd be playing the nice girl who didn't. At least, not until she'd tamed the bad boy she'd met in the first reel and the end-credits started to roll.

She had shoulder-length auburn hair, cut to the nape of her neck and waved so that it curled in a natural way. She had green-blue eyes and eyebrows that arched mischievously over them. She had a figure that would get Brigitte Bardot demanding a recount. She was wearing a jumper with red, white and blue hoops, and red slacks.

Little laugh lines crinkled around her mouth as her full lips parted in the kind of welcome smile I felt I could pay into the bank.

She certainly took my mind off the toffees.

The smile vanished as her gaze travelled from me to Sneath.

She looked at the lad in the way she might have looked at an old toad peeing on her peonies and said: "I've told you not to come in here when you've already spent your pocket money."

Sneath twitched a thumb in my direction and said: "This man is paying for me, Miss Staples. So I'll have two cream buns, a quarter of liquorice toffees, and three gobstoppers."

Miss Staples looked at me and her eyes widened with the question.

I nodded: "I guess buying all this sweet stuff must make me a sugar daddy."

She put the cream buns in a paper bag, weighed out the toffees into another bag, and added the three gobstoppers from one of the glass jars.

"I don't know about sugar daddy but it makes you one and nine pence poorer," she said.

Sneath grabbed his tuck from the counter as I handed over the money.

Miss Staples took the cash and put it in a drawer under the counter.

"He'll only stuff all that in one go and be sick," she said.

I turned to see what Sneath made of that. But he'd already hurtled outside.

I made towards the door. Turned back with my hand on the doorknob.

"Sneath sick?" I said. "Gives new meaning to: *'Sic transit gloria mundi'*."

Sneath was already fifty yards down the street by the time I stepped out of the tuck shop.

I called after him: "Wait!"

He turned clutching his paper bags.

I trotted up to him. "We need to find somewhere quiet to talk, Sneath."

He pointed down the street. "The churchyard."

About two hundred yards away, the tower of an ancient church rose above the roofs of the surrounding buildings. We walked towards it.

I said: "I can't keep calling you Sneath. What's your first name?"

"Ranfurly," he said. "But most people call me Snitcher."

"I can't think why. But Snitcher it is."

We entered the churchyard through an ancient lychgate. A gravel path led up to the church porch. But Snitcher pointed to a corner of the churchyard. A yew tree, that could have been a sapling when Cromwell was chopping off Charles the First's head, stood close to a crumbling flint wall.

We picked our way between the tombstones and crept behind the yew. There was a single grave up against the wall. Snitcher sat on the gravestone and opened his bag of buns.

I took a look at the headstone. It read: "Arthur Jeremiah Popplewell. Fell asleep 21st June 1883." I sat down and leant my back against the headstone. But not too hard in case Popplewell unexpectedly woke up.

Snitcher stuffed most of one of the buns into his mouth. He wiped some cream off his nose with the sleeve of his jacket.

I said: "You've got the pay-off. Now tell me what you know about Spencer Hooke."

"I suppose it doesn't matter now that he's gone. I wouldn't tell if he was still alive."

"Were you afraid of him?"

Snitcher stuffed the rest of the bun into his mouth. Crumbs sprayed out as he talked.

"Everyone was afraid of Hooke - if he had something on you."

"And he had something on you?"

"Might have done." Snitcher swallowed hard and reached for his second bun.

"What was it?"

"He found out that I knew Talbot Minor had cheated in a Latin exam. He'd written conjugations of Latin verbs up his arm. He wore a short-sleeve shirt under his jacket, so when he wanted to find something he only had to look up his sleeve."

"And he got away with it?"

"Old Masterson the Latin teacher used to fall asleep during exams."

"And the other boys didn't notice?"

"They're all swots. They were too busy translating a passage from Caesar's *Gallic Wars* into English. But I was sitting behind Talbot and I clocked what he was doing."

Snitcher finished the second of his buns and started on the toffees.

I said: "And you decided to put the squeeze on Talbot?"

"I don't know what you mean."

"You told him he'd have to pay up or you'd snitch on him."

"I was reasonable about it. I only asked for sixpence a week."

I said: "Talbot wasn't your first blackmail victim, was he? You didn't get your Snitcher nickname for nothing. How many others are there?"

Snitcher grinned, like he'd just won a medal in the school sports. "There's Herbert Jackson. He discovered that if he stood on his bed after lights out, he could see across the courtyard to matron's room. There was a gap in her curtains and he watched her going to bed."

"And what did his voyeurism cost him?"

"Nine pence a week and help with my maths homework. Then there's Timothy Pugh. I caught him stealing pencils from the stationery cupboard. He buys me a chocolate covered Turkish delight after school every Friday."

"That all?"

"There's Andrew Todd-Willoughby."

"And what was his indiscretion?"

"I hid while he wrote something on the wall in the lower corridor bogs. He didn't even spell it right. There are two Ts in that word."

"So he's paying you as well?"

"He gives me the pot of raspberry jam his mother sends him every month."

"And Hooke found out about your blackmail racket?"

Snitcher nodded and unwrapped the last of his toffees.

"How did you guess?" he asked.

"I didn't guess. Your career in crime is just starting, so you won't have heard the old saying: set a thief to catch a thief. In this case, substitute blackmailer for thief. I'm guessing that

Hooke was blackmailing too - but for bigger stakes. He'd have spotted the signs of your bungling efforts. Flush with pocket money other boys didn't have. Turkish delight and jam you couldn't afford. He'd have been worried that if your amateur racket had been uncovered, the headmaster might have spread the search wider. So he closed you down."

Snitcher stuck out his tongue at me. The liquorice toffees had turned it black. "You're wrong."

"I see. He didn't close you down. He took over your accounts - probably for higher amounts."

"And he paid me a commission if I found anyone else he could touch."

"Did you?" I asked.

Snitcher shrugged. "Tried some, but Hooke wasn't interested. And one day he went to Chichester. When he came back he said he'd hit the big time, whatever that was supposed to mean."

I knew what it meant. That Hooke had expanded his blackmail racket beyond the boys. Could he have found out secrets about some of the teachers? Perhaps even Steyning residents outside the school?

That "big time" comment meant he'd found a rich mug with a confidence to hide. And enough money to keep it secret.

Suddenly, it looked as though there could be a motive for running him down on his bicycle on a dark night. But who would have the motive?

And why?

Hooke's blackmail of the boys would be small beer. He'd terrorise them for minor misdemeanours around the school. Besides, I doubted that any but a handful of sixth-formers would have access to a car and know how to drive it. The manner of Hooke's death suggested an adult was the killer. And after what Snitcher had just told me, one of his grown-up blackmail victims could be in the frame.

If Hooke put the black on adults, it wouldn't be for cheating in Latin exams or writing on lavatory walls. It would be for serious stuff. The kind that puts people in mortal fear. The kind they'd pay big money to keep quiet. The kind that might drive them to kill.

It was clear that Hooke had had some kind of special relationship with Owen Griffiths. But, then, that would be natural as Griffiths was tutoring Hooke in the subject he hoped to study at university. But did the relationship go further? Griffiths had encouraged Hooke to join the bell-ringers' group. Could the killer be one of the bell-ringers? Or could it be another Steyning resident nobody suspected? Or perhaps somebody beyond the village? After all, Sneath said Hooke had visited Chichester.

I gave Snitcher my stern look and asked: "Do you know why Hooke was cycling over the Bostal?"

Snitcher reached for a green gobstopper. He shook his head. "No." He shoved the gobstopper in his mouth and his cheeks bulged like a balloon.

"Was it to meet someone?"

Snitcher shrugged.

"Did he mention the names of any people outside the school to you?"

Snitcher took the gobstopper out of his mouth. It had turned purple.

He said: "No." His mouth closed around the gobstopper again.

Snitcher was keeping schtum about something. There had to be a reason. He'd opened up about his own scams. He'd told me how Hooke had taken over his blackmail business and put him on commission. But there had to be something else. Clearly Snitcher knew about some of Hooke's operation. But Hooke would have been careful to keep the serious stuff - the black he had on any adults - to himself.

That would only have piqued the curiosity of someone like Snitcher. He wasn't the kind of little tyke to let that rest. He'd have ferreted away until he had something on Hooke. It would have been a blackmailer's honour thing. Even the score. Find their weak spot. Keep the secret in reserve for the day when the scams collapse. Then use it as a bargaining counter. The get-out-of-jail-free card.

I said: "You had something on Hooke. What was it?"

Snitcher levered himself off the gravestone.

I commanded: "Sit down!"

Snitcher shot me a look like he wanted the ground to open and swallow my body in an ancient tomb. But he sat down.

I said: "All this will come out one day. Now's the time to decide whether you want me as an ally or an enemy when it does."

Snitcher took the gobstopper out of his mouth. It was now yellow. He was frowning and a nervous tic had started up at the side of his mouth.

He said: "Hooke said he'd protect me."

"Hooke's lying in a mortuary. You're on your own Snitcher. Unless I decide to help you."

"Why would you help me?"

"Because it might lead me to a scoop for my newspaper."

"Will there be more tuck?"

"If you deliver what I think you can, you'll be the Henry the Eighth of the tuck shop."

Snitcher looked at his gobstopper. Thought about shoving it back in his mouth. Decided he'd save it for later. Wrapped it in a snotty handkerchief and thrust it into his pocket.

He said: "Hooke kept papers."

"What kind of papers?"

"I don't know. I never saw them."

"Then how do you know he had them?"

"Because I once followed him and saw him hide them."

"A resourceful scam artist like you would have returned and viewed them at your leisure."

"Hooke hid them somewhere I couldn't get them. But you could."

"You could show me where?"

"It would be dangerous."

"For you or me?"

"Both of us."

I said: "As Friedrich Nietzsche advised us, 'Live dangerously!'"

"Who's he?"

"Nobody you need to worry about."

"We'll have to do it at night."

"Tonight," I said.

A cloud of indecision passed across Snitcher's face.

"And you're quite sure there'll be more tuck in it for me?"

"If I find what I think we'll find, as much as you can eat."

Snitcher stuck out his hand and said: "Let's shake on it."

I said: "Let's not. Your fingers are covered in gobstopper goo."

Chapter 6

By the time Snitcher had climbed off the gravestone and scampered out of the churchyard, he was down to the red centre of his gobstopper.

I'd arranged to meet him late that night at a quiet spot near the school. He'd assured me he could sneak out and spirit me into the school unseen. At least I believed him on that. Snitcher was a boy who'd turned sneaking into an art form. I only hoped he was as good at the spiriting part. Otherwise, I was going to be in big trouble.

I'd spent a long time questioning him about his relationship with Hooke. I still wasn't sure that he'd told me everything. When you're dealing with blackmailers, you learn they always keep a little something back. They can't help themselves. It's as though giving up everything is like stripping themselves naked. I wondered what Snitcher was still hiding.

After he'd left, I'd spent a bit of time just leaning back on the headstone. It was a pleasant spring day with the world coming alive again after a long winter. A squirrel foraged in some leaf litter looking for cobnuts. A blackbird pecked up a strand of straw and flew off. By the church wall, a couple of jackdaws squabbled over a worm. Life in a country churchyard. All I needed was for Thomas Gray to stroll by and compose another elegy.

Not that it would have helped my predicament. Now that Snitcher had scarpered, I began to realise the implications of what I'd decided. I'd placed myself in the hands of someone who had the trust profile of a cornered rat. If Snitcher smuggled me into the school in the dead of night and we were caught, I'd end up as the mug in the firing line. After all, I was the supposedly responsible adult. And being fired from the *Chronicle* would only be the start of it. There'd be a police investigation and I could end up in court.

Perhaps in jail.

And all for a story which Figgis would run and forget about a week later.

But I was overlooking the most important fact. This was about more than a story. The cops had decided Hooke's death was down to a hit-and-run driver. A serious crime, certainly. But not in the same league as murder. Besides, Holdsworth had written off the chances of ever catching the driver. So, if it were murder, a killer would walk free. Perhaps to murder again.

That was wrong. I couldn't allow it to happen. Even if the victim was someone like Spencer Hooke who didn't sound like a shining example of humanity. In my book, that made this caper a risk worth taking. And if I ended up in court, I'd plead that I was doing the work the cops had flunked.

The squirrel cautiously crept closer, uncertain whether I had any food to offer. Decided I looked like a lost cause and scrambled up a beech tree. Wise decision.

I shifted uncomfortably against the headstone and looked up at the church's bell tower. I stood up and strolled around the outside of the church deep in thought.

Owen Griffiths had mentioned that Hooke had been allowed to join the bell-ringers. Perhaps one of them was Hooke's blackmail victim. Perhaps more than one. I needed to know more about those for whom the bells tolled. The person to ask would be the vicar. But I couldn't barge in and tell the reverend I thought one of his ringers might be a murderer. I needed a cover story.

And Hooke's untimely death provided one.

I found the name of the vicar - the Reverend Simon Purslowe MA - on a noticeboard inside the church porch.

The noticeboard presented a slice of village life. There was news about a book club (they were reading Ernest

Hemmingway's *A Moveable Feast*), a gardening society talk (Trouble with Artichokes) and a meeting about road safety. A sombre poster from the Royal Society for the Prevention of Accidents showed a sad-looking woman in a wheelchair.

There was also a photograph of the Reverend Purslowe. He had a domed forehead covered with a few strands of dark hair. He had bushy eyebrows over a pair of dark eyes that peered loftily into the middle distance. His thin lips were parted in what may have been a smile - or a prayer. I'd put his age at about forty-five.

The noticeboard helpfully provided the address of the vicarage. It was a couple of hundred yards away, connected to the church by a gravel path.

The vicarage was a double-fronted Queen Anne-style house built in red brick. It would have been put up in the eighteenth century when vicars were often the fourth son of minor aristocrats. (The first inherited the title, the second was elected to parliament, the third went into the army, which only left the church for the runt of the litter.)

The house was certainly not your humble hovel, but it wasn't a stately mansion either. It had two floors with a garret level let into the roof where the servants of the fourth son would have slept. These days the garrets were probably stuffed with old hymn books and unsold junk from church jumble sales. There was a sturdy front door painted deep red and fitted with a handsome brass knocker.

I raised the knocker and gave three imperious raps, like the bishop had come to call.

Heavy steps hurried up the hall and Purslowe opened the door.

His wire-rimmed spectacles were balanced on the end of his nose. He was wearing a light grey cable-knit sweater with brown leather elbow patches and blue corduroy trousers. Evidently not all the jumble sale stuff was in the garret.

Purslowe looked at me with sad eyes and said: "Oh dear. I can always tell when someone's suffered a sad loss."

I said: "Very perceptive, vicar. I haven't been able to find my Beatles' *Hard Day's Night* album since before Christmas."

Purslowe's bushy eyebrows knitted together like a pair of mating caterpillars.

"You're not here about a funeral?" he said.

"In a manner of speaking. But at the moment, it's just an unexplained death."

"You'll have to tell me more than that."

I reached into my jacket pocket, fished out a card, and handed it to him.

"Colin Crampton, *Evening Chronicle*," I said.

Purslowe shook his head. "I suppose you've called about that unfortunate Spencer Hooke."

"You could describe being knocked down by a car and left for dead as unfortunate. I'd call it a crime. Perhaps you'd prefer to think of it as a sin."

Purslowe rubbed his chin. "I might call it the hand of fate. But that would be too mystical for a man of the cloth."

I said: "I'd like to ask you a few questions. It will be completely off the record at the moment."

Purslowe shrugged. "I suppose if I don't ask you in, you'll hang around outside like those door-stepping reporters from the tabloid newspapers one reads about."

I grinned. "Won't look good if the rural dean comes to call."

Purslowe frowned but he waved me inside.

We walked up a long thin hall with a dark parquet floor covered with a worn Persian carpet runner. Purslowe led the way into a room that was obviously his study. It had French windows that looked out across a garden where the daffodils and crocuses were in bloom. There was an ancient desk with green leather inlay set at an angle to the window. No doubt Purslowe contemplated his garden while considering his next sermon. The desk was covered with a large writing pad and a litter of pages full of notes written in a spidery hand. There was a Bible open at one of the earlier pages - something from the Old Testament.

The wall behind the desk held an embroidered sampler which read: "In God we Trust".

I suppressed a smile. It reminded me of a similar sign I'd once seen in a rough boozer down by the docks in Newhaven. Underneath the publican had written: "All others pay cash".

Purslowe took the seat behind his desk and waved me towards the guest chair.

He gathered together the scattered papers on his desk.

"Notes for my sermon for the Mother's Day service," he said. "Always difficult to choose a text. This year I'm drawing on Exodus chapter two, verses one to ten."

I put my mind into gear and tried to remember lessons from school-day Bible classes. "Something about Moses?" I asked.

"How the Pharaoh's daughter found the baby Moses in a basket among bulrushes by the river Nile."

"Didn't the daughter give the baby back to the mother to nurse - thinking she was just a slave who did that kind of work?"

"You have the gist of the passage," Purslowe said in a snooty way.

I gave a small cough and sat up straighter, like I'd just been reprimanded by the headmaster.

I said: "These days, mothers are more likely to leave their infants in a supermarket trolley at the Co-op."

Purslowe frowned. "That is not a parallel I planned to draw. But can we get to the purpose of your visit?"

I said: "I believe Spencer Hooke was a member of your bell-ringers' group."

"He was introduced about four months ago after old Mr Deacon fell down the steps to the bell loft and broke his neck."

"And Hooke was introduced by Owen Griffiths."

Purslowe's caterpillar eyebrows wriggled a bit at that.

"You know Mr Griffiths?" he asked.

"I met him briefly. He seemed the teacher most likely to have known Hooke best - given that Hooke spent most of his time in the stinks lab."

"Yes, I believe Hooke was something of chemistry savant," Purslowe said stiffly.

"With a keen interest in bell-ringing. What did the other members of your merry band think about having a schoolboy savant amongst them?"

Purslowe cleared his throat nervously. "Whenever a new ringer joins there is always a period of adjustment. But Hooke seemed to have two keen supporters who won the others over."

Did he indeed? I knew that Griffiths had proposed Hooke as a member, but I didn't realise he'd had a second backer.

"Apart from Griffiths, who was the other Hooke fan?" I asked.

"Georgina Staples."

"Do you mean the young woman who runs the tuck shop?"

Purslowe raised an eyebrow. "You know Miss Staples?"

"And her cream buns," I said. "But I hadn't realised that she obviously knew Hooke well enough to support him as a member of the bell-ringing team."

"I'm sure the lad had met her when he bought sweets at her shop."

I'd already worked that out for myself. But Hooke would have needed a very sweet tooth to make him stand out from the other boys who visited the shop. Unless, I wondered, Georgina's interest in Hooke went beyond toffees and gum drops. But I wasn't going to make the vicar blush by pursuing that line of questioning. At least, not yet.

Instead, I said: "Who didn't want Hooke in the group?"

"There are six bell-ringers - five now Hooke has passed on. As I've mentioned Mr Griffiths and Miss Staples were supporters, but the other three were less keen - initially."

"They were hostile to him joining?" I asked.

"I wouldn't say any of the other members were actively opposed to the boy. Charles Fox, the leader wasn't keen, but Miss Staples persuaded him."

"He's a Fox with a sweet tooth, then?" Or a roving eye, I didn't add.

"He's a Fox who's a merchant banker," Purslowe said.

"From the family which owns Fox's Bank?" I'd heard Susan Wheatcroft, the *Chronicle's* business reporter, mention it. She sometimes wrote a piece about a new deal the bank had pulled off.

"The Fox family has supported the church for several generations. Charles is just the latest. So very generous with their time - and especially their money. I don't think the church would still have a roof without their magnificent benevolence. And Charles Fox takes a great interest in bell-ringing. Once he'd accepted Hooke, the remaining two fell into line, as it were."

"Who are they?"

Purslowe lounged back in his chair with his hands together as though he were praying.

He said: "One is Tom Hobson. He's a fisherman who lives locally in Mouse Lane, but runs a small trawler out of Shoreham harbour. Inshore mackerel mostly, I think. I'd heard that times were hard for fishermen but Tom seems to do well from it. There'll always be a pound note in the collection plate from him on a Sunday morning. But to get to the point, Owen Griffiths is friendly with Tom. He had a word with him about Hooke and that seemed to seal the matter."

"You mentioned two," I reminded Purslowe.

"The final member of the group is a maiden lady of mature years," Purslowe said pompously.

"Does this mature maiden lady have a name?"

"Of course. Clothilde Tench-Hardie."

"That's not a name, it's a fanfare."

Purslowe frowned. "Miss Tench-Hardie is a long-standing and widely respected resident of the village. Although perhaps not so much for the way she races around the streets in her Morris Minor. In any event, she was already a member of the bell-ringing team when I was appointed to this living. And she's always taken a keen interest in the church."

"Always down on her knees, is she?"

"Not at all," Purslowe said. "In fact, her interest in the church is more historical than religious. I believe she has a modest private income and has made herself something of the local historian. You'll find her always delving into books in the library or visiting the County Records Office in Chichester to dig through some dusty old documents. She has a fascination with aristocracy. She's always asking Mr Fox about his wife, Lady Evangelina."

"With a name like that I'll bet she's a real lady," I said.

"It's a courtesy title," Purslowe said. "Lady Evangelina is the daughter of the Earl and Countess of Herstmonceux. I should say the late Earl and Countess. His lordship died a year ago and the Countess a few months before that. In any event, Miss Tench-Hardie has always admired Lady Evangelina."

"Miss Tench-Hardie sounds like a real ferreter out of village secrets," I said.

Purslowe looked down his nose at me. "Steyning is not a village that has secrets," he said.

I didn't shatter Purslowe's illusion and tell him that the most shocking secrets are found in the least likely places.

Instead, I said: "You'll need a replacement for the bell-ringers, now that Hooke is dead."

Purslowe ran a weary hand over his forehead. "Yes. We don't seem to be having a great deal of luck with our bell-ringers lately.

"What with Mr Deacon's fall and Spencer Hooke's accident, being a bell-ringer seems like a death sentence."

Chapter 7

Three hours later I walked into Prinny's Pleasure, a run-down boozer in the North Laine district of Brighton.

I used the place when I wanted to meet someone on the QT. In this case, I'd called Detective Inspector Ted Wilson, my main contact in Brighton's police force. Correction, my only contact in Brighton police. I wanted to find out what he thought about the Spencer Hooke killing.

Prinny's Pleasure occupied a corner site where two streets of tiny terraced houses met. The pub had frosted glass windows, flaking brown paint, and a set of double doors which failed to meet in the middle.

A pub signboard hung from a rusting bracket above the doors. The board featured a portrait of Mrs Maria Fitzherbert, the eighteenth century courtesan who'd been the Prince Regent's top squeeze. She had a bouffant hair style, piercing blue eyes, fulsome red lips, and a tea-strainer moustache on her upper lip. Although that last could have been the kind of furry mould you sometimes see on rotten fruit.

Inside, the green flock wallpaper had turned grey. The carpet was marinated in a generation of beer slops. It made little squelchy sounds as you walked over it. The place smelt like a weasel had peed in the corner. Not surprisingly, few patrons made a second visit. But that suited me. When you're meeting a contact who's a cop or a crook, you don't want snoopers earwigging your talk.

Jeff Purkiss, the landlord, was behind the bar. He was sitting on a barstool. He was wearing a tee-shirt with a green stain around one armpit and a pair of jeans with a busted zip-fastener. So, sartorially, one of his better days.

He rested his elbows on the bar and held his head in his hands. He looked like a man contemplating the end of the world. Or perhaps he was just thinking about the cost of a new pair of jeans.

I walked up to the bar and said: "Snap out of that brown study and pour me a gin and tonic. One ice cube and two slices of lemon."

Jeff slid off the stool, grabbed a glass, and turned to the optics. He poured the gin and put it down on the bar beside a bottle of tonic water.

I said: "What's up? You look like a man who'd give depression a bad name."

He said: "Things couldn't be worse. It's the same every year at this time."

I said: "What time?"

"Mother's Day. It's this coming Sunday."

I reached over the bar and placed a consoling hand on Jeff's shoulder.

"Is it because you don't have a mother anymore?"

"Worse than that. I've got seven mothers. And they'll all be expecting a greetings card and a bunch of daffs."

I reached for the G and T and took a sip. "Nobody has seven mothers," I said.

"I blame my Dad."

"Just the one?"

"More than enough. He was a deckhand on merchant ships. You know what they say about sailors?"

"A girl in every port."

Jeff turned to the optics and poured himself a large Scotch. He took a generous pull at the drink.

He said: "It seems Dad arrived back in Liverpool after a long voyage from Argentina feeling a bit frisky. Well, you would, wouldn't you - cooped up in an old rust bucket with nothing but twenty tons of frozen beef for company? But he had a few bob in his pocket - his pay from the voyage. And he didn't see why the Liverpool lasses shouldn't benefit. My old Pop knew how to play the field when he had a couple of pounds to spend. From the Liver Building to the Anfield Stadium, no girl was safe. Anyway, a couple of days later, he was off on a boat heading for Valparaiso with a cargo of pig iron. And nine months later, I was born."

"But not to seven mothers."

"No. Just one. She left me wrapped in a blanket outside the tradesmen's entrance to the Royal Liverpool hospital. She'd tied a card round my left foot. It read: 'Return to sender'. I think she must've been an Elvis fan."

I suppressed a smile and said: "That's tragic, Jeff. But where did the other six mothers come into the picture?"

"That happened a few years later. Dad was back in Liverpool on a two-week layover. A Littlewood's collector gave him a football pools coupon and he filled it in. That Saturday, he was the only man in Britain with eight score draws and an invitation to Littlewood's head office to pick up a cheque for £75,000 from John Moores himself."

"He was rich," I said.

"What he hadn't bargained for was that there'd be a reporter and a photographer from the *Liverpool Echo* at the handover. His picture was on the front page of the paper that day. The reporter had done some digging and come up with the story of the baby left outside the hospital. Suddenly, Dad found himself being chased by seven women all claiming to be the mother and demanding back maintenance payments, lump sum compensation, and monthly shopping allowances."

"But surely he knew which one was the real mother?"

"I heard later it was none of them. They were all chancers. But after a few days being pursued by seven determined women, he couldn't stand it anymore. Although he was rich enough never to work again, he packed the money in fivers in a rucksack and signed on for another voyage to get away from them. Surgical appliances to Zanzibar. It was his last voyage. There was a typhoon in the Indian Ocean and the ship went down with all hands."

"And with all the money?" I asked.

"Yeah. So the story goes. Trouble is none of these women believed it. They all thought the money had passed on to me. They tried to adopt me from the orphanage where I lived. But I was having none of it. The only way I could keep them at bay was to strike a totally confidential deal with each in turn. I'd secretly agree to be their son if they'd keep it to themselves."

I drained my drink. "And they agreed to that?"

"They all thought I was hiding the money and that eventually they'd get their mitts on it. They still do. That's what blind greed does to you. So here I am. Facing up to Mother's Day - and seven mothers to keep happy. Does anyone deserve that? It would be free drinks for a month if anyone could tell me how to shake them off."

I said: "And you're sure none of them knows about the others?"

Jeff nodded.

"Then the answer's simple. Invite them all here on Mother's Day for lunch."

Jeff's eyes popped. "Together? They'd kill one another."

He paused. I could see his mind working, like rusty old clockwork. His eyes lit up with the answer. He grinned. "I see what you mean."

I didn't think they'd kill one another. If they took one look at the place, they'd know Jeff didn't have a prayer to bless himself with let alone a secret fortune. And when gold-diggers find there's no cash, they can't get out of the door fast enough.

I said: "I'll take another gin and tonic for solving your problem."

Jeff was about to say something when the pub door banged open.

Ted Wilson stood backlit by the street lamps outside. His hair was blown over his forehead by a stiff breeze. His beard looked shaggier than usual. He was wearing a grey worsted suit. The trousers bagged at the knee and the jacket was missing a button. There were two Bic pens in his breast pocket.

I said: "Better add a scotch to my order. But I'll pay you for that."

"Big of you," Jeff grumbled.

Ted and I sat at the corner table at the back of the bar.

The pub was empty, but we could see anyone who came in. We were next to the back door, so we could leave fast if anyone appeared we didn't want to see.

All very furtive but it added a frisson of excitement to our meetings. Besides, where would journalists and police be without a furtive side to their characters? They'd be stolid upright members of the community. The kind who clean the backs of their shoes even when they're not dirty and go to church every Sunday. The kind outwitted by every villain with his eye on the main chance.

Anyway, that's the way I see it. Furtive is up there with honesty, good manners and generosity in the pantheon of human qualities.

Ted slurped his Scotch and said: "There was a lot of talk in the station today about that killing up on the Steyning Bostal." He hoisted his glass and drained it. Thumped it back on the table. "I've assumed that's what you wanted to see me about."

I signalled to Jeff to bring Ted a refill. Did a little shaky motion with my hand to show I didn't want another. With what I'd planned for later, I needed a clear head.

I said: "With that kind of insight, Ted, you ought to be a detective."

Ted stroked his beard vigorously. He couldn't decide whether to laugh or frown. Worst of all, he couldn't think of a come-back.

He said: "You won't be so clever when you hear what I've got to tell you."

"Tell away. But I should mention, I've already interviewed Detective Inspector Holdsworth about the Bostal killing."

"You want to watch Holdsworth," Ted said. "He's the type who thinks a warrant card doubles up as a paying-in book at the bank. Seen too many of that sort in the Brighton force."

"You mean he's bent?"

"As a fiddler's elbow."

"And he gets away with it?"

"Too many higher up are happy to look the other way. They made their bundles on the way up. I guess Holdsworth doesn't see why he shouldn't join them."

I said: "Holdsworth has Spencer Hooke's death down as a hit-and-run, but I think there's enough evidence to start a murder enquiry."

I told Ted my theory. About the note in his pocket. About how his body had been dragged from the roadside.

I said: "Even if Holdsworth is crooked, I can't see why he doesn't treat the case as murder."

"That's because he's as ambitious as he is bent," Ted said.

"A big-time murder conviction would make his name."

"You're right. But he'd needs to make the conviction stick. I reckon Holdsworth thinks he has no chance of nailing the killer. That's why he wants to label the case a hit-and-run. Lower profile. No-one cares if he doesn't solve it."

"Except the family of the dead Hooke."

"Holdsworth has already worked out that Hooke had no close family. No-one around to raise a stink about his lax handling of the case. I reckon Holdsworth has his eye on a big promotion in this new Sussex Police Force the home secretary Sir Frank Soskice is setting up."

"That's the one they're creating by amalgamating the East and West Sussex forces with the borough forces in Brighton, Eastbourne and Hastings?"

Ted nodded. He was about to say something when Jeff arrived with his drink and thumped it on the table.

Jeff shot us a sly look and said: "I don't know what you're plotting, but if I'm questioned I'll plead ignorance."

"Like you were born to it," I said.

"And I thought you were on my side," Jeff said. He scowled and sloped off to the bar.

Ted said: "What was that all about?"

"Something we were talking about earlier. Nothing that will trouble the police."

"Why is it that when you say that, I just know I need to cover my back?" Ted said.

He picked up his new whisky and drained it with one gulp.

An hour later, a comely young woman in a dirndl skirt, with a bodice embroidered in multi-coloured silks, yodelled up to my table.

She plonked a steaming metal dish on top of a small oil burner and said: "*Yodellay-ee-ay. Fondue mit Emmenthaler Kase.*"

I looked at Shirley sitting opposite me on the other side of the table. Her eyebrows rose like a couple of high Cs. We were in the Swiss Restaurant, a new place which had just opened in Brighton's Queens Road.

I said: "Fondue with Emmental cheese. As you can see the cheese is melted and bubbling in the pot."

"Jeez," Shirley said. "That looks like something out of that Steve McQueen horror movie *The Blob* we saw a few weeks back."

"Except this blob won't eat you. Other way round. Dip some bread into the cheese using this long-handled fork - but be careful. The cheese is scalding hot."

"I'll need a longneck beer to wash this down," Shirley said as she tore some bread off a roll. She dipped the bread in the cheese, touched it to her lips to test the heat, put it in her mouth, and chewed thoughtfully.

Shirley put down her fork. "I think I'd rather eat the Blob," she said. "But I'm not really hungry."

"Something on your mind?" I asked.

"It's my mother," she said.

"Barbara? What's the problem?"

"I haven't heard from her like I usually do."

"I thought she wrote to you with the news from Adelaide regularly."

"Yeah. I'd get an aerogram every week. But I haven't had a letter for four weeks now. I tried calling her yesterday - took me forty minutes to get a line to Oz. But all I heard was a phone ringing."

"No answer? Perhaps your mother was out."

"Not at the time I called. She'd always be getting her supper. I'm worried, Colin. I think something's happened to her."

"What kind of something?"

"An accident."

"I don't think so. If Barbara were in hospital, she'd be able to tell someone where you were. They'd get in touch. Perhaps she's visiting someone."

"Then why doesn't she write?"

"I don't know," I said. "Perhaps the Blob has got her."

"That's not funny, Colin."

"Sorry."

I pushed the fondue away. I'd lost my appetite.

"I'll make some calls tomorrow and see if I can discover anything."

Shirley gave me a thin smile.

I'd no idea why Barbara had gone silent. And I didn't like to think about what I might find when I made those calls.

We left the Swiss Restaurant a few minutes later with the cheese still bubbling in its pot.

With the prospect of my clandestine visit to Steyning Grammar School ahead of me, I was too keyed up to eat. And Shirley was clearly worried about Barbara.

We climbed into my MGB in silence.

But once inside, Shirley rummaged in her handbag and produced a letter.

She said: "I forgot to give you this. It's addressed to you but it came to my flat."

I took it and looked at the printing on the envelope. "It's our tickets for the Press Ball," I said. "I had the tickets sent to your flat because our local postie has been ill lately and his stand-in too often delivers my mail to the wrong house."

I ripped open the envelope, took out the tickets, and put them in my pocket. I tossed the envelope into the back of the car.

Shirley glanced behind her. The jump seat was covered with a litter of old envelopes, discarded press releases and crumpled newspapers. My private trash pile.

She raised an eyebrow. "And you should clear out that garbage."

"I'll throw it all away tomorrow," I said. "Without fail."

"Yeah! I've heard that before," Shirley said.

I drove Shirl home and we parted at the steps to her basement flat. I promised I'd call her as soon as I had any news.

I hoped it was a promise I'd be able to keep. If the scam at the school went wrong, I could end up in jail bumming coins for the phone from an old lag in exchange for snout. Perhaps Figgis would provide me with some Woodbines to trade.

Which set me thinking.

I needed an alibi. Someone who would swear blind I was safely home in bed instead of sneaking among the shadows at a school. And I knew just the person to provide it.

My landlady Beatrice "the Widow" Gribble has her parlour on the ground floor for a very good reason.

It ensures she can monitor the movements of her tenants. It's nigh on impossible to enter or leave the building without her logging the event. And I should know. I've tried often enough.

So when I arrived back at my lodgings, I made no effort to tip-toe through the hall avoiding the table with the glass ornaments which tinkled when you knocked against them. Instead, I threw open the door and galumphed into the place like a marauding elephant.

I needn't have bothered. The Widow shot out of her parlour and cornered me by the hat stand before I could get my foot on the first tread of the stairs.

She'd put her hair in multi-coloured curlers. There was a net arrangement fixed over the curlers - like she'd captured a collection of small songbirds on her head. She was wearing an ankle-length pink dressing gown and pointy-toe slippers, each with a pompom on top.

I said in a loud voice in words clear enough for her to repeat in a witness box: "I'm very tired, Mrs Gribble, and I'm going upstairs for a long sleep."

Her hand fixed around my arm like a raven's claw.

"Before you do, Mr Crampton, I've had some terrible news."

"Always deal with bad news in the morning. Never late at night," I said.

"This won't wait," she said.

I sighed. It would be quicker in the long run to hear the Widow out.

"What is it?" I said.

"I've been expelled from the West Brighton branch of the Mothers' Union," she said. "It's a disaster. They were the heart of my social life."

I said: "As you don't have any children, why did they let you join in the first place?"

The Widow looked at the floor, and not just to study the stains on the faded Wilton. She was avoiding my steely gaze.

She said: "It was all a misunderstanding that went too far. It was about three years ago. That Mrs Mangan on the other side of the square asked me if I'd take her little nipper Wendy for a walk in her pram. All this was on account of she'd broken a bone in her foot when she'd dropped a glass ashtray on it. It happened when she rushed to get a final bottle of stout before closing time in the Flag and Trumpet. Mrs Mangan that is, not Wendy. Anyway, as you know I've got a charitable nature - I'm a fool to myself - and I agreed to push the pram as far as the Palace Pier and back."

"And you met someone who thought young Wendy was your own daughter." It wasn't hard to see the way this story was going.

"It was Mrs Thorpe-Henry, the chairwoman of the Mothers' Union. She'd made a few coochy-coo noises at Wendy. And then she invited me to join the Mothers' Union on the spot."

"And you accepted. Why on earth did you do that?"

"Well, Mrs Thorpe-Henry's husband is a company director and they've got a house in Palmeira Square. They've got a refrigerator with an ice box and a television set with a nineteen-inch screen. And they hold all those smart parties where people drink cocktails with olives on sticks. And they eat little bits of toast with dead things on them. My Hector never gave me any of that. I didn't see why I shouldn't have some of it now the old grouch has gone."

I'd seen the photo of her late hubby on her mantelpiece. He had the defeated expression of a bloke who wished he was somewhere else. But preferably not at a party with little dead things on toast.

The raven's claw tightened around my arm.

"But now they've discovered Wendy isn't my daughter," the Widow wailed.

"How?"

"They invited Mrs Mangan to join - and I couldn't hide the

truth any longer. Mr Crampton, you're a man with a devious mind. I want you to think of a way to get them to let me back in."

I brushed her hand away.

"You could always claim you had a real daughter," I said. "A secret one you've never spoken of."

"Why would I do that?"

"Because she was illegitimate."

"What? You mean I would have to confess to having a child born out of wedlock."

"Exactly. A love child. A nipper born on the wrong side of the blanket. *Nullia filia*, as the Romans put it."

The Widow's face flushed with anger. A bead of spittle appeared at the side of her mouth.

She stamped her foot. "That is an outrageous suggestion, Mr Crampton. I won't do it. And, furthermore, you will think up a sensible idea or your future here in my commodious apartments will be in question. That is all I've got to say to you. Now go to your bed for that long sleep you so clearly need."

She stormed back into her parlour.

Well, that's the alibi in the bag, I thought. I'd work out how to invent an unknown daughter for the Widow later.

Chapter 8

It was two o'clock when I parked my MGB in a narrow lane on the outskirts of Steyning.

It was a lonely spot - a rough track flanked by tall trees on either side. The wind crooned through their branches in a low moan, like a ghost in pain.

In the distance, the clock on St Andrew's church struck the hour.

Bong.

Bong.

I shivered and pulled my jacket more tightly around me. I jumped as bushes at the side of the road rustled. Something moved. I stared hard. A pair of green eyes stared contemptuously back, blinked and disappeared. A cat on the prowl.

I'd decided to park well away from the school and approach on foot. Now I wondered whether I should. But the last thing I needed was a late-night dog walker to spot the car near the school and put two and two together.

There was a real danger they'd make four.

I'd had no difficulty sneaking out of the Widow's place. I'd stayed awake and listened to her close her parlour door. Her feet clumped down the corridor to her bedroom. The hinges of the bedroom door squeaked as she opened and shut it. I heard her shoot the bolt behind the door. By the time I'd crept down the stairs and let myself silently out, her snores sounded like a set of steam bellows.

I'd dressed in dark grey trousers and a black polo-neck sweater. Shirley had given it to me during one her drives to smarten up my image. It made me look like a society cat burglar. But women never listen when they've decided what you ought to wear. I'd slid my hands into a pair of leather gloves that fitted like a second skin. I'd taken them from a dancehall gigolo who'd crossed my path a few months earlier. I'd put on a pair of soft shoes. All the better to creep quietly into places I shouldn't be.

In this rig-out, I felt I could crack the Bank of England.

I locked the car and listened to the night. Deep in the woods an owl hooted. Another, away in the distance, replied. Further down the lane, the lid of a metal dustbin rattled each time a gust caught it. But there was no sound of a car engine. No squeak of the pedals on an ancient pushbike. No crunch as boots scuffed gravel at the side of the lane.

I was alone.

I'd brought a torch with me - we wouldn't be able to switch on lights inside the school. But I decided not to use it as I made my way down the lane. There's nothing alerts people more at night than a light swinging from side to side.

I'd arranged to meet Snitcher Sneath at the foot of Burdock Slope, a side entrance to the school. He'd told me that's where there was a door into the school with a loose latch. A firm shove from the outside would usually open it, he'd said. I hoped he was right.

He'd assured me he'd be able to sneak out of his dorm without anyone giving him away. I had no difficulty believing that. No doubt Snitcher had enough goods on his fellow dorm mates to ensure their silence.

But after this escapade, Snitcher might get clever. He might decide he also had the goods on me. He might feel he'd outgrown a weekly Turkish delight. He might hanker for some serious money from a real grown-up, like his late mentor Spencer Hooke. He might decide he was ready to step into Hooke's shoes.

So at the end of our adventure I would make clear to him the peril of dead men's shoes.

A single street lamp shed a thin yellow pool of light at the foot of Burdock Slope.

I stood clear of the light and looked around me. The slope led up to the school grounds. At the top, I could make out the black silhouette of the school's buildings.

The street was silent. No late night loiterers staggered home from the pub. No lovers swapped kisses in the lamplight. No burglar, swag bag over his shoulder, lurked in the shadows.

I looked around anxiously for Sneath. There was no sign of the lad. I wondered whether he'd developed the frights and decided to call off this risky rendezvous. But Snitcher was a greedy type. He had too much riding on this caper to abandon it.

I whispered: "Sneath".

Answer came there none.

I moved around the pool of light to the other side of the slope and called again. This time loud enough to make me worry whether the sound had carried too far on the wind.

I glanced behind me. A stone flint wall turned in a dog-leg into what looked like an alley. The entrance to the alley was black. Then something in the blackness moved. Snitcher stepped forward and grinned at me. Like he'd just been playing cricket for the school eleven and scored a century.

He was wearing a dark navy raincoat and had blacked up his face with make-up.

I pointed at it and said: "Where did that come from?"

"The school drama society's make-up box. Last year, they did *Othello*."

"No doubt with you as Iago."

"Actually, I was in charge of the props." He giggled. "After the show, I snitched Othello's handkerchief. I wrap my unfinished gobstoppers in it."

I frowned. "And who said Shakespeare can't connect with the modern generation? But what were you doing in that alley?"

He said: "Taking advantage of the natural cover."

"It's time to stop playing hide and seek and show me where

Hooke stashed his papers."

A little dribble appeared at the side of Snitcher's mouth. "This way," he said.

We crept up the slope like hunters stalking a deer. At the top, we reached a path which led to a door. We edged our way along the path, sneaking glances over our shoulders. I wondered whether there were late-night patrols. It was a boarding school and there'd be teachers on duty most of the time. I should have checked more thoroughly.

We reached the door.

Snitcher whispered. "This isn't the main way in. It's not used much, so nobody bothers that the latch is loose."

I gave the door a tentative shove. The latch rattled like loose change in a Scotsman's sporran.

Snitcher said: "If you pull the handle upwards and lean your shoulder against the frame, it'll open."

I grasped the handle and heaved it north, shoved my shoulder onto the frame.

Nothing.

I tried again.

No dice.

I said: "It doesn't work."

Snitcher said: "You have to twiddle the handle while you lean with your shoulder."

Snitcher, the master cracksman.

I tried the lock another time. With extra twiddling. And a heavier push. And a fleeting thought that they never covered this in my journalist training course.

Clunk.

The latch snapped back. The door swung open. And I stumbled five yards into the building like a clown doing a pratfall.

Snitcher followed me and giggled. "That wasn't supposed to happen," he said.

I said: "We're not here to entertain each other." I pulled out my torch, switched it on and let the beam play over the walls.

We were in a corridor painted an institutional green. There was a worn wooden parquet floor. Doors led off the corridor on each side, every twenty feet or so into classrooms. At the far end, the corridor was crossed by another running from left to right to create a T-junction.

The place smelt of disinfectant. Dettol. The Widow splashes it around my bathroom every Friday. Apparently, it kills 99.9 per cent of all known germs. Not that that gives me any comfort. It's always the 0.1 per cent that gets you.

I turned to Snitcher and shone the torch in his face Gestapo style. He blinked and raised his hand to shade his eyes.

"Now let's have some straight answers," I said. "Where is Hooke's hiding place?"

He snickered and said: "Follow me."

We crept down the corridor and turned left at the T-junction. Ten yards along there was a door off to the right.

Snitcher pointed. "In there."

I knew what we'd find even before I opened the door. The Dettol pong left little doubt this would be a lavatory.

"The bogs," Snitcher announced unnecessarily.

I opened the door and we went in.

Snitcher said: "There are no windows in here, so you can switch on the light."

I shone the torch along the bottom of the door. There was a half-inch gap underneath it. The light would shine through the gap into the darkened corridor. I might as well set up a neon sign flashing "intruders at work".

But if we were going to study Hooke's secrets, there was merit in switching on the light. I shone the torch around the room. Along one wall was a set of urinals. Along the opposite wall there were four cubicles. At the far end a couple of washbasins. Each had a grimy towel hanging beside it.

I trotted across the floor, unhooked the towels and stuffed

them into the gap under the door. Then I switched on the light.

I said: "Right, Snitcher, let's make this quick. Where did Hooke hide his secrets?"

Snitcher twitched a thumb at the fourth cubicle, the one furthest from the door.

We crossed the room and pushed open the cubicle door.

Snitcher pointed to a spot on the wall above the lavatory cistern.

"See those white painted bricks?" he said.

I nodded.

"The third brick from the left is loose. There's a cavity behind it. Hooke's stuff is in there."

"Why haven't you had a look?"

"I tried but I'm too short to reach. You have to stand on the lavatory seat and reach over the cistern. I'm about a foot too short. There's nothing I could do about it."

I believed him. The cistern was a substantial porcelain item, big enough to bath a baby. It was held high on the wall by a pair of rusting brackets and operated by a chain which hung down from the lever which made it flush. The whole thing was a testament to the genius of Thomas Crapper who invented the floating ballcock which controlled the refill mechanism.

I looked at Snitcher. There was an eager light in his eyes. "So Hooke's secrets were so near yet so far? I bet that annoyed you," I said.

I put one foot on the lavatory seat and pressed down. It was a sturdy wooden job. It would need to be in a school with strapping schoolboys. I decided it would take my weight.

I levered myself up, taking great care not to slip sideways so my foot went into the pan. The last thing I needed right now was a shoe full of lavatory water. I'd need to soak my foot in Dettol. Besides, I'd leave a trail of footprints as I made my getaway. It would look like a one-legged bloke with a leaking foot.

I reached across the cistern. I could see Snitcher's problem.

The bulk of the cistern provided a considerable obstacle to reaching the loose brick. I inched along the lavatory seat and stood on tiptoe. My fingers barely brushed against the brick.

I flattened myself against the cistern and leant in as far as possible. My fingers closed around the brick and I felt it move a little. I worked my fingers into a gap. I loosened the brick, took it out of its place, and balanced it on the edge of the cistern.

I reached into the black hole left by the brick. My fingers closed around something cold and metal. I got a grip on it and pulled it out.

It was a cash box. The kind you used to see in small shops before cash registers became popular. The kind aged spinsters hide their savings in before stuffing the box underneath the bed. The first place any self-respecting burglar looks.

Like an acrobat making a dangerous move, I pirouetted off the lavatory seat.

Snitcher leaned into my face "What is it?" His breath smelt like an explosion in a sugar factory.

I said: "It's the kind of box we're not going to be able to open."

"Isn't there a key?"

"First, nobody keeps a key in the same place as the box holding their valuables. And second, this box doesn't operate with a key. It's the kind with a lock opened by a three-number code."

I pointed to a rotor arrangement on the side of the box. You needed to change the rotors so that they displayed the right three-digit number and the box would open.

Snitcher looked at me with defeated eyes. "That means there are nine hundred and ninety-nine possible combinations."

"One thousand," I said. "It's possible the three digits could all be zero."

"Just start at the beginning and try each number after the other."

"We don't have time for that. Besides, these boxes often have a cut out after so many incorrect tries. Usually three."

"We could have a lucky guess," Snitcher said.

"And with an unlucky failure," I said. "We need to think about what number Hooke might have used."

"What about 1, 2, 3?" Snitcher said. "Easy to remember."

"And too obvious. I think we can exclude any three consecutive numbers. That rules out nine possibilities, if we include 0, 1, 2 and 8, 9, 0 as consecutive sequences."

"Then it has to be three same numbers."

"Also too obvious. Hooke sounds like the kind who'd have been more subtle than that. I think it's more likely to be a number that's special to him."

"Like his birthday?"

"Not special enough. He'd know that other people knew it."

"What about his locker number in the changing rooms?"

"Also known by other boys. So I don't think so. What other number might have been special to Hooke? Think, Snitcher."

The lad's face creased with worry, his forehead wrinkled, then he grinned.

"I bet it's his highest score in cricket. But I know that he was really out leg before wicket before he'd scored. He claimed he'd nicked the ball before it bounced off his pad. The umpire believed him."

"What was his score?"

"One hundred and six."

"And you think he'd use that even though other people would know it?"

"I'm certain. He was always boasting about it."

I shrugged. There was nothing else. I shifted the rotors so the number read 1, 0, 6. I heaved on the handle. The lock creaked but didn't budge.

One chance gone.

"We have to think of something else," I said. "Isn't there anything about Hooke that would give us a clue? Come on,

Snitcher, it's about time you lived up to your name."

"I don't know," he whined. He scratched his head. "Wait a minute. I've remembered something. It was last year. I went into the library and Hooke was sitting in one of the alcoves reading a paperback novel. You're not supposed to do that during study time. I cheeked him about it. He told me to buzz off. But later he showed me the book and told me it was the best he'd ever read."

"How does that help us?"

"It was called *Fahrenheit 451*."

"The Ray Bradbury novel." I'd remembered it'd been around for a few years. It was the kind of dystopian tale I've never really taken to. Why invent weird new worlds when the current one is strange enough for anyone?

But perhaps Hooke had used the number on his cash box. I flicked the rotors - 4, 5, 1. I pulled on the handle. The box rattled. Didn't open.

Two chances lost.

We weren't going to crack this. I'd taken a big risk that wasn't going to pay off. Snitcher looked miserable.

"Think harder," I said to him. "Did Hooke have any other favourites?"

"He said he'd enjoyed the 1812 Overture in musical appreciation."

"Too many digits."

"In the summer, he always chose a 99 ice-cream from the tuck shop."

"Too few."

Snitcher slumped down on the floor. He held his head in his hands. I wasn't going to get any more out of him. And how could I guess the very personal number of someone I never knew?

I turned towards the door. It was time to go.

But wait a minute.

There was one thing I did know about Hooke. He was proud

of his bicycle. The one he was riding on the Bostal. I remember it was a special model. The model number had been painted on the front of the handlebars. It was a 77I. The I stood for Invincible. A great marketing name for a bike. Except it hadn't proved invincible for Hooke.

There were only two digits and one letter. But suppose that letter was interpreted not as an I but as a number 1. That would make the number 771.

My hand quivered with excitement as I twiddled the rotors. I pulled gently on the cashbox handle.

There was a click and the lid swung open.

Snitcher jumped to his feet. Hurried to my side. I pushed him back.

"I'll take a look at this privately first," I said.

Snitcher gave me a look like he wanted to see me boiled in oil. He slunk over to the washbasins and leaned sulkily on one.

I reached into the box and took out a book. It was a dog-eared Mayflower paperback with a pink cover. The book was *Fanny Hill, Memoirs of a Woman of Pleasure*. It had been written in 1748 by a bloke called John Cleland who had a way with words and a fantasy about wicked women. I'd read on the books page of the *Chronicle* that literary historians had tagged it as the first example of a pornographic novel. Only the previous year the police had seized copies of it from a London bookshop. The court had fined the owner for distributing an "obscene publication". But, evidently, not before Hooke had laid his hands on a copy.

Over by the washbasins, Snitcher sprang alive when he saw the book.

"I've seen that book before," he said. "Hooke used to charge boys a shilling to read it. I saved up my pocket money but he said I was too young."

I tossed the book to Snitcher. "Be my guest."

Snitcher caught the book, ripped it open, and buried his nose in the first page.

He didn't notice as I reached into the cash box and took out the only other item in it.

It was a passbook for the Sussex Coast Building Society. It had been issued by the Worthing Branch in the name of Spencer Hooke. I opened the book. There was a record of cash deposits going back at least two years. As I flipped the pages, I noticed that the number and size of the deposits increased. I made a mental note of the total: £1,793.17s.8d. It was a colossal sum for an 18-year-old boy to have on deposit. It would take me a year to earn that. But then I'd be doing it honestly.

I glanced at Snitcher. His ears had turned red and some yellow stuff had seeped out of his nose. His left leg was wobbling, like it was powered by electricity. He hadn't noticed me look at the passbook.

I slipped it back into the cash box.

I said: "Okay, Snitcher. There's nothing else in the box. Come over here and give me that book before you have a laundry accident."

Snitcher said: "Can't I keep it a bit longer?"

"It must go back in the box and the box must go back where it came from."

Snitcher gave me a surly sneer. But he sloped across the room and handed me *Fanny Hill* like he was losing a lover.

I put Fanny back in the box. Then I pushed my way back into the cubicle. I climbed back on the lavatory, stuffed the box back, and replaced the loose brick which hid it.

Snitcher watched me with resentful eyes.

"What do I get out of this?" he asked. He had a scowl on his face that could have clouded the sun.

I said: "The knowledge that you've helped one of Her Majesty's journalists in the performance of his clandestine duty."

"You think you're clever, don't you? But you'll find I'm cleverer," Snitcher snarled. "Wait until I let people know you've been sneaking around the school at night. The rozzers will put you in prison as one of those men who prey on young innocent boys like me."

"I don't think so."

"They'll believe me. You see if they don't."

"You've overlooked a couple of points, Snitcher. First, I've got an alibi. My landlady will swear blind she saw me go to bed this evening and not reappear until tomorrow morning. And, second, when the cops are tipped off that they'll find a porno book in the lavs, guess whose fingerprints they'll find on it? None other than young innocent Ranfurly Snitcher Sneath's."

"It'll have your prints, too," Snitcher wailed.

I held up my hands. "Ever wondered why I've been wearing these gloves throughout? The cops won't find any evidence to connect me to this. But plenty to nail you. Now beat it."

Snitcher looked like he'd swallowed a frog. Sounded like it, too, when he tried to speak. He turned, kicked the towels away from the door, flung it open, and stormed out.

I listened as the sound of Snitcher's running feet receded down the corridor. Then I switched off the light and flicked on my torch. I removed the towels from where Snitcher had kicked them. I rehung them on their hooks, and slunk silently into the corridor.

Around the bend in the corridor a door opened, then slammed shut. Feet shod in heavy leather-soled shoes clumped over the parquet. Not the feet of a boy. The feet of a man.

And they were heading towards me.

Chapter 9

I winced as the tendons in my arms and legs tightened, like an invisible puppet master had just yanked on the strings.

I couldn't move. The feet clumped closer. This was going to be the moment when Crampton's career ended in disgrace.

It was going to be difficult when this all came out - but I'd have to find a way to feel ashamed.

I could see the *Chronicle*'s own front-page headline: Rogue Reporter Jailed for Five Years.

If I was lucky, Frank Figgis would give me a goodbye gift of some Woodbines to trade as snout with my fellow inmates.

Mrs Gribble would gossip to her neighbours that she'd known I was a bad'un all along.

Shirley would slap my face, cry a bit, and then return to Australia where she'd marry a jackeroo with his brains in his saddlebag.

My life would be in ruins.

Nemesis was a pair of feet just ten yards away.

Their steady tread moved towards me. They were approaching along the main corridor. Towards the T in the T-junction. I was around the corner to the left.

Had Snitcher betrayed me in a fit of pique?

I stood rigid like I'd been nailed to the floor.

I was seconds away from being discovered.

I had nowhere to run.

I'd have no excuse for what I'd been doing. No clever explanation to offer.

My brain felt like a fog had descended. I could always see a way to talk myself out of a difficulty. But not this time. The fog obscured my view.

My heart had been colonised by drum majorettes pounding out a samba rhythm. Sweat pricked at my pores.

My body had closed down. Given up. Prepared to surrender. But then a lone brain cell sent a message to my hand. My hand twitched and I turned off the torch.

If my hand could work, so could my legs. I could run for it. But where?

With five more steps the feet would turn the corner. I felt the air move as the figure approached. I caught the whiff of something sharp. Like the stench of rotten eggs.

The smell kicked my senses into action.

Silently, I slid along the wall away from the approaching feet. I clung to the wall and prayed my figure would blend into the darkness. If Shirley's black polo-neck sweater kept me invisible, I'd even buy those summer shorts she'd been going on about.

I wished I'd blacked up like Snitcher.

I edged further along the wall keeping my eye on the T-junction. And backed into a set of lockers. I felt around them. They stuck out about two feet from the wall. If I could get to the other end of them perhaps I could hide myself.

I glanced back in the direction of the footsteps. The flicker of a torch appeared as the feet approached the junction. I tiptoed to the far end of the lockers. Crept behind them and pressed myself against the wall.

The footsteps reached the junction and stopped.

The torch beam flicked up the corridor towards me. It played over the floor and lingered over the lockers.

I held my breath like breathing had just become a luxury I couldn't afford.

My chest tightened as the little circle of light from the torch flicked around.

Then it moved away.

I breathed out. As silent as a dying saint.

The footsteps started again. This time walking away from me along the other leg of the corridor - leading away from the T-junction.

Cautiously, I peered round the corner of the lockers.

The figure was tall, cast in shadow, and swinging the torch in front of him. But I recognised that cocky walk.

Owen Griffiths.

Chemistry master.

And night-time prowler. At least we had something in common.

He wasn't looking for an intruder. I could tell that straight away. When you're hunting for someone you look right and left. Your eyes dart everywhere. You start and you stop and you move forward again. Tentatively. You watch your step. You only move when you've satisfied yourself you've drawn a blank on the ground you've covered.

But Griffiths wasn't walking like that. Snitcher hadn't tipped him off that an errant journalist was on the loose. Griffiths was striding ahead like he had to get somewhere fast.

Like a man with a job to do.

Like a man on a mission.

And I thought I knew where he was heading. The chemistry lab. It was where I'd interviewed him the day before. The place where he'd spoken highly of Spencer Hooke.

As Griffiths disappeared through the door at the end of the corridor, I stepped out from my hiding place behind the lockers.

I had two choices.

The sensible choice.

The stupid choice.

If I took the sensible choice, I'd head out of the school like I was wearing jet-propelled shoes. I would race down Burdock Slope and disappear into the night. Tomorrow morning I'd arrive at the office and file my copy. Life would return to what passed for normal in my world.

If I took the stupid choice, I'd follow Griffiths to find out what urgent business he had at three o'clock in the morning. I'd spy on him and hope I wasn't caught. I'd risk my career for a scoop.

What was it old Kipling wrote in his poem? "If you can make one heap of all your winnings, And risk it on one turn of pitch-and-toss." And if I lost, of course, I'd take Rudyard's advice and never breathe a word about my loss. I wouldn't get the chance. I'd be in jail.

I brushed myself down, switched on the torch, and shaded the beam with my hand. Then I headed down the corridor wondering what I'd find when I spied on Griffiths.

I pushed through the door at the end of the corridor and out into an open area.

I knew where he was as soon as I saw the lights on in the chemistry lab. Whatever he was up to, Griffiths was hiding in plain sight. No doubt he'd have an explanation ready in the unlikely event that someone happened along.

But who was going to appear on the scene in a grammar school in the middle of the night?

I knew the answer to that question.

The chemistry lab was at the end of a block of classrooms. No doubt the architect thought that if the place blew up, it would limit the damage to the rest of the building. Clever of him.

There was a bicycle shed opposite the chemistry lab. I crept into it and hid behind a bike draped with a tarpaulin. I could see one end of the lab well but had no view of the other.

Just my luck, Griffiths was up the other end. I crouched down behind the tarp wondering whether to move my position and risk being spotted.

I decided to chance it. But before I moved, Griffiths stepped into view. I didn't know what he'd been doing at the other end of the lab, but now he was focused on some equipment. It looked like the equipment I'd seen him setting up the day before. There were flasks and beakers and test tubes. There was a Bunsen burner and a tripod.

Griffiths disappeared again into the part of the room I couldn't see. When he returned, he was wearing a white lab coat. He took a small packet out of the lab coat's pocket and cut the top of it with a pair of scissors.

He picked up the conical glass flask with a spout I'd seen before. He shook a little powder from the packet into the flask. Then he plugged the narrow neck of the flask with a cork which had a glass tube running through the middle of it. He fixed a rubber tube to the spout of the conical flask and shoved another glass tube into the other end of the rubber. Then he put the glass into a test tube which was half full with a clear liquid.

Watching Griffiths reminded me of the chemistry lessons I used to snooze through at school.

This time I was riveted by the action.

Griffiths returned his attention to the glass tube sticking out of the neck of the conical flask. He took a small funnel and inserted it in the top of the tube. Then he picked up a bottle containing a dark misty liquid. He poured a few drops of the liquid into the funnel.

He leant over and looked closely as the drops rolled down the inside of the glass tube and dropped onto the powder in the conical flask. Within a few seconds a grey smoke started to rise from the powder.

Griffiths blocked off the top of the tube with the funnel so the smoke could only escape through the spout of the flask. It drifted up the spout and through the rubber tube and down the glass tube into the clear liquid in the test tube. The liquid bubbled as the smoke passed through it - and then slowly became opaque.

Griffiths looked up from his experiment and smiled.

The kind of sinister grin Bela Lugosi sported in those old nineteen-thirties horror films still showing on TV.

Griffiths rummaged in a drawer under his test bench. He took out a sheet of paper and an envelope. He spent several minutes writing something, folded the paper, and put it in the envelope. He wrote something on the envelope - presumably the name of the recipient.

I was willing to bet it wasn't a note for the milkman asking him to leave an extra pint and some yoghurt.

Then he dismantled his apparatus and poured the contents down the test bench's sink. He washed the flasks and tubes in running water and left them to dry on the bench.

He disappeared from sight and a moment later the lights of the lab went out. I heard a door open and Griffiths hurried across the yard towards Burdock Slope. I crept out from behind the tarp and poked my head around the side of the bike shed.

Griffiths was at the bottom of the slope. He'd taken a torch from his pocket and he used it to give three quick flashes up the road. I heard the low growl of an engine spark into life. A moment later, a grey van appeared at the foot of the slope.

It was an old wreck of a van. There was rust under the door, blotchy marks on the paintwork, and a dent in the rear wheel-arch.

The driver's window wound down. It was dark inside the van and I couldn't see the driver. But his hand appeared at the open window. Griffiths stepped forward and handed in the envelope. The window wound up.

The driver revved the engine and it backfired twice. I recognised the sound. My first car, an old banger, did the same. It happened when the petrol didn't ignite in the combustion chamber. The fuel seeped into the exhaust and fired late. The local garage's mechanic told me I was running the car on the wrong air and fuel mixture. Too much air, too little fuel. I remember him telling me that every car backfired differently. Just as everyone could be identified by their own cough.

These thoughts flashed through my mind as the van backfired twice. Then it pulled away from the kerb and drove off.

Griffiths hurried back up the slope, crossed the yard, and disappeared into the school.

There was no point in following Griffiths. His night's work was done.

***

I had plenty to think about as I drove back to Brighton.

I'm no chemist but it wasn't difficult to work out what Griffiths's clandestine experiment was all about. He was testing the purity of drugs. It could have been heroin, cocaine or some concoction I'd never heard of. But, sure as hell, it wasn't sherbet.

And it was illegal.

This put the Spencer Hooke murder in a new light. Griffiths had looked like a careful man. He'd conducted his tests at night and cleared up afterwards. There wouldn't be any evidence for the police to find. But, perhaps, Griffiths hadn't been careful enough. He'd told me that Hooke was a bright pupil. The star of his chemistry A-level class. Expected to go to Cambridge University. Perhaps Hooke was clever enough - or just lucky enough - to have stumbled on Griffiths's secret.

Snitcher had told me how Hooke had graduated from minor blackmail of his fellow students to grown-ups. Perhaps Griffiths was the first of them. The stash in Hooke's account was big enough to be funded by drugs money. If that was the case, Griffiths had to be a top suspect as the car driver who left Hooke dead on the Bostal road.

But Griffiths wasn't the only person involved in the drugs caper. I'd seen him pass an envelope to a man in a van. I couldn't see who it was. And from where I was hiding, I hadn't been able to log the number plate. But I was guessing that the van man was a messenger to take news about the quality of the drugs back to the Mr Big behind the operation. Perhaps the van man had killed Hooke. Or Mr Big. Or persons unknown, as the cops liked to call them.

I was sitting on a story that would put a grin on Figgis's face - and make the national papers. The only trouble was I couldn't write a word of it. If I did, I'd be asked where I'd got the information.

I couldn't say without incriminating myself.

Nothing about this story was going to be easy.

Chapter 10

I arrived in the newsroom the following morning after not enough sleep and not enough breakfast.

Correction, after no breakfast. I'd slept through my alarm. By the time I'd woken up, I was late. So I had to hustle to reach the office in time to write a story before deadline.

First, I picked up my telephone and called the number I'd seen on the chemical society card Owen Griffiths had shown me.

The phone was answered by a man with a brisk voice: "Fletcher."

I said: "Good morning, Mr Fletcher. I'm calling from the *Evening Chronicle* and I was hoping to get some information about the meeting you held earlier this week on polymers."

"Didn't realise a popular newspaper would be interested in a technical matter. But you're out of luck. Meeting was cancelled. Professor Williamson, the speaker, had a bad attack of shingles."

"Sorry to have troubled you. Perhaps another time."

The line went dead.

So Griffiths had lied about attending the meeting. Perhaps he'd also lied about his car being in for a service. I'd need to speak to him again. But if he'd lied once, he'd lie twice. Best if I pursued other lines of enquiry before I tackled him.

But what lines?

I yawned a couple of times and thought about that. This was a case for Crampton's legendary cunning. If Detective Inspector Bernard Holdsworth had sight of the riches in Spencer Hooke's building society passbook, he'd have to take the idea of murder seriously. He'd have to reopen the case. Then I would have a story. So I needed to find a way to put Holdsworth in the picture while keeping me out of it.

I'd lain awake in bed puzzling over the problem. And as the

thin light of dawn crept between the gaps in my curtains I'd hit on a way to do it.

Hooke had held his account at the Worthing branch of the building society. He had a record of his deposits in his passbook, but the branch would also hold a record of the deposits and the balance in his account.

If the branch manager discovered that Hooke had died a violent death and the police were investigating the case, he'd be bound to tell them about the account. Holdsworth would then have a motive for Hooke's murder he couldn't ignore.

I reached for the telephone directory and looked up the building society number. Then I crossed to one of the telephone booths on the opposite side of the newsroom.

Years ago, Frank Figgis had had them built. He'd intended reporters to use them for confidential calls to contacts. But what Figgis didn't know was that most of the time reporters used them to make dates or place bets with bookies.

But not me. At least, not this time. I was inside the booth at the far end because I needed to practice a little deception. "Oh! what a tangled web we weave when first we practice to deceive." I could almost feel the ghost of Sir Walter Scott grinning beside me.

I dialled the building society number.

The phone was answered after three rings by a young woman with a plummy voice. "Sussex Coast Building Society. Who is speaking?"

"I'm calling on behalf of Spencer Hooke who has an account at your branch."

"Are you Spencer Hooke?"

"Mr Hooke is dead."

"I'm so sorry."

"So is Spencer."

"May we tender our condolences?"

"Very kind. But it would be even more useful if you could

tender the information about Spencer Hooke's account to Detective Inspector Holdsworth at Shoreham Police Station."

"Information about our clients is confidential even when they have passed on," she said.

"That must give them a lot of a reassurance in the after-life. I can just hear Spencer now: 'Well, St Peter, it's a bit of a choker being dead, but at least I've the comfort of knowing no-one can snitch a peek at my building society account'."

"This is not a matter for sarcasm."

"I agree. A serious crime is suspected."

"A crime?" Plummy voice sounded alarmed.

"Yes, Spencer Hooke was killed by a hit-and-run driver. It's a police matter."

"Are you at the police station?"

"Frequently."

"I'd like to know who I'm talking to."

"Me, too. But please make sure the information about the £1,793.17s.8d in Spencer's account is passed to Mr Holdsworth this morning. Obstructing the police in their enquiries is a very serious matter."

I replaced the receiver before she could ask me again for my name. I pushed out of the booth and headed back to my desk feeling pleased with myself. If I knew how much Hooke had in his account, the building society would worry about who else had the information. They'd be on the blower to Holdsworth before you could say "compound interest".

I sat down at my desk and thought about my other problem. I'd promised Shirley I'd try to get some information about her missing mother. I glanced at my watch. It was just after nine. I vaguely recalled that in Australia time was about eight hours ahead of Britain. At least, parts of the country were. The rest of it was about fifty years behind. (Of course, I'd be cautious about saying that in front of Shirley. Call me a coward, but I'm as attached to my balls as the next man.)

I leaned back in my captain's chair, picked up the phone, and asked for the international operator. There was a ninety-minute wait for a line to Australia, I was told. My stomach was rumbling like a grumbling volcano. That reminded me I hadn't had any breakfast. So I stood up and headed for the tea room.

When I pushed through the door into the tea room, Susan Wheatcroft, the paper's business reporter, was over by the drinks table.

She was pouring coffee into a mug.

I ambled over and said: "Mine's white but strong."

Susan said: "So I'd heard. But how about your coffee, honeybunch?"

She guffawed at her joke and made her chins wobble. Susan had a big personality to match her figure.

I grabbed a mug and Susan handed me the coffee thermos.

"Got anything for the midday edition?" Susan asked. She reached for a bun and took a giant bite out of it.

"Nothing much. How about you?"

"Possible big deal brewing with one of the county's banking magnates."

"Magnates? Do you find they attract you?"

Susan pulled a face. "Pardon me while I don't laugh," she said. "I'm talking about a merchant banker. And that's not rhyming slang. Although it could be in the case of this shyster."

I poured coffee into my mug. "Anyone who's crossed my path?" I raised the mug to my lips.

Susan stuffed the rest of the bun into her mouth. "Doubt it. I reckon this fellow has sailed close to the wind a few times, but he's always managed to tack out of trouble. Charles Fox."

I looked up from the mug so quickly, I spilt my coffee.

I said: "You mean the Charles Fox from the Fox banking family?"

"Fox by name. And foxy by nature."

That had my attention. Charles Fox was one of the names the Reverend Purslowe had mentioned as one of his bell-ringing group. The good vicar had practically canonised the banker for the money he'd lavished on the church.

I said: "What more can you tell me about Fox?"

"How long have you got?"

"How long do you need?"

Susan winked. "How about the rest of your life?"

I winked back. "How about we sit at the table over there while we drink our coffee and you give me a five-minute briefing?"

Susan shrugged. "Guess I'll have to put the rest of my life on hold." But she headed for the table and I followed.

I took a swig of the coffee and asked: "I'm guessing from your reaction, Charles Fox is not just another money man on the make?"

Susan gave her coffee a desultory stir with her spoon. "The guy likes to play the pin-striped banker image, but he's really got the business ethics of a back-street bookie."

"Fast and loose?"

"Any looser and those pin-striped trousers of his would fall round his ankles." Susan grinned, then leaned forward more serious. "He took over as chairman of the bank from his father Richardson Fox five years ago. The bank was founded in the eighteenth century as a place for wealthy Quakers to stash all that cash they made from selling porridge oats. They didn't like anyone poking noses into their financial affairs, so the bank's watchword was discretion. Imagine a bank with a 'keep out' sign over the door and you'll get the idea. There are only two branches - one in Gracechurch Street in the City of London and one in Brighton. You won't know where the branches are because they don't have name plaques on the buildings. They say unless you can smell the money, you'll never find your way there."

"That rules me out."

"Me, too," Susan said. "Richardson had run the bank on the same careful lines as his father and his father before him. They looked after the money and kept their names out of the headlines. A discreet mention in the *Financial Times* when the annual general meeting came round, but that was about it. But when Charles took over it was like a hustler had replaced a hermit."

"Too many big ideas?" I said.

"Too many crooked ideas," Susan said. "Not that anything was ever proved. Charles was as sharp as a shark's tooth. But he didn't realise that when you're swimming with sharks, you may get eaten."

"And did he?"

"Almost, if the rumour mill had it right. Remember that dodgy seafront casino project the crooked property developer Septimus Darke was behind?"

"That was three years ago," I said. I'd faced down Darke after a long investigation and he was still serving time in Lewes prison.

"Charles put up more than a million for the project. Lost the lot. It nearly brought the bank down. If it hadn't been for his wife's money, probably would have done."

"That would be Lady Evangelina," I said.

"You've heard of her?" Susan said.

"Apparently it's a courtesy title because her daddy was an earl. I heard he died a year ago."

"I wrote a story about his death," Susan said. "The Earl's title died out because there was no male heir and a woman couldn't inherit. But Evangelina picked up a pile of the folding stuff. As you know, wills are published and I made a point of looking up the sum - it was more than seven hundred thousand pounds. But the money is in a complex trust fund set up only for the Earl and Countess's natural daughter. The terms of the fund are tighter than a mouse's arsehole. They're designed to make sure that nobody outside the family gets their hands on a penny. Evangelina gets the income from it rather than the capital. I wrote a story, but Figgis spiked it. Said people didn't like reading stories about rich people scooping even more boodle. It just depressed them."

I said: "Figgis was wrong about that. It may stimulate jealousy, but that's a powerful emotion and emotions sell newspapers."

Susan nodded. "That's as maybe, but there was an interesting twist in the will. Charles and Evangelina have a nineteen-year-old daughter called Christabel - and she inherited the family mansion, Natterjack Grange."

"I know the place. It's that Victorian pile just north of Sompting village."

"But I bet you don't know this. Since Christabel moved in, she's turned the place into a commune. I've heard it's dropout heaven over there."

I raised an eyebrow at that. "What kind of dropouts?" I asked.

Susan shrugged. "Beatniks, hippies, whatever they call themselves these days."

"I thought beatniks had gone out with Jack Kerouac's beat generation ideas."

"Seems they're still around. But I think the hippies are taking over. At any rate, Christabel has moved a bunch of people into the old house and it's all peace and love. Mostly love, apparently. But that's all I know."

Susan picked up her mug and drained the last of her coffee.

She said: "I can't sit around here any longer unless you're going to propose marriage to me, honeybunch."

"It would be fun, but I don't deserve so much happiness," I said.

"Yeah! I heard Frank Figgis say exactly the same thing about you."

Susan stood up and headed for the door. She was still giggling as she went through it.

But I had a frown. What she'd told me about Charles Fox had made worrying thoughts scamper around in my mind like rats in a sack. Spencer Hooke would have known Fox through the bell-ringers' circle. Blackmailers can sniff out a crook like a vulture smells a rotting corpse. When you're looking for the culprit of a crime, a sound adage is to follow the money. And of all the people Hooke knew, Fox would be the richest. He'd be an ideal target. A rich man with dirty secrets. A blackmailer's perfect sap.

It all led me to a sombre conclusion. Could Fox be the killer who'd run Hooke down on the Bostal road?

He wouldn't do it himself. He'd be rich enough to pay a professional assassin.

It would take some looking into - and with a moneybags like Fox that wouldn't be easy. I'd need to penetrate a defensive circle of secretaries, personal assistants and accountants. Perhaps Fox even had a bodyguard.

I glanced at my watch. There was still half an hour before my line to Australia would come through.

I hurried back into the newsroom, sat down at my desk and looked up Fox's number in the telephone directory. I dialled the number.

The phone was answered by a woman. A voice like the crack of a whip said: "Lady Evangelina Fox speaking."

I turned on my friendly tone and said: "Good morning, Lady Evangelina. This is Colin Crampton, a gentleman of the press."

"I wasn't aware the press had any gentlemen."

"I work for the *Evening Chronicle*."

"Is that supposed to impress me?"

"It cheers me up most mornings. But the reason for my call is I need to speak to your husband, Mr Charles Fox."

"I know who my husband is," the good lady snapped.

I said: "I was just confirming that I know who your husband is."

"As you're calling to speak to him, I'd assumed that."
"Then could you put him on the line?"
"No."
"Why not?"
"He's not here."
"Do you know where I can reach him?"
"Not at present. But I suppose this evening he'll be with those dreadful bell-ringing people."
"But he's out of contact until then?"
"That's what I've just said. Anyway, why do you need to speak to him? I trust this isn't more muckraking about my husband's banking affairs."
"At the *Chronicle* we don't deal in muck. And if any unexpectedly comes our way we never rake it. I wanted to talk to your husband about Spencer Hooke, his bell-ringing companion who was killed in an accident on the Steyning Bostal road."
"I'd heard something about that. But I doubt whether Charles would be able to help you. He rings bells with the others, but doesn't socialise with them. Not our sort. Neither are journalists."

The line went dead.

I sat back for a moment and thought about that. Lady Evangelina sounded like she cared nothing for bell-ringers - or much for her husband.

I was pondering that when the phone rang again. The operator said she had a line to Australia and did I want to make a call?

I hurriedly reached for my copy of *Willings Press Guide* and turned to the Australian newspapers. The Adelaide paper with the largest circulation was called *The Advertiser*. It would be the paper most likely to have a crime reporter. I gave the operator the number.

When I was put through, it took a couple of minutes to persuade the newsroom secretary that I was a reporter calling from England. She finally agreed to connect me to a guy she called the "police and courts reporter".

A brisk voice said: "Bill Freeman."

"Colin Crampton. Crime reporter on the Brighton *Evening Chronicle* in merry old England."

"G'day Colin. So you're calling from the old country. Has there been a murder round the maypole?"

I gave a diplomatic laugh. "No. It's something else I'm calling about. A missing woman."

I waited for Bill to reply.

The line crackled and I thought I'd lost the connection.

Then Bill's voice, a lot less jokey, said: "What did you say?"

"I said I'm looking for a missing woman."

"In Brighton or in Adelaide?"

"In Adelaide."

"That's what I feared."

Something was wrong. I said: "Why do you fear that?"

"Because here in Adelaide, we've had two women go missing in the past three months. And both turned up murdered."

If blood could run cold, mine would have turned into an Alpine glacier.

I heard my voice quaver as I asked: "Do you have names for these women?"

"Engraved in my memory. I covered the stories. Delia Waters and Alice Kemp. Both middle-aged women in their forties and fifties."

I sighed with relief. Neither was Shirley's mum.

I said: "Have the cops caught their killer?"

"No. And the blue meanies believe he'll kill again. That's why my ears turned into radar dishes when you mentioned a missing woman. Who is she?"

"She's Mrs Barbara Goldsmith."

I explained about Shirley's mum. About the letters Shirley received every week. About the fact there hadn't been a letter for five weeks. And about the fact that Shirley hadn't been able to raise her mum on the telephone.

"I was wondering whether you could call at the house, perhaps talk to the neighbours, pick up any information."

Bill said: "If it's what I fear I'll be round there in an hour."

I gave Bill Barbara's address. He promised he'd check it out as a priority. But he warned that the time difference meant he might not be able to get back to me until tomorrow.

I replaced the receiver with a shaky hand. My heart thumped in my chest and I shivered.

I sat at my desk and stared blankly at my typewriter. I couldn't believe that Barbara Goldsmith had been murdered. There were plenty of other reasons why she could have gone missing. I tried to construct scenarios to explain why Shirley hadn't received the weekly letter from her mum.

But every time I came back to a murdered woman. The cold urgency of Bill's words kept repeating themselves in my head. "If it's what I fear, I'll be round there in an hour."

And another thought was pounding in my brain: what should I tell Shirley?

Chapter 11

Sometimes it can be kind to tell a lie.

Like when the mother of the bride has a giant boil on her nose and asks you whether she's ever looked better.

Like when your grandmother asks whether the black lump on your plate which looks like a cremated toad isn't the most delicious scone you've ever eaten.

Like when your girlfriend is ten thousand miles from her mother and wants to know why she hasn't been in touch.

An hour after I'd put down the phone to Bill Freeman I met Shirley for lunch at Marcello's.

I had a mushroom omelette. Shirley had a ham salad.

I had a secret. Shirley had a worried frown.

Shirley picked at her food while I explained how I'd contacted Bill Freeman on *The Advertiser*. I kept it as upbeat as I could without giving Shirley any false optimism. But I didn't mention the serial killer - or hint that was the reason why Barbara hadn't been in touch.

I felt bad about not telling Shirley about my fears. But perhaps they'd prove groundless and she would only worry needlessly.

Shirley speared a piece of tomato with her fork and said: "I guess we'll have to wait until Bill checks in tomorrow. He's an ace cobber doing this when there's nothing in it for him."

I swallowed a mouthful of omelette and said nothing.

"Cat got your tongue?" Shirley said.

"I just burnt my mouth on a hot mushroom," I lied.

"I'll sure be relieved when I hear from my Ma," Shirl said.

"Until then, try and find something to take your mind off it."

Shirley finished her salad and clunked her knife and fork back on the plate. "As it happens, there is something. I've had another work offer in the post this morning."

"That's great," I said.

For the past year, Shirl had been working as a photographer's model - mostly fashion shoots for small magazines. In recent weeks the work had become more regular.

"Is the money good?" I asked.

"Very good. Trouble is I can't decide whether this is the kind of work I want to do."

"What kind of work is that?"

"It's modelling for a clothes catalogue."

"You've done that before."

"Not this kind of catalogue. The catalogue is called Night-time Whispers."

"And I'm guessing whoever reads it won't be whispering their prayers."

"Yeah. Let me put it this way. The kind of gear they want me to model wouldn't keep you warm on a cold night."

Shirley rummaged in her handbag and fished out something about the same size as a thin paperback book.

She pushed it across the table.

I looked at the cover. It showed a statuesque blonde wearing a pair of black lace panties, peek-a-boo bra and a saucy smile.

I said: "I've just decided what I'm buying you for Christmas."

"Forget it, buster. And that's just the more respectable gear."

I flicked over a few pages. There were baby-doll nighties trimmed with feathers. There were basques sculpted like egg-timers. There were panties trimmed with faux mink. There were bras that could hoist watermelons. There were stockings with fishnets that could catch a salmon. There were lacy garters that would snap anyone to attention.

I put the catalogue down.

I said: "I can imagine you modelling this gear, but I'm not sure I'd want other people seeing you in it."

Shirley grinned: "You say the nicest things - sometimes."

"So what's the verdict?"

"I'll turn them down." She picked up the catalogue. "I'll bin this."

"Yes. Better not leave it for Marcello. He'll go blind if he reads this."

Shirley dumped the catalogue upside down on the table.

I glanced at the back cover. A headline read: Fifi Le Bonbon models our Naughty November collection.

The colour picture showed a young woman with auburn hair styled in curls. She was wearing a transparent pink nightie with black stockings and red suspenders. But it wasn't the bedroom gear that had me riveted. (Honest!) It was the face. The woman had rouged cheeks and carmine lips. She wore heavy blue eyeshadow and had long false lashes, like rare spiders. She had piercing green-blue eyes which looked direct at the camera as if daring the lens not to fall in love with her.

I thought of Andrew Marvell's poem To His Coy Mistress. But there was no false modesty about this girl. Old Marvell would certainly have allowed one hundred years to praise her eyes and two hundred to adore each breast. And there was no need for this madam's coyness to turn to dust. It had the moment she'd put on the gear.

Because I'd met her just the day before.

When she wasn't parading in her underwear, Fifi Le Bonbon was better known as Georgina Staples, proprietor of the Steyning tuck shop.

As I powered the MGB towards Steyning, I couldn't get the picture of Georgina in her pink nightie and black stockings out of my mind.

But not for the reason you're thinking.

If Spencer Hooke had seen the picture as well, he'd find a way to turn it to blackmail. He'd put the screw on Georgina. And he wouldn't be satisfied with a bag of toffees or a few gobstoppers. Hooke would have wanted hard cash.

The tuck shop relied on sales to boys from the school. If the headmaster heard about Georgina's saucy side-line, there's no saying what he might do. But, most likely, he'd ban boys from using the shop. Georgina would watch her little business melt away like an ice-cream sundae on a hot day. She'd have a strong motive to keep her modelling secret. But would she resort to murder?

I slowed the car as I drove through the narrow street in the mediaeval village of Bramber. Hunched timber-framed cottages with leaded windows crowded alongside the road. I glanced at the ruined castle which loomed over the place. It seemed like an emblem of what the Hooke murder story was all about - ruin.

Reputations in tatters.

The Night-time Whispers catalogue lay on the passenger seat beside me. I'd persuaded Shirley to lend it. After I'd confronted Georgina with it, there was no telling what she might do.

But I was determined to find out.

I parked the MGB a few yards down the street from the tuck shop. I stuffed the catalogue in my jacket pocket and climbed out.

It was early afternoon, a brisk day with fluffy white clouds scudding across a blue sky. Further down the street, I could see a couple of elderly ladies strolling arm-in-arm towards the church. They didn't look the Night-time Whispers type.

I walked towards the tuck shop wondering how I should handle the interview. If Georgina wanted to pose in her undies for a catalogue, that was her affair. It wasn't a crime. If I questioned her about it, she'd be entitled to tell me to mind my own business and show me the door.

But when I reached the shop's door, a sign in the window read: "Closed". There was a blind pulled down behind the door.

I rapped on the door.

Not like a schoolboy wanting some sherbet lemons.

More like a cop with a search warrant.

The blind was pulled aside and Georgina peered out. Those crystal-clear eyes widened in surprise and her jaw dropped just enough to let me see the pearly white teeth. She looked like a Parisian gamine who'd just flicked a teasing wink at a boulevardier outside the *Moulin Rouge*. If I'd had a camera, I'd have adjusted the focus and clicked the shutter. And to hell with the bustiers and the suspender belts and that wispy thing on page forty-one which might have been a tiny pair of knickers or a pair of shoelaces.

The blind fell back and I heard a chain rattle as it was released from its hook.

She opened the door and said: "We don't open until four o'clock when school's out."

I said: "I've got a free period so I came earlier."

A tiny frown wrinkle appeared on Georgina's forehead. She said: "Then you'll have to come back later. I don't do anything when the shop is closed."

"That's not what I'd heard."

"What do you mean by that?" Georgina snapped.

"Can I come inside?"

"What for? If this is an attempt to make a pass at me, I can assure you I'm well practised in seeing them off."

"Off being the operative word."

"Now you're talking in riddles."

"I've got something to show you."

"Then show it to me here."

"This is not the kind of thing you flash around in the street."

"Why not?"

"It's a clothing catalogue."

"Mrs Emerson from Shooting Field comes round with the Littlewoods' catalogue but I've got everything I want to wear."

"Including underwear, I bet."

"Now you're being impertinent."

She tried to shut the door. But I was too quick for her. I shoved my shoe in the gap between the door and the jamb. Just like a rent collector avoiding the brush-off.

Ouch!

That hurt. Georgina may be gamine but she knew how to slam a door with force.

She said: "Take your foot out of the door or I'll break it with the next shove."

I said: "Before you do, take a look at this." I yanked the Nighttime Whispers catalogue out and pushed it through the narrow gap left by the part-open door.

"Even though it's daytime, I thought we could have a whisper about it, Georgina. Or should that be Fifi Le Bonbon?" I added.

The door opened and Georgina glared at me. Those crystal-clear eyes had turned to ice.

She said: "Come in and close the door behind you."

I obeyed. It's the gracious thing to do when you've won a small advantage but want to press home your point.

Georgina flipped the door-chain back on the hook. She turned and marched through the shop. She pulled aside the curtain over the door behind the counter and stepped into a small parlour.

I followed her.

She turned and faced me with arms akimbo. Not so gamine now. More like a female wrestler (lightweight) ready for a rumble.

She said: "Are you some kind of pervert?"

I said: "No, I'm some kind of journalist."

"Where did you get that catalogue?"

"In the normal course of research for a story." I wasn't planning to bring Shirley's name into what was shaping up as a fraught encounter.

"What do you want?"

I said: "In an interview, I normally ask the questions. And, at the moment, I have only one. Were you being blackmailed by Spencer Hooke?"

For a brief second those confident eyes flared. Then the light died in them. The crystal clouded. The gamine crumbled. And Georgina slumped down in a chair. Her delicate fingers trembled. Her lips quivered.

I sat on a chair opposite and waited for her to regain her composure.

She looked up at me. No hatred in her eyes. Just resignation. She said: "How did you know?"

I said: "Let's just say I've been looking into the affairs of the late Spencer Hooke. He was a young lad with a less than healthy eye on the main chance. When did the blackmailing start?"

"It was last year, just before Christmas."

"I suppose he'd got his sticky hands on a copy of the catalogue?"

"No. It was a magazine."

"A girlie magazine?"

Georgina nodded. "I'd been doing some… well, I think it's known as glamour modelling. I bought this shop with a mortgage. I thought it would be a lovely life dispensing sweets to children. But I soon realised that children aren't big spenders. When they've spent their pocket money it's gone - and so you have no more takings until they get more. I simply needed to make more money to pay my bills here."

"But why girlie magazines and sleazy catalogues?"

"For the money, of course. A couple of years ago, I'd visited London to see an old friend. After she'd left, I went to a café in Soho - a place called *Le Macabre*. The tables are all black and in the shape of coffins."

"Sounds like a bit of a dead-end place."

Georgina ignored that and said: "The café was full and a couple sat down at my table. We got talking and I discovered he was a photographer and she was a model. He asked me whether I'd ever done any modelling before, said I'd look great through his viewfinder. Gave me all the chat. Well, one thing led to another. As his girlfriend was modelling, it seemed like it was something to do. And when I heard the money I could make - well, I swallowed my pride."

"And your modesty?" I added.

Georgina's eyes flashed angrily. "Yes, my modesty," she said. "And then that loathsome Hooke found one of those magazines. He told me that unless I paid him ten pounds a week, he'd arrange for it to be left lying on the table outside the headmaster's study."

"No doubt, alongside his copy of the *Times Educational Supplement.*"

"I had no choice. I had to pay the money. It's almost broken me."

Georgina's head drooped. She reached for a hankie and patted her eyes.

"You must have hated it when Hooke joined the bell-ringers," I said.

Georgina gave a thin smile. "I loathed his presence. But what could I do? I couldn't say he shouldn't join or the others would want to know why I felt that way. Instead, I had to pretend I supported having him. I hated going to meetings when he was there, but I wasn't going to give in."

"What did the other ringers think about Hooke?"

"I think most of them tolerated him. Owen Griffiths seemed keen he should join. But at first Clothilde - that's Miss Tench-Hardie - seemed to take to Spencer. I hated her for it. I believe she had him round to her cottage for tea sometimes. But she lives by herself and I think she's a bit lonely. She bores everyone with her local history research so most people try to avoid her. But Spencer didn't seem to mind."

I said: "Do you have a car?"

Georgina nodded.

"Did you drive over the Steyning Bostal two nights ago?"

Georgina shook her head. "I haven't driven my Ford Anglia

for several days now. The price of petrol these days…"

"Where do you keep your car?"

"In the lane at the back of the cottages. It's quite safe. No-one ever goes there."

"Where were you two nights ago?"

"Here. I had an evening in. Most nights I have in."

"Alone?"

"With a friend."

"Who was that?"

Georgina gave me another sharp look. "That's none of your business."

"A gentleman friend?"

"I won't say."

I nodded. "It may not be important."

"I suppose you're going to write about all of this. I hope you'll be proud of yourself."

"No. As far as I'm concerned you're entitled to pose wearing what you like - as long as it's legal. That won't make copy in my paper - unless I discover you've lied to me."

Georgina let out a deep sigh. Some of the sparkle returned to her eyes. "Is that a promise?"

"One that I will keep," I said.

***

And when I left the tuck shop a few minutes later I fully intended to do so.

I walked round to the lane where Georgina had said she kept her Ford Anglia. I found the car parked against a stone flint wall. It had a grey-green paint job that made it fade into the background and the first signs of rust around the front door trim.

I took a close look at the car. The front licence plate was bent inwards at a sharp angle.

I leant on the wall and thought about it. The damage could've been caused by hitting Hooke. But there'd be no way to prove it. And if it had been, Georgina would already have a lie ready to explain it.

I trudged back to my MGB feeling that I'd not learnt a lot more.

And I'd left the Night-time Whispers catalogue in Georgina's parlour.

Chapter 12

I unlocked the MGB and opened the door.

But I didn't climb in. I stood there thinking about what Georgina had said about Clothilde Tench-Hardie.

Hooke was stinging Georgie for a tenner a week. So it was no shock to find she hated anyone who treated the lad like a buddy. The question running round my mind, like a bunny in a burrow, was why the extravagantly named Tench-Hardie lavished praise on the young scammer.

If she'd taken the boy under her wing, she can't have known about his extra-curricular blackmail. Perhaps she was a maiden lady with a thing about young men who had the oily charm of a lounge lizard. But wait a minute. Perhaps Hooke had a line on Clothilde as well. Perhaps the protective mothering stuff was her defence mechanism. Whatever the truth, it was time I found out.

And no trouble either. Tench-Hardie's cottage was just a couple of hundred yards from where I'd parked the MGB.

The cottage turned out to be a whistle and toot from the railway station. The place wasn't the kind of roses-round-the-door idyll you see on the front of chocolate boxes. It was more like the kind of workmen's cottages that were put up in Victorian times to house farm hands and their families. Not so much "the rich man in his castle", more "the poor man at his gate". Except that there wasn't a gate, just a short path up to the front door.

The path was fringed with red and yellow tulips. There were a few of those variegated ones which start off purple and develop white tips on the ends of the petals.

I'd paused to admire the display when a woman marched around the corner of the cottage. She stopped when she saw me. She stood with arms akimbo and her hands on her hips. She was in her early sixties. She had deep-set eyes and a broad nose.

Her lined face had deep creases which plunged like ravines on either side of her mouth. Her dark hair was streaked with silver. But it curled luxuriantly around her face and fell to her shoulders. A deep fringe hung over her forehead, like a theatre curtain about to fall.

She was wearing a tweed hacking jacket, brown corduroy trousers and gardening gloves.

She had a pince-nez hanging from a lanyard around her neck.

She took off her gloves and said: "If you're the swine who raided my garden for a dozen tulips last night, you can hand over one shilling and sixpence. That's what you'd have paid at the florists."

I said: "For that money, I'd expect them to be wrapped in cellophane paper and come with a gift card."

Clothilde raised the pince-nez and perched it on her nose.

"Ah! I see you're not the blackguard I suspect of the dastardly crime," she said. "Sorry about that. What is it you've come about? If it's about second-hand clothes for the church jumble sale, I'm wearing them."

I reached in my pocket and pulled out a card. I handed it to her.

I said: "Colin Crampton, *Evening Chronicle*, at your service."

She took the card, looked at it, and wrinkled her nose.

She said: "You're here about that poor Spencer Hooke. I wondered how long it would be before the newshounds were on my trail. I suppose if I don't invite you in, give you a cup of tea and as much fruit cake as you can eat, you'll write horrid lies about me."

"I'm already making notes." I flashed her one of my most winning smiles.

She pulled an unimpressed face and tramped towards the door.

"Follow me and don't forget to wipe your feet on the mat," she said.

Clothilde led the way through a narrow passage into one of those comfortable kitchens you feel you could live in.

The warm aroma of fresh baking hung in the air.

I had a good look round. There was a fat Aga cooker, glowing warm, with a kettle simmering on one of the hobs. There was a Welsh dresser along one wall with a fine display of willow-pattern crocks - plates and bowls and cups all in neat rows. The centrepiece was a huge soup tureen as fat and round as Buddha's belly.

There was a large deal table in the middle of the room loaded with a jumble of stuff. There were jars of pickled onions, pots of fig jam, stained recipe books, packets of seeds, a bottle of prescription pills from a local pharmacy. There were dog-eared cookery magazines, a heap of soup ladles and serving spoons, a dish of custard, a biscuit tin.

Half-a-dozen odd chairs were arranged around the table. Clothilde waved me to one of them.

I sat on the chair and studied the stuff on the table while Clothilde spooned Darjeeling into a brown teapot. She poured on the boiling water. She set out cups and saucers, fetched milk from a pantry, and poured some into a jug. She returned to the pantry and brought out a rich fruit cake, its crown encrusted with glazed nuts.

I let her pour the tea before I asked: "When did you hear about Spencer Hooke's death?"

She paused cutting a monster slice of the cake and gave me a hard look.

"It was the morning after the accident," she said. "The Reverend Purslowe called on me. He was very upset by the news. He wanted to cancel the bell ringing for the Mother's Day service. But I told him the congregation would be disappointed."

Clothilde handed me a plate with a huge wedge of the cake. "Will that ensure me good coverage?" she said.

"For at least the first couple of paragraphs," I said. "How did you come to know Spencer Hooke?"

Clothilde spooned sugar into her tea. She frowned while she thought about how to answer my question.

"It was when Owen Griffiths introduced him to the bell-ringing circle," she said finally. "On the second, no third, meeting I happened to mention to Spencer that my main hobby was local history. He said he was interested in that even though his main school subject was chemistry. I told him how my own interest had been kindled by the story of St Cuthman."

I'd once heard the name mentioned by Sidney Pinker, the *Chronicle's* theatre critic. Apparently, Cuthman was one of those holy blokes in Anglo-Saxon times - way back in the eighth century. But, then, if you believe the Venerable Bede, they were all at it in those days, converting heathens and illuminating manuscripts. Cuthman's gimmick was pushing his sick mother around in a wheelbarrow. He got canonised for it. She got a bruised bum. Cuthman had built the first church in Steyning. Pinker was interested because Christopher Fry had once written a stage play about Cuthman called *The Boy with a Cart*. Fry had even got Richard Burton to star in it and John Gielgud to direct. According to Pinker, it wasn't a show with many laughs.

I said: "Seems a strange story to interest a teenage lad in the Swinging Sixties."

Clothilde said: "I think it was Cuthman's devotion to his mother that moved Spencer."

"I'd heard Spencer's mother was dead."

"Yes. But I think he revered her memory. He'd had a difficult upbringing in boarding schools with no normal home life."

I wondered whether Hooke's orphan boy act was genuine or a ploy to engage Clothilde's sympathy.

I asked: "Did Spencer ever speak about his family?"

"No. But he did say that when you don't have a family of your own, you become more intrigued by other people's. I think that's what sparked his enthusiasm for my local history research."

"So it was just a general interest?"

"Not entirely. He also asked me whether I was working on any project at the moment. I told him I was researching some of the early tradesmen's families in the village. As he seemed interested, I invited him round one day after school. I showed him some of the family trees of local people I'd compiled over the years."

I took a bite of the cake and considered that. The young blackmailer must have thought he'd landed in easy street. Files which would no doubt include the by-blows of some villagers and it was being handed to him on a plate - no doubt alongside a slice of the monster cake.

I said: "Did you see much of Spencer?"

Clothilde frowned again. "He came almost every week. He asked some very searching questions about how the family trees were compiled. I told him about Somerset House, which keeps records of births, marriages and deaths. But I also mentioned that some of the most revealing files of family papers were held in the County Records Office in Chichester. He said he'd like to go there himself one day. I offered to take him on one of my own trips. I drive there about once a month in my old Morris Minor. But Spencer thanked me and said he suffered from car sickness."

Yes, I thought. The lad ended up car sick in a way he hadn't bargained for. But I didn't say that.

Instead I asked: "Did he ever say he'd made a visit to the Records Office?"

Clothilde took a sip of her tea. She put the cup back in the saucer with exaggerated care. As though she was deciding how to answer the question.

"A few weeks ago, he told me he'd made a couple of visits during the half-term holiday," she said.

"Did he say what he'd been researching there?"

"I think he was just fascinated in looking through personal papers in the archives of our great county families," Clothilde said brusquely.

I bet he was, I thought. No doubt looking for some indiscretion he could turn into a regular few quid each week.

I sipped my tea while I considered where all this was leading. Was Clothilde just helping the lad out, like an honorary aunt, or was there more behind it all?

I still wasn't convinced Hooke hadn't had the black on Clothilde. But I couldn't ask outright whether she'd made payoffs.

So I said: "When I was speaking to some other boys from the school, they told me it was often tough for them to get by on the amount of pocket money they're allowed each week. Did Spencer ever ask to borrow money from you?"

Crampton, the crafty questioner.

I caught a flash of suspicion in Clothilde's eyes. But it may have been the way the sun's rays through the window caught her face.

"What a strange question," she said.

"It's a strange crime," I said.

Clothilde arched an eyebrow. "Strange crime?"

"Hit-and-run," I said. "Strange and despicable."

Clothilde looked down at her teacup. Moved the spoon from one side of the saucer to the other. "I suppose you're right," she said softly.

"Will you be able to ring the bells on Mother's Day now that you're a ringer short?"

"Mr Burton from the butcher's is always willing to stand in when someone is away. In fact, we're having a practice this evening at seven o'clock."

"Spencer is away permanently," I said.

Clothilde nodded. "Yes, he is."

I took a last bite of the cake. If I ate any more of it, I was going to end up with a stomach like the soup tureen on the Welsh dresser.

I said: "Thanks for answering my questions. You've helped me understand a little more about Spencer Hooke."

I stood up and moved towards the door.

Clothilde shot a disapproving glance at my plate. "Aren't you going to finish your cake?"

"Sorry. It was delicious but you were too generous by far."

For the first time, Clothilde smiled. It was a wide hungry grin like when a wolf closes in on a lamb.

"Too generous? That's exactly what Spencer told me a couple of days before he died," she said.

But generosity for what, I wondered. Helping out a lad with no parents? Handing out giant-sized slices of cake?

Or paying up like a patsy to keep a dreadful scandal secret?

Clothilde waved me off as though I were heading on a round-the-world voyage.

I returned the waves as I ambled down the road towards the railway station. I kept on walking away from the house after she'd shut the front door. I had a feeling that she'd be twitching the net curtains to spy on me.

Clothilde had mentioned she'd offered to drive Hooke to Chichester in her old Morris Minor. I'd spotted a car parked across the road from her cottage when I'd stepped outside. But I didn't want to show too much interest in it if she was peering at me from behind the window drapes.

After I'd vanished for a few minutes, she'd conclude I'd left the street. She'd leave the window and head back to her kitchen. Probably to bake another monster fruit cake. I'd sneak back to the Morris Minor and take a quick peek to see if it had any damage consistent with a hit-and-run. It seemed unlikely as Clothilde had left it parked on the street. But Clothilde struck me as a wily old bird who didn't always take the expected course of action.

To kill a few minutes, I strode into the railway station and sat in the waiting room to think about what to do next.

I was mulling over some advice a barrister once gave me. He'd just sprung an old lag with a string of previous convictions from the dock.

"Always visit the *locus in quo*," the barrister told me when I asked him how he'd pulled off the acquittal.

The lag had been accused of climbing through the lavatory window of a house in Ovingdean and stealing the owner's jewellery box. His lawyer had told the jury he couldn't have done it, because he was more than six feet tall and weighed twenty-two stone. The window was only eighteen inches wide.

If my barrister friend hadn't visited the *locus in quo*, the place in question - where it happened - he wouldn't have realised his client couldn't possibly have climbed through the window.

I decided it was time I visited the *locus in quo* - the place on the Bostal Road where Spencer Hooke had died.

But first I had to check out Clothilde's Morris. There was no sign of twitching curtains in her cottage when I walked back up the street. The car was one of the older Morris Minors, the kind that were around in the nineteen-fifties. It was shabby but there were no dents or bumps consistent with a hit-and-run.

I strolled around the car taking a close look. The old jalopy needed some vigorous action with a wet chamois leather. The wheel arches were encrusted with dark yellow sandy mud. But I was convinced the car hadn't been used to run Hooke down.

I walked back to my MGB, climbed in, and headed for the Bostal.

The sun was shining but a brisk wind was blowing in from the west by the time I pulled the MGB into the verge on the Bostal road.

I'd taken care to park a few yards away from the place where Shirley and I had originally found Hooke's bike. Not that I needed to bother. There was no police tape around the scene - another sign of Holdsworth's sloppy investigation.

I climbed out of the car and shivered. The wind was cold up here. I buttoned my jacket and thrust my hands into my pockets.

It had been raining hard on the night of the accident. But the sun and the wind had dried out the mud in the grass verge. There was a churned-up area where the bike had crashed. But it had been trampled by the clod-hopping footprints of the cops.

But about ten yards further back, there was a depression from car tyres. The car had evidently driven off the road. The tyre track extended towards the trampled area and disappeared into it.

I walked in the opposite direction, past the churned up stuff. And there it was again. The tyre track extended for about three yards as the car must have swerved back onto the road.

I stood there feeling cold and thinking about that. Surely, even Holdsworth would have seen the tracks and deduced they came from the car that hit Hooke. Perhaps he'd taken a plaster cast impression of them - but I wasn't placing a big bet on that.

I walked back along the road in the direction the car would have come from. There was a copse of trees about a hundred yards away. It would provide some shelter from the wind while I considered what to do next. By the side of the copse there was a muddy lay-by which led into a field. The lay-by would have been hidden from the road to anything coming from Steyning - as Hooke did on the fateful night.

Like the grass verge, the lay-by would have been slick with mud on the night of the killing. And there were tyre marks of a car in the dried mud. I trotted back along the road verge and took a closer look at the tracks there. They had a distinctive zigzag marking. Then I hurried back to the lay-by, knelt down and looked closely at the tracks. The same zigzag pattern. I was as certain as I could be that both sets of tracks came from the same car.

I stood up and looked at the shape of the tracks in the lay-by. One set swept back in a curve, while a second set headed straight out into the road. It was as though the car had reversed into the narrow lay-by and then accelerated out of it.

I had a good think about that. If the killer - or killers - knew Hooke planned to cycle across the Bostal, they'd want to lie in wait for him. They'd want to choose a spot where the car wouldn't be seen. So as Hooke cycled towards it, he would never have known that death lurked behind the trees. Perhaps that was just as well.

If my reasoning was right, Holdsworth should open a murder case. A random hit-and-run driver wouldn't have parked just yards from the accident spot. Generally, they were tearaways who drove too fast.

I was about to walk back to my car, when I noticed another mark. About a foot outside the tyre tracks on the driver's side of the car, there was a series of small holes in the ground. They advanced in two lines, rather as though a large bird with stumps for feet had been walking. Right foot, left foot, right foot - and so on. I followed the line of holes alongside the tyre tracks towards where the back of the car would have been. The holes looped around where the tyre tracks ended. Then they came up on the other side of them - what would have been the passenger side as the car was parked. They ended as abruptly as they'd started.

I couldn't make anything of it. I stood there as the cold wind chilled me and tried to think of an explanation. But I couldn't come up with anything that made sense.

I still couldn't think of a reason for the holes as I drove back to Brighton.

Chapter 13

An hour later I was back in the newsroom at the *Chronicle*.

I sat at my desk and leafed through messages which had come in while I'd been out. There was the usual nonsense - improbable leads from contacts eager to earn some tip-off cash. Nothing that matched the headline potential of the Hooke killing. Nothing to touch the drama of a drugs ring bust.

There was no news from Bill Freeman in Adelaide about Shirley's mum. But perhaps he hadn't had managed to find her yet. Or perhaps he had and couldn't bring himself to tell me the dreadful truth about what he'd discovered.

My telephone rang. I lifted the receiver.

Frank Figgis said: "Come in here for a minute."

I asked: "Will the sixty seconds run from the moment I knock on your door or the time I enter the room?"

He said: "If you don't watch out, it'll run from the moment I boot your bum out of the building."

"In that case, perhaps I should meet you downstairs in the lobby. Not so far for me to fall when I hit the pavement."

The line went dead.

I strolled round to Figgis's office, knocked once and entered.

Figgis was emptying his ashtray into his wastepaper basket. A small cloud of dust billowed above the rim of the basket, like a minor volcano erupting.

I said: "Are you sure all those fag-ends were out?"

Figgis slammed the ashtray back on his desk. "Of course they were," he snapped. "Anyway, you're the one playing with fire."

I gave Figgis my innocent-eyed look and said: "I can't think what you're talking about."

"This hit-and-run incident which you claim is a murder. The cops say they haven't got a shred of evidence to back that up."

"That's because they haven't looked. Besides, if I'm playing with fire, it's because you handed me the matches. You gave me two days to look into the case. The second day hasn't ended yet."

"And what have you got to show for it?"

I told Figgis about Georgina Staples aka Fifi Le Bonbon. But I had no evidence to challenge Georgina's denial that she'd killed Hooke in revenge for blackmail.

I told him about my meeting with Clothilde Tench-Hardie, the dotty old dear who'd shown kindness to Spencer Hooke. And who may have been repaid with blackmail. Again, no proof.

I told him about the tyre tracks I'd seen on the Bostal road. I described the curious line of holes around the tyre marks in the lay-by.

He said: "You've got no evidence for a murder, only a theory based on a bunch of facts which are open to different interpretations."

"So how do you explain the car tracks in the lay-by? Who parks up in a lonely spot on a filthy night?"

"A courting couple. For them, it wasn't only a filthy night outside the car."

"And what about the holes around the tyre tracks?"

"Made by a walking stick I'd say. Perhaps one of them got out of the car during their love making."

"In the pouring rain?"

"It was obviously steamed up in the car."

"So, in a fit of passion, one of the lovers jumped out and went for a stroll, leaning so heavily on the walking stick it made lasting impressions in the mud. That's the most improbable theory I've ever heard."

"That's what the cops say about your murder idea."

I shrugged. I had to admit it to myself - I wasn't going to make the Hooke murder story stand up.

But I did have a potential story on a drug smuggling ring. Owen Griffiths had to be testing drugs when I spied on him in the school chemistry lab.

I told Figgis what I knew about Griffiths and the mystery man who'd driven away in the van.

Figgis lit up a Woodbine and asked: "Have you tackled Griffiths about what he was doing in the lab?"

"No. He'd cook up some plausible excuse and he'd know I was on to him. He'd be extra careful in the future. I need more evidence before I question him again. Like finding the driver of the mystery van."

Figgis glanced at his watch. "Your sixty seconds seem to have been up some time ago," he said.

"According to Albert Einstein, time is a relative concept anyway."

Figgis sucked on his fag and blew out a long stream of smoke.

"What's not relative is that the deadline for you producing a story expires at midnight tonight. In just over seven hours. You'll never do it in time. I said you were playing with fire."

I stood up and headed for the door.

"And I'm not the only one," I said as I opened the door. "I said you shouldn't have tossed those dog-ends in your waste basket. It's burning."

I stepped smartly outside and closed the door behind me.

When I got back to my desk, I found Cedric had left a copy of the night final edition draped over my typewriter.

I glanced at the front page. The paper led with a story about a row in Brighton Council. That may have fascinated the people who worked there, but it would bore most readers. What they wanted was human interest - like a good murder story.

But, if Figgis was right, I didn't have one.

With the night final on the streets, the newsroom was winding down for the day.

Most reporters had already quit their desks. Sally Martin finished a telephone call and put down the receiver. Phil Bailey collected up an untidy pile of papers and shoved them in a drawer. Susan Wheatcroft tucked her chair under the desk and slung a shawl around her shoulders.

She sidled up to me: "Hiya, honeybunch. Would you let a big girl show you a good time?" she said in voice loaded with laughter.

I grinned. "What had you in mind?"

"Well, we'd start by taking our clothes off and then hold a vote on the next move." Her two chins wobbled as she chuckled.

"By proportional representation, I hope."

"If you've got the representation, I've got the proportions, honeybunch."

"At least that doesn't need a recount," I said. "But, on second thoughts, I think I'd better spend the evening at church."

Susan pulled a disappointed face at that. "Well, if your knees get sore from too much kneeling, you just let Susan kiss them better."

She pushed through the newsroom doors and I could hear her laughing as she clattered down the stairs.

But I hadn't been joking about the church.

With so little time left, I'd decided the best chance of making my story stand up was to visit St Andrew's. Clothilde Tench-Hardie had told me the bell-ringers were holding a practice this evening.

It would be the first time they'd met without Spencer Hooke. I wanted to see their reactions.

It was twilight by the time I drove into Steyning.

I'd used the journey from Brighton to think of the best way to approach the evening. The bell-ringers were arriving to practice for the Mother's Day service. They wouldn't want a journalist hanging around.

They'd know I was on the prowl for scandal, so I'd be as welcome in the church as Old Nick himself. Besides hanging around in the nave - a knave in the nave, I thought - wouldn't get me anywhere. The bell-ringers would be in the bell tower. No admittance to non-ringers. Especially crime reporters.

So my only option was to fall back on the old reporters' trick of door-stepping. But that wasn't going to be easy. When I'd looked around the church in the afternoon, I'd noticed at least two doors in. I had no idea which one the bell-ringers used.

In the end, I parked my car about fifty yards down the street from the church so it wasn't too obvious. And waited.

Clothilde had told me the practice began at seven o'clock. I glanced at my watch. Twenty to seven. I guessed they'd turn up a bit before. Did bell-ringers wear special kit like Morris dancers? I had no idea.

I sat in the car and gazed at the church. Its grey flint walls and brown tiled roof stood as a stark outline against the darkening sky behind. The Normans had knocked up the place after they'd invaded the country in 1066. Good of them, as if we couldn't have built our own churches. Still, they'd made a solid job of it. It was still standing nine hundred years later. Mind you, they'd had to add a couple of buttresses on the outside of the bell tower to stop it falling down.

I was thinking about this when I spied Georgina Staples hurrying down the street. She was wearing a three-quarter length coat over a brown pleated skirt with a hem just below the knee. This was not the time to speculate whether there was exotic underwear beneath the modest outfit. For all I knew, she had a pair of bottle-green bloomers especially for bell ringing.

The wind had blown her hair over her face and she brushed it back as she stepped inside the church porch.

We'd said our piece to one another earlier in the afternoon, so I kept my head down in the car. I didn't want to attract her attention.

A couple of minutes later Owen Griffiths appeared, walking eastwards along the street. He raised his hand to wave and, for a moment, I thought he'd spotted me in the car. But I glanced over my shoulder through the back window. Clothilde Tench-Hardie, dressed in a tweed jacket and skirt, was striding along from the opposite direction. I slunk down in my seat as I didn't want to speak to either of them just yet.

The pair met at the church gate. Griffiths gallantly kissed Clothilde on both cheeks. Clothilde took Griffiths's arm and the pair walked up the path and into the church. Griffiths said something. Clothilde nodded and laughed. Perhaps Griffiths had told a joke. Or perhaps he was offering her drugs at a knock-down price. It seemed unlikely but I was getting to the point where I thought anything could be true.

I was musing on this when there was movement at the end of the road. A large grey Bentley moved silently up the street like it owned the place. There'd only be one bell-ringer with a Bentley. Charles Fox. The merchant banker with the ethics of a back-street bookie, Susan had told me.

The car nosed into the side of the road outside the church and pulled up. The driver's door opened and a tall man stepped into the street. He stood by the Bentley and looked about as though he was expecting a round of applause. He had deep-set eyes, a beaky nose and thin lips. His dark brown hair was swept back from his forehead, cut around his ears, and fell to his collar in an upturned curl. The sort of haircut which looked like he'd done it himself but probably cost ten pounds in Trumper's of Mayfair.

He was dressed in an open-necked shirt with blue stripes fastened with gold cufflinks. He wore a pair of pillar-box red moleskin trousers. A tweed jacket completed the ensemble. He could have modelled for one of those fancy fashion catalogues you see with clothes you can never afford. And wouldn't buy even if you could. He had a thick cigar - a real Winston Churchill job - wedged between his lips.

Fox reached into the Bentley and collected a case with a long strap. It was a kind of satchel. He looped the strap over his shoulder, locked the Bentley, and headed for the churchyard lychgate. I climbed out of the MGB and scooted up the road after him.

He was halfway up the path to the church door by the time I raced through the lychgate. The satchel bounced on his back as he strode along.

I puffed up behind him and called: "Mr Fox."

He glanced over his shoulder and snapped: "I'm not giving another penny to your charity whatever it is."

I said: "It's good news. I've left my collecting box for the Home for Broken-down Journalists at home."

Fox turned and faced me. "Just as well. I wouldn't even give that one the time of day. All journalists are liars."

"And all bankers are crooks."

Fox's pale cheeks reddened and his eyes turned as hard as chips of granite. "I hope you're not implying…"

"Merely demonstrating the dangers of generalisation. By the way, I'm Colin Crampton from the *Evening Chronicle*. And seeker after truth."

Fox harrumphed. "Yes, well perhaps I spoke a little hastily."

"As it happens, I'd like to ask you a couple of questions about Spencer Hooke."

"Hardly knew the fellow."

"But you met him at the church?"

"That doesn't make me his bosom pal. He was a schoolboy, damn it. We rang bells together. We didn't play conkers."

"What did you make of him?"

"Bright lad, clever, perhaps too clever. But mustn't speak ill of the dead."

"Did you ever meet him away from bell-ringing?"

"What would I have in common with a schoolboy? Now if you'll excuse me, I'm late."

Fox turned away and stalked into the church.

I shuffled back down the path, scuffed at the gravel, and

The Mother's Day Mystery

wondered whether I'd learnt anything from that encounter.

I glanced around. I'd seen no sign of Tom Hobson, the fisherman bell-ringer, or Mr Burton the butcher stand-in Clothilde had mentioned.

But then the church clock struck seven. And within seconds, the bells sounded as the ringers moved into their first peal. So Hobson and Burton must be in the bell tower. Perhaps they'd come in through another door. Or perhaps they'd already been in the church before I arrived.

I walked back to the MGB wondering what to do next. I decided I'd wait until the bell-ringers left and see if I could waylay Hobson then.

Ho-hum. It was a tedious wait. I sat in the car as the twilight turned to night and the grey mass of the church became black.

I made a mental note never to live in a house close to a church with a bell tower. After an hour, I felt the bells were ringing inside my head.

At then, suddenly, in a descending peal they fell silent. There was a light in the lychgate at the entrance to the churchyard. I'd be able to see whether Hobson was among the leavers. Fox was first, striding down the path, swinging his arms like he'd just lifted a steamroller. He headed for his Bentley. Then a burly figure I didn't recognise wheeled a butcher's bike out of the church porch and cycled away. Mr Burton heading back to his lamb chops. He was followed by Owen Griffiths, Georgina Staples and Clothilde Tench-Hardie in a group. They strolled to the gate and paused to exchange a few words. Clothilde bustled off to the left. Griffiths and Georgina strolled the other way, arm-in-arm.

The street was deserted. There was no sign of Hobson. He must have come out of another door and disappeared into the night. I decided that I'd have to track him down at Shoreham Harbour if I wanted to speak to him. But I doubted whether it would yield any useful information.

Damn Figgis and his arbitrary deadlines. I was going to miss a scoop because Figgis wouldn't give me enough time.

One thing was for certain. My visit to Steyning had been a waste of time. I'd picked up no new information on Hooke's killing. Tomorrow I'd have to admit as much to Figgis. I only hoped he wouldn't make me eat a slice of humble pie as large as Clothilde's fruit cake.

I started to wind up the car window, when I heard another vehicle's ignition fire. The sound came from a road off to the right about a hundred yards ahead of me. The vehicle's engine failed to catch at first firing, then backfired twice.

Just like the van I'd seen on the night Griffiths had given an envelope to the driver.

I wound the window open again. The vehicle ignition sparked again with the same double backfire as the van. The engine caught and turned over with a rough throaty roar. And then the vehicle appeared. It paused under a street lamp while the driver checked the junction for other traffic.

It *was* the same van I'd seen the previous night.

It had the same rust under the door, the same blotchy marks on the paintwork, the same dent in the rear wheel arch.

And I was willing to bet the driver was salty fisherman Tom Hobson.

Suddenly, I wasn't feeling so tired. I felt good. Fired up. Figgis's midnight deadline was fast approaching. But now I thought I would make it with a story after all. I grinned at myself in the rear-view mirror. I breathed in deeply, let the air out slowly. Gripped the steering wheel with renewed determination.

Then I fired the MGB's ignition and took off in pursuit.

Chapter 14

I followed the tail-lights on Hobson's van humming the theme tune from Wagner's *Ride of the Valkyries*.

Dum-di-di-dum-dum. Dum-di-di-dum-dum. DUM-DI-DI-DUM-DUM.

In case you've never come across the Valkyries before, they're the Norse girls who decide who'll die in battle. So it's good to keep on their right side. I had a feeling I might need them before the night was out.

Hobson backfired his way out of Steyning and took the main road to Shoreham-by-sea. I gave him a ten-second start and then turned the corner after him.

I didn't think he'd suspect he was being followed. After all, he'd just attended an innocent bell-ringing practice. Ding-dong merrily on high. And not a naughty thought in anyone's mind.

Not like the previous night, when he was messenger boy for Owen Griffiths. If I was right, Hobson would have been taking the results of Griffiths's tests to the drug ring's Mr Big. He'd be the man who handed over the money to pay for the new consignment.

If Hooke had discovered Griffiths's role, the top man would have had to be told. And top drug smugglers are ruthless. I'd bet it was he who arranged Hooke's execution. So if I could nail the humble Hobson, the police could force him to reveal who the man at the top was. They'd collar a drug smuggler and a murderer in one swoop.

But, perhaps, Hobson's role in the operation wasn't so humble. If, as I suspected, Griffiths was the tame chemist, Hobson could be more than a message carrier.

I remembered what the Reverend Purslowe had told me. Hobson ran a fishing boat out of Shoreham harbour. The gang would need a way to smuggle their drugs into the country. A fishing boat loaded with rank smelling mackerel could be the safest way. Police and customs officers used trained dogs to sniff out drugs. What better to put the doggies off the scent than a hold full of stinking fish?

If I was right, the transfer - money for drugs - took place at sea outside the three-mile limit. That would make it safe from police and customs officers. Nobody would question a fishing boat sailing out into the English Channel in search of a catch.

Hobson had driven off with the message from Griffiths about seventeen hours ago - in the early hours of the morning. It would take time for the buyer to assimilate the news. If Griffiths's tests had been a success, the buyer would then assemble the money. Drug deals, I assumed, were done in cash.

No cheques. No building society passbooks. And definitely no IOUs.

All this would take a little time. In any event, I assumed - as I accelerated and closed the distance with Hobson's van - there was no hurry. Dirty deeds are done at night. Under cover of darkness. So, perhaps, there would be action tonight. If Hobson were more than a messenger boy, perhaps he'd organise the hand-over.

Money for drugs. Far out at sea on his fishing boat.

But I was speculating. Perhaps Hobson was heading home for a quiet evening by the fire watching *Z-Cars* on TV.

Up ahead, Hobson's van passed the Red Lion pub on the outskirts of Shoreham. He didn't stop for a quick one. He looked like a man with business to do. But what business?

Z-Cars or a drug deal? I would soon find out.

Hobson drove into the harbour and disappeared behind a large warehouse.

I was a hundred yards back and I was certain he'd had no idea he'd been followed. I slowed the MGB and turned into the same entrance Hobson had used. I stopped in the lee of the warehouse. Even if Hobson was just around the corner, he'd not know I was there.

I opened the car door, stepped out and listened. Further along the wharf, I heard the gunshot sounds of Hobson's van backfire as he brought it to a halt. For a man on clandestine business, he certainly made enough noise about it.

I peered around the edge of the warehouse. Two hundred yards down the wharf, the lights on Hobson's van switched off. The wharf was dimly lit so I could just see Hobson open his van door and climb out. He had something in his hand, but I couldn't see what it was. He slammed the van door and waved to someone out of sight. He walked towards the unseen person with a limp which favoured his right leg.

I was thinking hard. My brain was ticking over like a Formula One racing car. I ought to report my suspicions to the cops straight away. But then I'd miss the action - and my story. Besides, Holdsworth would probably think I was wasting his time. He'd told me nothing happened in Shoreham harbour that he didn't know about. Well, he didn't know about this.

I climbed back into the MGB, pressed the starter button, and put the car in gear. I had no intention of driving away. I was turning the car round. Ready for a quick getaway, if necessary. I tucked the MGB up against the wall of the warehouse, where it would be in shadow and not easy to see.

Then I climbed out and crept on to the wharf. I wasn't too worried about being noticed. Hobson didn't know who I was. And because the comings and goings at harbours are governed by the tides, it's not unusual to have sailors, dockers and fishermen walking around at hours when most people are snoring in their beds.

A Russian timber ship had moored alongside the wharf. The *Joseph Stalin*. A red flag with the hammer and sickle fluttered from the stern. If I was challenged I'd pretend to be a Russian sailor.

Dobryy vecher, tovarishch.

Good evening, comrade.

That should stop any English passers-by pursuing the conversation. And if they happened to be Russian, they'd just think I was some eccentric Brit trying to be friendly.

With this bold thought in mind, I stopped creeping and strode boldly along the wharf to where Hobson had parked his van. When I reached it, I had a quick look in the driver's window, but it was too dark to see much. Besides, if Hobson was a key go-between for a drug smuggling outfit, he wouldn't be so stupid as to leave incriminating evidence in view.

I looked around but could see no sign of Hobson. But at the far end of the wharf, there was a dockers' hut. Lights blazed inside. Through a small window I could see figures moving around. I counted five of them including Hobson.

I strained my eyes to see what they were doing. But then, unexpectedly, the door opened and Hobson limped outside.

I moved like a jackrabbit surprised by a hunter and dodged down behind Hobson's van. Dumb move. If Hobson drove away I'd be as exposed as a Windmill Theatre stripper without her G-string.

But Hobson didn't drive away.

Instead he waited while a second man emerged from the hut. The second was more than six feet tall. He had long black hair which fell in tangles to his shoulders. He had dark eyes, a large nose and thick lips. He had a bushy Zapata moustache which drooped on both sides of his mouth. He wore blue jeans with bell-bottoms and a leather jacket. He had the stub of a smouldering cigar between his thick lips.

He was carrying a conical basket arrangement. I used my deep knowledge of maritime matters to identify it as a lobster pot. There was something inside the pot. Not a lobster. It was a package tightly wrapped in oilskin.

He handed the lobster pot to Hobson.

He said in an American accent: "You take good care of that little baby, Tom."

Hobson hefted the pot towards his shoulder. "Yes, Zach," he said. "I've netted the money from the big fish on the way. Now it's going to sea for the first time. Bet you never had so much fun in New York."

Zach gave him a flinty look.

He said: "You talk too much, Tom."

He gave Hobson a dismissive nod, and strode away. I watched as he tossed his cigar butt aside and disappeared around the side of the hut.

Hobson turned to move off down the wharf.

As he did so, three more men came out of the hut.

One of the men shouted after Hobson: "Tom, you'll need a boy."

Hobson turned: "I've got one, Steve."

Steve looked like the gaffer among the three. He was about forty and overweight. He wore a jacket and tie, and had a clipboard under his arm.

"They'll need to see the boy at night." Steve said.

"Leave that to me," Hobson said. "They'll see the boy a league away. I've scraped its bottom."

Ah, they were talking about a buoy. Not a boy.

Steve pushed the other two men forward and said: "Jock and Toby could give you a hand to load up."

Jock was a six-foot stevedore type with biceps like basketballs. He had a square chin and cow eyes that reminded me of Desperate Dan in *The Dandy*. Toby was shorter by six inches and looked like he'd been made out of wire and rubber. He had a whippy frame and a face with a disappointed mouth. He had a pointy nose which made him look like a frustrated ferret.

Hobson waved them away. "I've loaded all the gear," he said. "I'll head out on the high tide."

He turned and limped off down the wharf towards wherever

his boat was moored.

Jock turned to Steve and said: "What do we do now?"

"Just what Zach has told us," Steve said.

"Tom keeps Captain Morgan in the back of his van," Toby said.

"Who?" Steve said.

"Captain Morgan rum," Jock said.

"Yeah! We deserve a drink," Toby said. "Let's have a knockout shot."

Steve shrugged. "Bring the bottle but let's make this quick."

I crushed myself smaller behind the van. This wasn't going to end well.

There was no way Toby could grab a bottle from the van without spotting me crouching behind it.

I looked behind me. Nowhere to hide.

To the right. Nothing.

To the left. Zilch.

Perhaps I should make a run for it.

But that would be an admission of guilt.

Perhaps if I stood up and strode towards them, I could play my Russian sailor act. Perhaps they wouldn't realise I'd been hiding behind the van. Perhaps they wouldn't think I'd earwigged their conversation.

There were too many perhapses.

Toby was walking towards the van. He was the whippy one. The one I wouldn't want chasing me if I ran.

I wasn't bothered about Jock. He was a lumbering giant. It would be like being chased by a steamroller in first gear.

Steve was an unknown quantity. But he was a man with a big belly and a clipboard. Not a pair of running shoes. I'd take my chances with Steve.

Toby approached the rear doors of the van. He stretched out his arm to open them.

I stepped around the side of the van. His eyes widened in

shock.

I said: "Captain Morgan at your service. Try this for a knockout shot."

Then I hit him on the nose. Not hard enough to break bones. But hard enough to put him on his back. Hard enough to discourage pursuit.

I felt the soft tissue give way under my blow. Toby's eyes popped. Blood spurted from his nose. And he tumbled backwards.

I didn't wait to watch him hit the cobbles.

I turned and took off.

Behind me, I heard something clatter as Steve dropped his clipboard.

Then Steve yelled at Jock: "After him, you ape. I'll cut him off."

Jock aka Desperate Dan had moved closer to the van than I'd expected. He swerved inwards to block my escape route.

I slipped on the cobbles as I changed direction. I felt a rush of air as a hand the size of a bunch of bananas tried to grab my jacket collar.

Dan grunted in frustration. I forced my legs to move faster.

Behind me a rough engine growled into life. But not Hobson's van. It didn't backfire. I didn't waste time looking back. If they were trying to run me down, the further along the wharf I could run, the safer I would be.

Hobson had disappeared. Perhaps he'd already stowed his lobster pot with the oilskin. Perhaps he was already putting to sea.

So Hobson was out of the picture. Desperate Dan only yards behind me was very much in it.

I felt hot air burning in my lungs as I increased my speed. The dull clump of Desperate Dan's footsteps receded behind me as I put distance between us.

I listened for the engine noise that had started up behind me.

If I heard it coming closer, I'd take evasive action. But the engine growl had faded.

If I could reach the MGB, I could get myself out of this. After all, I'd turned the car round just so I could make a rapid getaway.

Crampton, man of foresight.

I pounded on towards the warehouse. Behind me Desperate Dan shouted like he wanted to break my bones. I ignored that and raced on.

I was ten yards from the corner of the warehouse. I risked a glance back. Dan was more than twenty yards behind. I'd have time to jump into the car, fire the ignition, and race away.

I swerved round the corner of the warehouse as I reached for the car keys in my pocket. I grabbed them, hustled to the driver's door, and thrust the key in the lock.

I unlocked the door, but before I could climb in, the rough engine growl I'd heard back at the hut grew louder. Steve swung around the far corner of the warehouse to block my getaway. He was driving a forklift truck like he was Stirling Moss at Silverstone. And he was aiming it at me like a guided missile.

I shot away from the MGB leaving the door swinging open.

I ran back the way I'd come but Desperate Dan lumbered around the corner. He panted like he'd just climbed Everest with a grand piano on his back. He looked at me like he'd decided I'd make me the *hors d'oeuvres* before a cow pie.

I was trapped like the meat in a sandwich.

Steve in the forklift truck closed in from the right. The two forks on the front - the arms which lift the heavy stuff - looked like sabres.

Dan flexed his basketball biceps and closed in from the left.

But Steve made it first. He floored the accelerator or whatever you do on a forklift truck. The thing surged towards me.

The two forks threatened to trap me between them. They couldn't miss. One would hit me and break my legs. Or my hips. Or my backbone. I was going to end up like one of those crash victims in hospital. Wrapped in bandages and suspended by ropes from the ceiling. I'd be fed on rice pudding by a nurse with a starched uniform and a starched manner.

I glanced at Steve. His face grimaced in a malicious sneer. There was a gap in his grey teeth. His tongue squeezed through, like an old snail creeping out between stones. He was going to enjoy every moment of this.

The forklift roared closer. I looked for a way out. There wasn't one.

In just a second, the prongs would catch me. They'd toss me aside like an old package. Like a broken mannequin.

I jumped.

No, I did more than that.

I leapt.

Like a ballet dancer auditioning for the Bolshoi. I flew through the air. If Rudolph Nureyev had been around, he'd have fitted me out in those tights which always get girls giggling about packed lunches and signed me up for the corps de ballet.

Relief flooded my body as I soared through the air.

And then it faded.

Because I didn't make it.

I landed on the left-hand fork of the truck. The forklift careened across the wharf at thirty miles an hour. I clung to the fork like I was gripping the handles of a roller-coaster.

The forklift swerved to the left. It dealt Dan a glancing blow and he tumbled to the ground.

Steve snarled at me as we rumbled across the cobbles. He pushed buttons and pulled levers. Suddenly I felt the forks rise. I was heading into the air. Steve had started the damned forklift. But he didn't know how to control it.

Or stop it.

We trundled across the wharf as the forks descended. Steve pulled a lever and we swerved to the right. We were inches from the edge of the wharf. This was getting dangerous.

What was I thinking?

It had been dangerous from the moment I'd decided to follow Hobson.

Steve pulled another lever and the truck turned a circle like it wanted to dance the waltz. My head spun. I looked down. The fork was closer to the ground. If I chose my moment I could jump.

Steve yanked another lever and the forklift swerved right.

I leapt for it.

I tumbled onto the cobbles. Steve glared at me as I scrambled to my feet.

But he should have looked ahead. He'd oversteered. The forklift headed for the edge of the wharf. At thirty miles an hour.

Steve yanked on a lever, but nothing happened. He looked frantically from side to side. He had a face like a child who's played with fire and knows he's burnt himself.

And then the forklift plunged over the side of the wharf.

A fountain of water sprayed into the air as the truck hit the surface. But I didn't stop to see whether it sunk or floated. And I didn't care what happened to Steve. After all, he'd tried to kill me.

I raced towards the MGB.

Freedom.

I rounded the corner of the warehouse and screeched to a halt.

Freedom was postponed.

Desperate Dan was back on his feet. Worse, he'd rummaged in my car and foraged a mass of old paperwork from the back seat. He looked at me and then at the papers like a man who's not sure what to do next. Like a man who's rescued a trophy and won't give it up.

I wasn't bothered about the papers. I was going to throw the stuff away anyway. But I had to get Dan out of the way.

I said: "Steve is drowning. He drove the forklift off the edge of the wharf."

Dan's mouth dropped open. He said: "What should I…?"

I said: "If you rescue him, you'll be a hero. If you don't, the police will be along in a minute to arrest anyone on the scene."

Dan said: "We don't want no rozzers." He took off. I heard his giant feet clump on the cobbles as he ran.

I grabbed the key out of the car door, jumped inside and fired the engine. The tyres squealed as I took off towards Brighton.

It's surprising what an evening's bell-ringing can lead to.

Chapter 15

Frank Figgis studied the two folios of copy I'd handed him, then tossed them on his desk.

He said: "I was expecting a story about drug smuggling not dangerous driving."

The story I'd given Figgis told how a man had been rescued by port workers after driving a forklift truck into the harbour.

I said: "I picked up the details in a routine call to the cop shop last night."

After I'd driven away from the harbour, I'd made the call. The harbourmaster would have alerted the cops after the fracas with the forklift. The cops told me an unnamed man - I knew him as Steve - had been fished out of the water. He was under observation at Southlands Hospital in Shoreham. He had severe bruising and suspected internal injuries. The police had dismissed the incident as a drunken prank that went wrong. And, I suspected, when the cops interviewed Steve, he wouldn't say anything to spoil that story.

It was no use me explaining to Holdsworth that Steve was a bit-part player in a drug ring. Jock - Desperate Dan to me - and Toby, the frustrated ferret, had vanished. And Hobson had not sailed his boat back into Shoreham harbour since the incident. Jock and Toby would have used ship-to-shore radio to warn Hobson of the trouble. He would have diverted to another port - possibly Newhaven or Littlehampton - to steer clear of the cops and an angry harbourmaster.

I explained this background to Figgis. He shook his head and lit up a Woodbine.

He said: "You're no closer to landing the drug ring story - or the Hooke murder, if there was one. I'm beginning to think the cops were right and it's a tragic hit-and-run."

I said: "I'm sure there's more to this. There are just too many people who'd have a motive to see Hooke dead. If Hooke had put the black on Owen Griffiths or Tom Hobson, that would link the killing to the drug running. We'd have a national story on our hands."

Figgis gave a smoky sigh. "Where have I heard that before?"

"So I can take some more time on the story?"

"Would it make any difference if I said 'no'?"

I didn't have time to answer that question because Cedric put his head around the door and said: "Call for Mr Crampton."

I said: "I'll take it in the newsroom."

"For this relief, much thanks," Figgis said.

Back at my desk I picked up my telephone.

A voice with an Aussie twang said: "Bill Freeman."

Bill was the reporter on *The Advertiser* in Adelaide who'd agreed to track down Shirley's missing mother.

I said: "Good to hear from you, Bill. Any news?"

"Not good," he said. "I've been round to Mrs Goldsmith's house three times. No answer on any of them. There's a pile a post just inside the front door - you can see it through the window. The house is at the end of a track leading out of town so there are no near neighbours. But I asked further down the street and a couple said they hadn't seen Barbara Goldsmith for weeks."

"What about police and hospitals?"

"Did the usual checks, but came away with a big zero."

"At least that means she's not seriously ill."

"Not in an Adelaide hospital. I can't check the whole damned country."

"Of course not. Thanks for your help, Bill. Much appreciated. If you've got any missing mothers in the UK, don't hesitate to give me a call."

I replaced the receiver and sat still thinking for a minute.

I'd have to tell Shirley but it wasn't going to be easy.

***

"You didn't invite me to a bonzer breakfast for no reason," Shirley said.

She seized her knife and fork and attacked a plate of eggs, bacon and tomatoes.

It was an hour later and we were in Marcello's. The early morning rush had finished but the heavy musk of fried food still hung in the air. Marcello was wiping down his espresso machine ready for the next customers. An old man at the corner table poured a dollop of brown sauce into his sausage sandwich.

I'd called Shirley and suggested we meet up after putting down the phone to Bill Freeman.

I said: "I thought you might need some comfort food to cushion the news I've got."

Shirley dropped her knife and fork on her plate. She stared at me with worried eyes.

"You've heard from that reporter guy in Adelaide," she said. "It's not good news."

"It's not bad news," I said. "In fact, it's really no news. Bill visited Barbara's house three times but she wasn't in. There was a pile of mail in the hallway, which suggests she's been away for a few days. Most likely explanation is that she's taken a short holiday."

"For five weeks?" Shirley said. "That's not a holiday. That's a disappearance."

"The good news is that the police and hospitals have no bad news - if you see what I mean."

"But it's still worrying with no news."

"I understand," I said. I reached across the table and held Shirley's hand. "The lack of letters may have a simple explanation. Perhaps there's been a postal strike somewhere along the line - or perhaps sacks of letters have gone astray. It does happen."

Shirley gripped my hand harder. "Thanks. You're great for

morale - even if it is all bullshit."

She grinned and picked up her knife and fork. Cut a piece of bacon and popped it into her mouth.

"I should be grateful I've still got a mother, even if she is missing. Hell, Colin, I must be as dumb as a box of rocks to say that. I'd forgotten that your own Ma is dead."

"It was a long time ago."

Shirley reached across the table for my hand. She took it in hers and squeezed gently.

"It must still hurt when other people talk about their mothers."

"Not so much now. She died during the war. A lot of people did. And the folks they left behind had to get over it."

"And have you got over it?"

"Her death, yes. But the manner of it still hurts. Especially as my Dad had been killed only two months earlier. For years, Ma had suffered with a weak heart. The doctor said there was nothing that could cure it and it would get worse, but she took pills to relieve the pain. And she tried to live a normal life - as normal as we could in south London during the war. She used to help out at the local church hall, making tea at Women's Institute meetings and things like that. She refused to give up her WI meetings, even though my Dad said it would be the death of her. He was right. A doodlebug landed on the hall."

Shirley's eyebrows lifted. "A doodlebug?"

"A V1 flying bomb. It hit the hall. She was the only person in it. She'd stayed behind to wash up the cups and saucers after the Institute's monthly tea party."

"That's terrible. That she stayed behind, I mean. Not the tea party."

I forced a smile. "By all accounts, the teas were pretty grim as well. But in war terrible things happen. But let's eat our breakfast."

I tucked into my scrambled egg.

I said: "Anyway, the Bill Freeman call is not the only news

I've got to tell you. I had a bit of an adventure last night."

"I wondered why I hadn't heard from you."

I told Shirley about the fracas with the forklift truck.

Her eyes widened. "Jeez. You crazy bastard. What made you jump on the forks?"

"It was a knife-edge decision," I said. "At least it's given me some copy for today's paper. But I haven't cracked the big stories on the drug ring and the Hooke killing. I'm beginning to think the two may be linked. If Hooke had tried to blackmail Owen Griffiths, he could have found himself hunted by the drug baron behind the racket. But I've no idea who that is. Figgis is riding me hard. If I don't deliver soon, he'll shut down my investigation."

Shirley mopped up the last of her egg yolk with a piece of bread. "So what's your next move?"

"I think I've got to go back to square one. I've been thinking about the note I found on Hooke the night he died."

"Some kind of message, wasn't it?"

"Yes. It read: 'Hollow Bottom Barn. 7.30 tonight. Don't be late.' I assumed Hooke was on his way to meet a girl. It's about the only thing that would compel an eighteen-year-old boy to cycle along a lonely road in pouring rain."

"He had the hots for some totty and needed to get his rocks off badly," Shirley said.

"I'm not sure that's the way Figgis would describe it - but you get the idea."

"But which girl?" Shirley asked.

"We might be able to answer that question if we knew where the girl came from."

"But that road is pretty lonely."

"It is - but there is one house about three miles further on from where we found Hooke. Natterjack Grange."

"Strange name," Shirley said.

"And these days, stranger people."

I told Shirley the information I'd picked up from Susan Wheatcroft. About how Natterjack Grange was the ancestral home of the earls of Herstmonceux. How it had been inherited by the Earl's granddaughter Christabel. And how she'd turned the estate into a hippie commune.

"Plenty of girls there, if what Susan tells me is correct. Peace and love. And not hard to know which of those Hooke would have been after."

"What makes you think the mysterious girl comes from there?"

"I'm willing to bet an egg sandwich to an earl's coronet that Hollow Bottom Barn is somewhere on the estate."

"You're sure as hell gonna look like some square cat when we pitch up at this commune," Shirley said.

"I can't see what the problem is," I said. "I'm wearing what I always wear for work - jacket and tie, grey flannel trousers. Nobody's complained before. And as a reporter I've met everyone from dukes to dustmen. The dustmen are usually better dressed than the dukes, by the way. But none of them has ever objected to what I'm wearing."

"These cobbers won't object," Shirley said. "They'll just laugh - that's if they notice, 'coz most of them will be so spaced out they could be flying round the moon."

We were in the MGB heading along the road towards Natterjack Grange. Shirley had insisted she should come as the culture shock might prove more than I could handle. I agreed as I thought it might take her mind off her missing mother.

I said: "What should I have been wearing?"

"Kaftan, perhaps. Or bell-bottom jeans."

"If I turned up at the office in a pair of bell-bottoms, Figgis would think I was auditioning for a part in *HMS Pinafore*."

I glanced at Shirley. She was wearing a denim jacket and a mini skirt with white leather boots.

She caught my glance. "Yeah, I know I look good," she said.

I said nothing - but she was right.

The entrance to Natterjack Grange was at a sharp turn in the Bostal road, just as it loses height along the ridge of the South Downs and descends towards the Sussex coastal plain. There were two tall pillars on each side of the entrance. They'd have been erected years earlier and were encrusted with yellow lichen. The pillars would once have held gates. Big wrought-iron jobs designed to keep the peasants out.

No need for the gates now. The peasants were inside. But perhaps that was an uncharitable thought. Someone had stuck a hand-painted sign on one of the pillars. It read: "Enter in peace and love."

I said: "We could pull into the side of the road and make sure we're up to date on the second of those."

Shirley grinned. "Keep your feet on the pedals and your hands on the wheel, buster."

The driveway into the estate wound between a copse of old trees – oak, hazel and beech. The copse was overgrown with brambles and ivy. There were clumps of bluebells. Here and there scarlet toadstools grew on fallen branches.

We drove round a curving bend into a hollow where a spring bubbled up from the earth. The water had left a pool of sandy mud across the driveway. I felt the wheels slip as we splashed through it.

It was an unexpected entrance to the land of peace and love.

I swung the car around a bend and we came out of the copse. Ahead Natterjack Grange stood like a black inkblot against the sky. The place looked as though it had been put up in Victorian times. It was a squat three-storey building with a crenellated arrangement around the roof to make folks who didn't look too hard think it was a castle. The house had been built out of cheap grey stone, probably by a builder who'd put in the lowest estimate. It was never going to be one of the great stately homes of England. Nikolaus Pevsner would not rhapsodise about the poky windows with rotting frames. Or the rusting drainpipes that left brown iron stains on the walls. Or the roof clumsily patched with different coloured tiles. It looked like a house that had long ago given up on its owners. I wondered whether that was the reason the late Earl had left it to his errant granddaughter.

Not a gift, but a curse.

I pulled the MGB up on to a wide driveway in front of the house and switched off the engine. To the left of the house, the driveway led into a stable block surrounding a cobbled courtyard. A beaten-up old coach - the kind of charabanc you'd have seen on seaside outings in Brighton years ago - stood in the centre of the courtyard. Except you wouldn't see this coach bringing trippers to the beach. The thing had been painted in all the colours of the rainbow in sweeping swirls. It had been decorated with skilful paintings of red birds, and yellow butterflies, and green fish. It was an explosion of colour to dazzle the eyes and confuse the senses. Beside the coach, two young hippie types - a man and a woman - dressed in jeans and smocks were painting an old Austin Cambridge car in the same theme.

They looked up at us as we climbed out of the MGB and waved.

"Let the sunshine in," one of them called to us.

We waved back.

"Cool car," Shirley shouted to them.

They laughed, hugged one another, and went back to their painting.

To the right of the driveway there was a crumbling red brick wall. It had an arch in the middle. We walked towards it and stepped through the arch into a garden. A gravel path looped around the garden and up to the house.

The garden was filled with huge rhododendron bushes, but

there were flower beds between them. Daffodils swayed in a light breeze. There were white, blue and purple crocuses. There were snowdrops which drooped their heads like a shy girl at a dance. There were yellow primroses that clustered around the roots of the rhododendrons.

I said: "When they talk about flower power, it looks as though they mean it. This garden is out of this world."

Shirley said: "Just like that pair sitting over there."

A man and woman slumped on a garden bench. He wore a shirt dyed in an eye-strain of psychedelic colours and a pair of brown moccasins. She wore a shift dress in striped primary colours. Her hair was braided with beads. The pair had thick reefers between their lips. The sweet smell of cannabis drifted across the garden.

The woman rose from the bench when she saw us and drifted across the garden. She picked a daffodil, looked at it and giggled. She walked up and handed the daffodil to me.

"Look at its face, my friend," she said. "It's smiling at you."

I said: "At least something is pleased to see me. Where can I find Christabel?"

The woman looked at me through blank unblinking eyes.

"Who?" she asked.

"Christabel Fox," I said. "The woman who owns this place."

"We all own the earth and the moon and the skies," she said.

"Listen, sister," Shirley said. "Who puts out the rubbish when it's the day for the bin men to collect?"

The woman's dreamy eyes moved slowly from me to Shirley. She didn't understand. She turned and drifted away, humming tunelessly to herself.

Feet crunched on the gravel behind me and I turned around.

A young woman approached. She was tall and had a slim figure. She had luxuriant blonde hair which fell to her waist, like you see in those shampoo adverts. It would've made Rapunzel dead jealous. Her face had a kind of wasted beauty, like some of it had been used up by hard living. Her green eyes were dreamy as though some soft and soothing music were playing inside her head. Her wide lips had the lightest touch of blue lipstick. No other make-up, but I guess with blue lipstick, you don't need it. She was dressed in a kaftan decorated with red, yellow and blue petals and open-toed sandals.

She crossed her arms and said: "I am Christabel Fox. We ask people to come here in peace and love, but you look as though you have come in neither."

Chapter 16

I said: "There doesn't seem to have been a lot of peace and love to spare in this area recently. Especially for young Spencer Hooke."

Christabel moved closer. The dreamy look in her eyes had faded. She wanted to give me a flinty look, but she couldn't manage it. She was on something. And it wasn't aspirin.

She said: "Who are you?"

"Seekers after truth - just like you."

The ghost of a smile passed over Christabel's lips. "There is no truth - only perception," she said.

"That's the gospel according to Dr Timothy Leary, is it? Nothing is real, particularly when you're spaced out on an acid trip with LSD. But it's not the gospel according to Frank Figgis."

"I know no Figgis."

"I wish I didn't most of the time. He's my news editor."

"And a big-time smoker like your pals over by the rhododendron bush," Shirley chipped in.

"Except Frank's poison is a Woodbine," I said.

"Not a spliff as thick as a kangaroo's todger," Shirley added.

Christabel's cheeks flushed in anger. "And you've come to print lies about us?"

"I thought you just said there was no truth."

"I did."

"In which case, there can't be any lies," I said. "I'm Colin Crampton. I'm from the *Evening Chronicle* and I'm not interested in even the perception of lies."

"I'm Shirley Goldsmith," Shirl chimed in. "And as straight as an Aussie state line."

I said to Christabel: "And, yes, we come in peace and love. Even for peace and love. A piece of cake and we'd love a cup of tea." I grinned. "Why don't we start this conversation again?"

Christabel thought about that for a moment and then shrugged.

She said: "Follow me."

She moved towards the house like she planned to float there.

Christabel led us into the house through a side door. In the earls' days, it would have been the servants' entrance. The door led into a scullery. There were three huge stone sinks each with a wooden draining board. Plates and cups monogrammed with elaborate coats of arms were stacked by the sinks. Whoever was on washing-up duty had bunked off early.

The scullery led into a kitchen. The walls had once been whitewashed but they'd yellowed with age. At one end of the room a blackened cooking pot hung from a chain above an open fireplace. It was the kind of place where you'd expect to see a group of peasants roasting an ox.

A large deal table dominated the centre of the room.

On the far side a kettle simmered on the hob of an ancient Aga. Christabel busied herself looking out a teapot and cups. She spooned tea from a caddy into the pot and topped up with boiling water. She fetched a bottle of milk from the pantry and gave it a discreet sniff before pouring some into a jug. She went back to the pantry and came out carrying a plate with small cakes. They had crimson icing which looked like it was radioactive. She put everything on a tray.

She said: "We'll go into the library."

I said: "For a talk rather than a read, I hope."

"Follow me."

She carried the tray and led us down a dark passage. We turned a corner and came to a large door left ajar. Christabel pushed her way in and we followed.

The library was an impressive room lined with floor-to-ceiling bookshelves. The shelves were filled with leather-bound volumes, many in sets. I saw a six-volume quarto edition of Gibbon's *Decline and Fall of the Roman Empire* and a two-volume early edition of Johnson's *Dictionary of the English Language* with raised bands on the leather spine.

To one side of the room was a handsome walnut writing desk. It held a large blotter and crystal inkstand. There was a wooden stationery tidy holding writing paper and cards. I wandered over for a closer look.

On the other side of the room, there was a fireplace with a marble surround. A group of red leather armchairs was gathered around a coffee table. The table was piled with a drift of papers. Some had floated onto the floor.

Christabel hovered around the table wondering where to place the tray.

Ever helpful, I hurried forward and gathered up the papers. While Christabel put the tray on the table and busied herself with the tea things, I carried the papers to the other side of the room. I had a quiet rummage through them as I went. (Well, what did you expect me to do?) There were letters from a firm of solicitors about the house, a big envelope stuffed with papers from the Sussex Coast Building Society, and some correspondence from a bank. If Natterjack Grange was the home of peace and love, the bank manager hadn't received the message.

I stuffed the papers into a space on a bookshelf and walked over the fireplace.

A picture of a young man and woman on their wedding day hung over the fireplace. He was tall and ascetic looking. He had a handlebar moustache and a look of complacent arrogance in his deep-set eyes.

The woman was shorter. A Thumbelina to her husband. She wore a pair of shoes with six-inch heels, but that only brought her up to her husband's shoulder. If she'd wanted to whisper sweet nothings into his ear, she'd have needed a pair of stilts. She probably had to climb a stepladder to kiss him goodnight.

"My father and mother," Christabel said.

She waved us to the chairs. She poured the tea and handed round the cups and saucers. We declined the radioactive cakes.

She said: "Thank you for moving those papers to make way for the tea."

Christabel smiled. It was a wan effort, but genuine I thought. "I should have welcomed you with the peace and love we aspire to."

"But you've been pestered by journalists before," Shirley said.

"And can't 'bear to hear the truth you've spoken, twisted by knaves to make a trap for fools'," I added.

Christabel took a sip of tea. "Yes, when I moved in here five months ago, the national newspapers thought it was a story. Earl's granddaughter turns stately home into a hippie commune. Well, you only have to look around. The place wasn't that stately when Grandpapa died."

I looked at the well-filled bookshelves. "This room is handsome," I said.

Christabel nodded to accept the compliment. "It is now. When I moved in, the room was packed with boxes of old family papers. I think Grandpapa had been sorting them when he died. I've no idea what was in them. I sent them straight to the County Records Office in Chichester. They take a pride in cataloguing the papers of the aristocratic county families. But don't be fooled by this room. The rest of the place is falling down."

"And you've been angry because journalists have written stories about the earl's granddaughter living a drug-fuelled high-life with a bunch of hippie freeloaders?"

"Something like that," she said.

Shirley piped up: "Some reporters are real bastards. Not Colin, of course."

"And you don't want newspaper headlines about wild drug orgies?" I said.

"There are no illegal drugs here," Christabel said. "I insist on that. Everyone here knows I won't stand for illegal drugs."

"Including the two muggle-heads in the garden?" Shirley asked.

"I shall speak to them when you've gone."

"But you take LSD here - lysergic acid diethylamide, to the boffins." I said. "Also known to the hip-heads as golden dragon, window pane, and yellow sunshine."

"I said I won't tolerate illegal drugs. LSD is still legal in Britain. We can use it, as though it were aspirin, without breaking the law."

"But you can't buy it at the pharmacy, like aspirin. And you can't do that because it's a powerful hallucinogenic. Or as the headline writers have it, a mind-bender. What I'd like to know is how an earl's granddaughter got in with the psychedelic crowd."

"If I tell you, will you print the truth?" Christabel asked.

I grinned. "If you'll accept the perception of truth."

Christabel nodded. "I suppose I asked for that. But, anyway, I think it's all down to my mother and father trying to make me do things I didn't want to. Last year, when I left Roedean, they wanted me to go to a finishing school in Switzerland. I ask you! Switzerland would be enough to finish anyone."

"Not unless you want to watch the Gnomes of Zurich counting their money," I said.

"I persuaded Mama and Papa to let me go to the United States. The idea was that I would travel around and see the sights. I was in a bar in California one night when I met a girl called Carolyn Adams. She told me about a group of people planning a road trip across America. It sounded great - see the sights. Just what Mama and Papa suggested. Carolyn said the trip was being organised by a man called Ken Kesey."

"Someone we should know?" Shirley asked.

"Kesey wrote that book *One Flew over the Cuckoo's Nest*, which came out about four years ago," I said. "I'd heard he's good mates with Timothy Leary, the LSD champion."

"The following day Carolyn took me to see Ken and meet his friends," Christabel said. "They were a wild crowd, like no-one I'd ever met before. They called themselves the Merry Pranksters and they lived life right up to the edge. I used that phrase to Ken and he told me it was possible to live life beyond the edge - with some help from California sunshine."

"He offered you LSD?" I asked.

Christabel nodded. "I wasn't sure but Mountain Girl - that's what we used to call Carolyn - said I had to try it. She said it would bring me closer to the group. I was frightened but I took my first trip that night."

"Jeez! What happened?" Shirley asked.

"It was slow at first, but then I felt like I could hear the colours. I felt I was walking through a wood and the brown of the tree trunks was played on a trombone and the green of the leaves on a violin. I felt happier than I'd ever felt in that forest, but at the same time sad that the happiness wouldn't last. I walked on, even though my feet never seemed to touch the ground. Then everything faded and the trees and the leaves became silent in my head. And finally, I must have fallen asleep. A few days later, we all left on the road trip in this crazy psychedelic painted bus we called Further.

"I learnt a lot on that road trip. We took more acid as well while we were on the road. It helped me to see so clearly what was wrong with us and what was right. It's true what Ken says - if we all took psychedelic drugs we could transform the world into the beautiful visions we see."

"But in the meantime, we have to rely on Harold Wilson and Lyndon B Johnson to do the job," I said.

"A few days before we were due to end the trip in New York, I learnt that my Grandpapa had died and left me this house. I decided I was going to build a community here that would live up to the ideals of the Merry Pranksters."

"So it's peace and love for all," I said.

Christabel shrugged. "It hasn't turned out quite like that."

I said: "Like when Spencer Hooke was killed. The lad seems to have been an enterprising type. Had he ever been here?"

Christabel gazed into the fireplace as though there was cheery blaze of pine logs. The grate was empty. Perhaps in her drug-addled mind the fire crackled and the smoke drifted up the chimney.

"Not while I was around," she said.

I glanced at Shirley. I'd been convinced Christabel had told us the truth about her American adventures. But now she'd just lied.

"Was Spencer here when you weren't around?" I asked.

"He may have been."

"Many times?"

"We live freely here – people come and go as they please."

"On the night he died, Spencer was cycling to Hollow Bottom Barn. Is that on this estate?"

"Yes," Christabel answered. "It's on the edge of Runciman's Field, just beyond the wood. But nobody ever goes there. I can't think why Spencer should."

Christabel had lied again. She'd told me nobody went there. I hadn't asked whether they did. Liars, like Christabel, give too much information because they're nervous. They think if they please their interrogator, they'll be believed. Yes, Christabel was a liar.

I said: "It is a truth universally acknowledged that a single lad without a bean to his name must be in want of a woman who's loaded."

Christabel flashed angry eyes at me. "I'm not loaded. And even if I were, what possible interest could I have in a schoolboy chemistry swot?"

"So you know he was a chemistry savant," I said. "Even though you say you've never met."

Christabel blushed. "I think someone must have mentioned it when we heard about his death. But I had no interest in Spencer Hooke. I have a boyfriend."

"One of the Merry Pranksters?" I asked.

"No, he's a wonderful guy I met in New York, before I flew back to Britain. He'd followed the exploits of the Merry Pranksters in the press and said how much he'd admired them. I told him about my plan to bring their vision of life to Britain and he just wanted to be part of it."

I bet he did, I thought. Penniless Yank would like to meet aristocratic Brit with own stately home. With a view to living a life of ease. No doubt he was a street-corner hustler who thought he'd hit the jackpot.

I said: "Have your parents met him?"

Christabel nodded. "I think they approve. At least my father likes him."

I said: "Can we meet him?"

"It would be great if we could say 'G'day'," Shirley said.

"I'm afraid he's out. He had to arrange a delivery of feed for the farm animals," Christabel said.

"At least tell us the hunk's name," Shirley said.

"It's Zachariah," Christabel said.

"Jeez, Colin, I thought your blood had drained down to your boots," Shirley said.

"For a moment it felt like it," I said.

We were sitting in the MGB parked in a lay-by on the Bostal road a mile from Natterjack Grange. A stiff breeze rocked the car on its springs.

"When I was at Shoreham harbour last night, there was a man who looked like he was the boss of the outfit. He was an American and one of the others said he came from New York. They called him Zach."

"Then why didn't you tell Christabel about that?"

"Two reasons. First, I can't be one hundred per cent sure that the Zach at the harbour and her boyfriend Zachariah are the same person."

"They have to be," Shirley said. "How many crazy parents name their children so they spend their life sounding like an Old Testament prophet?"

"I agree there are ninety-nine chances out of a hundred the two are the same - but there's still one chance that they're different. I have to be sure before I start throwing serious accusations around. But the second reason is even more important."

"Why?"

"Because I can't be certain how much Christabel knows about this."

"She has to know," Shirley said. "She met the guy in New York - she must have seen what he was into there."

I twisted in my seat to face Shirley. "I'm not so sure. We know Christabel takes LSD and has some kind of weird conviction that it can save the world. But she said she strongly opposed illegal drugs."

Shirley nodded. "Yeah. She could have meant what she said."

"She seemed genuinely annoyed when we pointed out two of her flower children were smoking pot. If Zach is the lynchpin in a drug smuggling operation, he could be doing it under her nose. She's so spaced out she could be flying round Venus."

"But she lied about knowing Hooke," Shirley said.

"Yes, he'd been there. Several times, too. Which makes me wonder whether he'd worked out what Zach was up to. Perhaps he'd tried to put the black on him. But he'd have made a mistake there. If Zach is what I think, he'll be ruthless. He wouldn't think twice about killing Hooke."

I shifted in my seat and turned on the ignition. I fired the engine and put the car into gear.

"Perhaps he wouldn't think twice about killing us," I said.

***

By the time I'd parked the car outside Shirley's flat it was late afternoon.

It had been a sombre return journey. We'd driven back to Brighton by a country route. Both of us needed time to think about what we learned at Natterjack Grange. Or what we thought we'd learned.

I suspected Figgis would've been prowling the newsroom. He'd want to know where I'd gone. He'd find out soon enough. I was determined to crack the Hooke murder story - and the more I learnt about it, the more I was certain I would.

Even if Zach posed a new danger.

We trotted down the steps to Shirley's basement flat. She opened the door, stepped inside, and let out a whoop of delight.

I followed her in. "What is it?" I asked.

Shirley picked a letter off the doormat. "It's from Australia. My Ma's writing."

She hustled into the sitting room, threw herself into an easy chair, and ripped open the envelope.

I watched as her eyes raced over the pages and the smile on her face faded.

I said: "What's wrong?"

"Ma's coming to England. She says she won some money unexpectedly. Decided to spend it on a surprise visit. But according to this letter, she was sailing on a ship that was due to arrive in Southampton early this morning."

"That's good isn't it? But why didn't she tell you earlier?"

Shirley waved the envelope at me. "Look at the stamp. She sent the letter by surface mail. She's never done that before. She always used aerograms. They only take five days from Oz."

"Why would she do that?"

Shirl shrugged. "I don't know." She picked up the envelope she'd thrown on the floor. "Look. She's written 'By air mail' on the envelope', but she's only paid for surface postage. I guess she must have run out of aerograms."

"The letter must have come on the same ship as your Ma," I said. "So she'll be here soon. That's good news, isn't it?"

Shirley ripped open the letter and began to read.

She said: "If this letter came on the same ship as Ma, where is she?"

"You weren't here to let her in."

"She knows I leave a key under the flowerpot by the front door. She says in her letter that she'll let herself in if I'm not here."

"So where is she?" I wondered.

Shirley stood up. She headed for the bedroom. "Perhaps she's fallen asleep."

I went into the hall. Looked at the front door. There was another letter which had fallen to one side. It had become lodged behind the doormat so we'd not spotted it as we'd walked in.

I hurried up the hall and picked it up. There was no envelope. Just a sheet of foolscap paper folded twice. I opened it.

Shirley came into the hall.

I looked at her.

She stared back at me. "What's wrong now?" she said.

My hand shook as I held up the note.

My mouth had turned as dry as a dustbowl. I swallowed hard. I couldn't think of any way to soften the blow that was coming.

"Your mother's been kidnapped," I said.

Chapter 17

Shirley threw back her head and laughed - a raucous belly-shaking guffaw.

"Now I know you're tugging my titties," she said. "It'd be easier to kidnap a boxing kangaroo."

I moved up the hall and showed Shirley the letter. "It's true," I said.

Shirley grabbed the letter. Her eyes raced over the words. Her jaw dropped and her eyes misted. Her hand began to shake.

She dropped the letter on the floor and folded herself into my arms. She sobbed on my shoulder. I felt her body against me throbbing with fear.

"It can't be possible," she said between gulping sobs. "It can't."

I picked up the letter and led Shirley into the sitting room. I sat her in a chair. I fetched a glass of water and said: "Drink this."

She put the glass on the table undrunk. She rummaged a handkerchief from a pocket somewhere and blew her nose. Wiped a tear from her eye. She was white and her lips quivered.

She said: "Read the letter to me."

I read: "*You've been sticking your nose in where it's not wanted…*"

Shirley held up her hand. "They can't mean Ma."

I said grimly: "They mean me."

I read on: "*We mind our business. You mind yours. Just to encourage you, we've taken the lady as our insurance policy. Keep out of our affairs and she comes back to you when we've completed our business. And no police. Repeat, no cops. We shall know if they're informed. Then all deals are off. You won't see her again. Remember: stay away from the cops.*"

I put the letter down. It had been typed on an old typewriter with a black and red ribbon. The ribbon had been poorly fitted so that the lower parts of some capital letters appeared in red.

Shirley said: "I don't understand. They came to kidnap you?"

I nodded: "It looks like it. This comes from the crowd I tangled with last night. They came for me, but they took your mother instead."

"But how did they get this address?"

A picture flashed in my mind.

Shoreham harbour. I'm racing back to my car. I've left the door open. And Jock - Desperate Dan - has grabbed the papers from the back seat. They're mostly the old newspapers and press releases I should have chucked out. But there's also the envelope that held the Press Ball tickets. The one I'd had sent to Shirley's flat. The one I'd tossed into the back of the car. And the one I definitely should have thrown away.

I explained. "They came to kidnap me. Or kill me."

Shirley's face grew grim. Her eyes flashed angrily. "I told you to chuck that," she snapped.

"I slung it in the back of my car. I meant to get rid of it. I'm so sorry."

"This is your fault," she screamed. "Why didn't you throw that old crap away? You idiot."

There was a moment's silence. It felt like an electric shock.

Then a voice said: "We must go to the police."

It was my voice. I never thought I'd hear myself say that. But with Shirley's Ma in danger this was beyond serious.

Shirley jumped up from the chair and squared up to me. "No police. The letter says no police."

"Kidnappers always say that. They won't know we've been in touch if the cops are discreet."

"Yeah! I can just see those discreet cops now. They'll charge in with their size tens and my Ma ends up taking a horizontal ride to the stiff's store."

Shirley slumped back in the chair. I'd never seen her look so furious.

I thought about what she'd said. Perhaps she was right.

Detective Inspector Holdsworth had shown about as much enthusiasm for feeling collars as for beating his own head with his truncheon. But perhaps detectives didn't have truncheons. I was getting off the point. I had Holdsworth down as a lazy no-hoper who wouldn't shift from his chair to save his bum from blisters. But perhaps there was more to it than that. The kidnappers had emphasised in the letter that they'd know if we approached the cops. As I'd told Shirl, they'd say that anyway. But perhaps this time it was true. Perhaps Holdsworth was welded to his office chair doing nothing because he'd had a sweetener. "A policeman's lot is not a happy one." Perhaps Gilbert and Sullivan's song wasn't always true. Perhaps Holdsworth's lot was a very happy one. Perhaps he had the joy of a fat bank balance, courtesy of a drug gang's pay-offs.

I said: "OK. No cops. We sort out this problem ourselves."

Shirley shot me a flinty look. "How?"

"We don't know who made the snatch, but my guess is that it was the two slow-brains Jock and Toby," I said. "I saw them last night at the harbour. They seemed the only muscle in the operation. Because this is Saturday, I can just see them confident they'd find me at home washing the car or trimming the hedge. They didn't realise I don't even live here. And then they blunder in and find your mother. They're working under orders from the boss - that's Zach. He looked like a tough cookie, so they won't want to go back empty-handed. But there's a problem if they take your Ma. They've brought a ransom note with them - but it's all about kidnapping me. They can't leave it, because it will make no sense. We'd just dismiss it as a hoax. So back they troop to their Mr Big and get a new note typed out. Then they return to deliver it. That suggests to me that someone associated with this operation has a base in Brighton or nearby. Otherwise, they wouldn't have had time to make the round trip - hide your mother wherever, and race back here with the note."

Shirley had been pacing around the room while I spoke. She

turned towards me and said: "So how does that help us?"

I said: "It gives us an idea of the organisation we're dealing with. There's a chain of command and a chain is only as strong as its weakest link. We tackle that weak link and we can break the chain and rescue your Ma."

Shirley stared hard at me. "And who is the weakest link?"

"Owen Griffiths," I said.

Shirley said: "If this goes wrong, I'll string up your lights along Brighton prom like summer illuminations."

I said: "That'll give the tourists something new to moan about."

We were in my MGB heading towards Steyning. I planned to confront Griffiths in his lab before he realised what was happening.

Shirley said: "Why have you tagged Griffiths as the weak link?"

"He's got more to lose than the others we've seen - a career as a schoolmaster at a respected grammar school. I'm not sure how he got into this, but I expect it was money. It's usually the sniff of riches. With drug money swelling his bank balance, he'd feel like he'd solved the alchemists' puzzle and found a way to transmute base metal into gold."

"He's not going to admit he's on the take."

"Griffiths strikes me as the nervous type. I think he'll have been drawn into the racket one step at a time. He was in too deep before he realised it."

"The guy stinks as much as his experiments," Shirley said.

"And he lied to me about his alibi. He said he'd attended a chemical society meeting – but it had been cancelled."

"Perhaps he's the man who killed Hooke," Shirley reminded me.

I had nothing to say to that. I pressed my foot down on the accelerator and the tyres squealed as we sped round a bend in the road.

The lessons had long ended and the chemistry lab was dark by the time we reached the school.

But we tracked Griffiths down to a small private sitting room he occupied in one of the boarding houses.

When he opened his door and saw us, he stepped backwards in surprise. I used the opportunity to barge inside and Shirley hustled after me.

Griffiths stuttered a bit but realised there was no way he could throw us out without making a scene. He shrugged his shoulders and closed the door.

The room was a cosy little haven with an easy chair and a small divan. An occasional table next to the chair held a telephone. There was an Indian rug on the floor and a bookshelf loaded with tomes about organic this and inorganic that. A couple of Agatha Christie's finest evidently provided his lighter reading. Which was handy. He was just about to discover what it feels like to be the suspect in a whodunit.

An old Bakelite wireless stood on a small table in the corner of the room. It was tuned into the Home Service and *Saturday-Night Theatre* was about to start. It sounded like tonight's show was a Sherlock Holmes tale.

I pointed at the radio and said: "You can switch that off. You're about to discover how you just won a starring role in your own drama."

Griffiths started to protest, thought better of it, and clicked the radio off just as Carleton Hobbs started on *The Sign of the Four*.

Griffiths pointed at Shirley and said: "Who's she?"

Shirley said: "Watch your mouth, whacker. I'm the girl who's gonna squeeze your nuts until they pop like rotten plums."

Hastily, I said: "Miss Goldsmith is the paper's court reporter - temporary post. She wants to get a good look at you before she sees you standing in the dock."

Griffiths stood up straighter. Clicked his shoulders back. Jutted out his chin. He was doing his best to look affronted. He moved towards the door.

He said: "I'm calling the headmaster."

I said: "I wouldn't do that. Unless you want to be sacked on the spot."

"Very well. I'll give you five minutes. What's this all about?"

"Shall we sit down?" I said.

"If we must."

He slumped into his easy chair. Shirley and I perched on the divan.

I said: "In the interests of saving time, let's dispense with the cat-and-mouse tactics and cut straight to the facts."

"Suits me. If you have any facts," Griffiths said sourly.

"I know the part you play in a drug smuggling ring," I said.

"That is a preposterous..." But I held up my hand before Griffiths could finish.

"I know what you're going to say," I said. "Gross libel. Defamation of character. Slur on your good name. I've heard it all before. Usually from people whose names had already turned rancid. Just listen and perhaps we can do one another a bit of good."

Griffiths frowned but I could see the cogs in his brain turning over. He knew he was in a corner and wondered whether there might be a way out.

"And listen good, whacker, because my Ma's life is at stake here," Shirley butted in.

"We'll come to that in a moment. First, let's start at the beginning. A few months ago - I'm not sure how many, but you can fill in the details later - you were recruited into a drug smuggling ring. Your role was a vital one - you were the quality assurance manager. The one problem with drug smuggling is that you have to deal with crooks. Buying illegal drugs isn't like nipping down to the chemists for a packet of aspirins. You know what you get in the pack - and the strength is helpfully printed on the label stuck to the bottle. With illegal drugs, you could be buying anything. You think you've got a pound of pure heroin, but you don't know whether it's been cut with half a pound of baking powder. Your seller is taking the rise out of you in more ways than one. Your role in the racket was a vital one. It was to test a sample of the product before the money was handed over for the goods."

"That is a slanderous fiction," Griffiths blustered.

"In the early hours of yesterday morning, I watched you in the school chemistry lab performing the tests. And very professionally done, if I may say so."

Griffiths slumped lower in his chair. "I didn't see you," he muttered.

"You wouldn't - when I don't want you to."

"You have no evidence. You can't prove it. It's my word against yours. The respected schoolmaster against the gutter journalist."

"If you don't watch your mouth, buster, you'll find out faster than you expected who's in the gutter," Shirley said.

Griffiths bristled. "Don't threaten me in my own room."

I held up both hands in a calming gesture. "Let's all cool down, shall we?"

I turned to Griffiths. "The fact is it won't be hard to find the proof you're involved in this dirty business. If the cops raid your lab, they'll find chemicals you wouldn't usually use in your lessons - but you would use for drug testing. If they raid your room, they'll find your bank books - and they'll want to know where unexplained sums in your account came from. And there'll be more. You're no career crook - you won't have covered your tracks like one. But your future doesn't hinge on whether I can prove you were testing illegal drugs in the lab the other night."

"Doesn't it?" Griffiths looked worried.

"It hinges on whether you can provide information which helps us to rescue Shirley's mother. She's been kidnapped by the tough guys in this business. And that's an even more serious crime. I'm betting you're deep enough in the smuggling ring to know who'd try a desperate scam like that."

"I might do," Griffiths said petulantly. "But what's in it for me?"

"The admiration which only a newspaper can lavish on a true hero."

"Hero - I don't think I can be a hero," Griffiths stammered.

"Don't worry, we're not asking you for fisticuffs - just information."

"Jeez, I've seen jellyfish on Bondi beach with more backbone," Shirley chipped in.

Griffiths rubbed his hands together. He was thinking there might be a way out for him. But the gesture made him look like Uriah Heep.

He said: "There's a man called Zach."

"I know," I said.

"You've met him?"

"That's a pleasure still to come."

"Zach handles the organisation. He's the link between Tom Hobson who brings the drugs ashore in his fishing boat and whoever sells them on land."

"And who's that?"

"I don't know. Tom is a member of the bell-ringing group, but he keeps himself to himself. I've asked him who else is involved, but he's warned me off asking too many questions. He says it's dangerous to know too much."

"What do you know about Zach?"

"Not much, except that he showed up shortly after Christabel Fox returned from America. There was quite a scandal at the time about her open support for LSD users. I was asked for my opinion - as a chemist - and I pointed out that lysergic acid diethylamide isn't illegal in this country. At least, not yet. I said we shouldn't criticise anyone who's doing something that's legal."

"And after that someone - I'm guessing Zach - approached you with some ex-curricular work."

"How did you know?"

"Because Zach would have been attracted by your free-and-easy views about drugs. Why did you accept his offer?"

Griffiths looked down and fiddled with the frills on a cushion.

"Money problems," he said. "I'd been gambling on the horses. Rather heavily, I'm afraid."

"And rather unsuccessfully," Shirley said.

Griffiths nodded. "I'd borrowed money and the creditor was - how shall I put it - pressing for payment."

"Have you met Zach often?" I asked.

"Only when he has a sample he wants me to test."

"I'm betting he doesn't bring it to the school."

"No, I meet him at a cottage on the Natterjack estate. There's an old woodsman's place - Gingerbread Cottage - about half a mile from the house in Cissbury Wood. It's isolated and hard to find, unless you know where it is."

I looked at Shirley.

She nodded. "It's worth a try."

I turned to Griffiths. "Get your coat, you're coming with us."

"But…" he quavered.

"No buts. Now it's payback time. You want redemption. This is the way. Shirley will take you down to the car. I'm going to use your phone to make a call."

Griffiths stood up like a man who hasn't got anything better to do.

Shirley said: "This way, buster, and don't try any of your tricks with me unless you want to feel your balls pop out of your ears."

Griffiths shrugged reluctantly into an old jacket. Shirley grabbed his arm and hustled him outside. I watched him go, then reached for his telephone.

Chapter 18

Fifteen minutes later, I swung the MGB onto the drive leading to Natterjack Grange.

I pulled up outside the house. Two glass jars with flickering candles stood on either side of the front door.

Shirley said: "If my Ma's not here, I don't know what I shall do. After I've croaked you, that is."

I said: "It won't come to that."

"You'd better hope…"

In the jump seat, Griffiths said: "I've got cramp in both my legs and a crick in my neck that'll take days to straighten out."

I said: "Stop moaning and consider yourself lucky to be here."

"How lucky?" he whined.

"About five years of time in jug lucky."

Shirley said: "We don't even know whether that Zach is here - let alone whether he's with Ma."

"We're about to find out," I said.

Shirley and I climbed out of the car.

I leant through the open door and said to Griffiths: "You stay there and do something useful."

"What can I do that's useful jammed into this tiny seat?"

"Massage some life back into your legs. You're going to need them."

I closed the car door and locked it.

Shirley and I didn't look back as we walked up the steps to the front door.

I tried the door and it opened first time.

We stepped into a big hallway. There were oak-panelled walls and moulded ceiling cornices with little cherubs in the corners. Tasteful. In the old days, there would have been a couple of liveried footmen with powdered wigs. The place was lit by thick church candles which guttered in the draught from the open door. The heavy musk of burning incense hung in the air.

From somewhere in the house the twang of a stringed instrument sounded a few discordant notes. It didn't think it was a guitar. Or a banjo. The instrument fell silent and voices started up a low rhythmic chant.

Aaaah-um, aaaah-um, aaaah-um.

I couldn't see the number making the top ten.

I motioned to Shirley and we walked silently towards the chanting.

We entered a large room with a high vaulted ceiling and a stone-flagged floor. There was a large circular Persian rug in the centre of the room but no furniture. Dim lighting came from candelabra standing on the floor around the edge of the rug. A billowy white smoke arose from an incense burner in the middle of the room.

Nine young women sat crossed legged around the burner. They held their hands together in front of their noses in a praying posture. The women wore colourful saris in bright reds, yellows and purples. The saris had extravagant designs with stars and planets, clouds and rainbows.

The twangy notes started up again. They came from an old man sitting at the far end of the room on an elevated platform. He had a bald head and a beard that came down to his navel. He looked like he'd put his head on upside down.

The notes came from a sitar - an instrument with a long neck which looked like a banjo that had grown up. George Formby would have been impressed. But I couldn't see the bald bloke knocking out *I'm Leaning on the Lamppost at the Corner of the Street*.

Not that he planned to try. He plucked a few more strings and everyone started on the *aaaah-um* routine again.

I looked around the room. I had to find Christabel. I couldn't see whether she was one of the women sitting around the burner.

Shirley whispered: "So what's the plan now, big brain?"

I said: "Let's see what happens."

The session was becoming more intense. The sitar player's fingers worked up and down the neck of his instrument. The notes came faster and more discordant. The *aaaahs* and the *ums* grew louder. The cross-legged women swayed from side to side as they chanted.

And then the sitar man thrummed some heavy chords.

And everyone fell silent.

They sat and bowed their heads.

The incense smoke billowed towards the ceiling.

A lamp shone a circle of pink light onto the podium.

Christabel stepped out from behind a curtain. She was wearing a long white shift dress which fell to her ankles. She moved slowly, one graceful limb at a time, like a stalking cat. She had that dreamy look in her eyes. She held a gold oil-lamp in her right hand. The lamp burnt with a tiny blue flame.

She held the lamp above her head and chanted: "I am Mnemosyne, the goddess of memory."

"You are Mnemosyne, the goddess of memory," the cross-legged bods on the floor chanted back.

Shirley leaned towards me and whispered: "She's mad. She's got a 'roo loose in the top paddock."

I nodded. "She's got a happy head stuffed with drugs."

Christabel chanted: "You are the nine muses. You are the daughters of my lover Zeus. You are my daughters. Your power comes from my memory. And I am the goddess of memory."

Christabel pointed at one of the muses. "Acknowledge my power, Calliope, muse of epic poetry."

A blonde woman wearing a blue sari decorated with mauve stars stood up: "I acknowledge your power, Mnemosyne."

"Acknowledge my power, Clio, muse of history."

A slight dark-haired girl in a scarlet sari rose: "I acknowledge your power, Mnemosyne."

"Acknowledge my power, Melpomene, muse of tragedy."

A young woman with teardrops painted beneath her eyes rose: "I acknowledge your power, Mnemosyne."

"How long is this pantomime going to last?" Shirley whispered.

"We don't have time for nine muses now," I said.

I stepped towards the podium and said: "I am Crampton, the muse of deadlines. And if you don't listen to what I've got to say you'll all spend the next few years in a prison cell. As the muse of slopping out."

The collective intake of breath sounded like a rush of wind as a fat old lady tightened her corsets. The neat circle round the incense burner broke apart as the bodies shuffled round to get a better view.

Christabel stepped down from the podium. She glided towards me in her Greek goddess get-up.

Her eyes were dreamy but her mouth was tight with anger.

She came up to us and said: "You must leave. Your presence here upsets the gods."

I said: "My presence here may well avoid the cops. Your pal Zach is in line for one of Zeus's thunderbolts. And you're standing in exactly the right place to suffer the collateral damage. Now do I have your attention?"

Christabel's brow furrowed.

"Come into the library," she said.

She waved her hand at the room. "Resume the position of penance and remembrance," she said.

The muses shuffled back into a cross-legged position with their hands together in front of their faces.

Christabel signalled to the sitar player. "Play something calming, Stanley."

"After all this excitement, I've lost my muse," Stanley wailed.

We left him looking for it as we headed for the door.

***

"When I first saw Zach, I thought he would be Zeus to my

Mnemosyne," Christabel said.

"You can't rely on Greek gods like you used to," I said.

We were outside the house on the track leading into the woods. The nine muses had formed up into a line, one behind the other. Each carried a lantern attached to a pole.

Stanley on sitar brought up the rear.

It had been half an hour since Shirley and I had marched Christabel into her library for a frank talk. She'd sat sullenly by the empty fireplace as I laid out what I knew about Zach. Her eyes were dreamy. At moments her mind seemed like it was in another place. Perhaps to talk philosophy with Socrates in a Greek olive grove. Perhaps to commune with the gods amidst the snows of Mount Olympus. Or perhaps to wonder how she would pay the rates bill on the mouldering pile of a house.

At first, she'd resisted the idea that Zach was a drugs dealer who'd abused her hospitality. But I piled up the evidence until she couldn't ignore it. I told her how I'd seen him give orders to other members of the gang. I explained how he was a key contact to other people in the smuggling chain. And I pointed out that she was barely an inch the right side of arrest as all this was happening on her doorstep.

I think I nearly got to her. But months of drugs had addled her brain. She could only see the world with a smiley face.

Had it not been for Shirley, we'd have lost her.

Shirley piled in with a passion which shook Christabel out of her acid torpor. Shirl reminded Christabel that if she were banged up on a drugs charge, they'd throw away the key. But if kidnapping was added, there wouldn't even be a key.

That got Christabel's attention.

"What can I do?" she'd wailed. "There's only ten of us - me and the nine muses."

"Don't forget Stanley," I'd said.

"Oh, he doesn't count," she'd said.

She was probably right. Here we all were and Stanley was

complaining that one of the strings on his sitar had broken.

But we had a plan.

In the house, Christabel had been leading the ceremony of remembrance. Apparently, they all sat in a circle, listened to Stanley play the sitar (broken strings permitting), sucked on the spirit of remembrance (LSD), and summoned up all the knowledge of the world (even stuff not in *Encyclopaedia Britannica*).

A cynic (not me) might say it was just an excuse to get smashed.

Anyway, it seemed that in the summer instead of holding the session in the house, they held it in a glade close to Gingerbread Cottage. That was the place Griffiths had suggested Zach could be holding Shirley's Mum.

It was a chilly night and the muses would feel a bit of a draught up their saris, but they were going to do the ceremony in the glade tonight.

The idea was that Christabel would get Zach aka Zeus and any other drug dealer/Greek god lookalikes in the cottage to join in. She thought it wouldn't be too difficult to persuade them. I mean what man is going to turn up the chance of taking a mind-bending drug with an attractive muse for company? Anything could happen.

While the ceremony took place, Shirley and I would nip into the cottage through the back door and rescue her Mum. Always assuming, of course, her Mum was there. But we didn't have a better plan.

I'd originally decided we'd take Griffiths with us. He'd eagerly clambered out of the car. He could identify any illegal drugs on the premises. But I changed my mind when I noticed him taking more than a fatherly interest in Terpsichore (muse of dance). So I told him to wait in the car and not touch anything. He pulled a face like a spoilt child. But I guessed he was going to have to get used to taking orders. From prison officers.

So that's how the Goddess of Memory and nine muses - not forgetting Stanley - happened to be standing in a line holding lanterns on a breezy night.

And just at that moment, the clouds broke, and a full moon illuminated the scene.

Christabel turned to the sky and raised her arms. She chanted a bit of Greek. The muses raised their hands and wiggled their heads from side to side. Stanley played a moonbeam riff on his sitar.

Actually, I thought it sounded better with a busted string.

Apparently, the general opinion was that the moon was a good omen.

So how could this plan possibly go wrong?

I felt a bit like a general giving his army an order to advance when I said: "Let's go."

Christabel spread her arms in a hallelujah gesture and the muses started up on the *aaaah-um* chant. Stanley twanged something on the sitar.

It soon became clear that this wasn't going to be a brisk trot through the woods. Every few yards Christabel turned round and said something in ancient Greek. One of the muses would bow her head and chant something back.

But step-by-step we made our way along the path towards Gingerbread Cottage. A little brook chuckled beside the path. I pointed to it and Christabel said it led to an ancient well further on in the woods.

As we approached the clearing in front of the cottage, Shirley and I slunk into the shadows at the side of the path. I wanted to find a way to skirt round to the back.

The procession of muses reached the edge of the glade. Shirley and I crept closer and peeped out from behind the trunk of a big beech tree.

We could see the cottage about fifty yards ahead and slightly off to the right. It was the kind of place you read about in children's books of fairy stories. The kind of place with a witch and a black cat. It was a squat little one-storey structure built out of those round cobbles they call flints in Sussex. There were tiny latticed windows at the front and side. Too small, I was pleased to see, for anyone to climb through. The roof was thatched and moss grew over it. There was a crooked red brick chimney. A weather vane in the figure of a cockerel was fixed to the chimney. A small path ran around the edge of the cottage. I guessed that led to the back door.

Candles were burning and all the windows were lit. As we watched, the silhouette of a man moved across the side window. And then another.

"At least two people inside," I whispered to Shirley.

But as I said it, the front door opened and a third figure stepped out. He stood in the pool of light thrown by the muses' lanterns. It was Zach. He had the taut body posture - clenched shoulders, balled fists - of a man who's been interrupted from something more important.

He stepped towards Christabel. "Hell, Christie, what is this circus?" he asked.

Christabel moved towards him and entwined her arms around his neck. She moved to kiss him on the lips. He accepted the kiss like it was loose change rather than a hundred-dollar smacker.

She said: "Join us, my god Zeus, in the ceremony of remembrance. Take some purple haze with us. Let us lie together as our minds grow as vast as the universe."

Zach pushed Christabel away. "Hey, you know I'm no god. It ain't a good time for this. I've got some boys – Jock and Toby - over for poker."

Christabel pushed closer again: "I've got the yellow sunshine with me now." She pulled something from within the folds of her gown and handed it to him. "Think what you will feel like with this inside you and you inside me."

His eyes opened wider and he moved his head to one side

while he thought about that. Decided it wasn't an unattractive offer, after all.

"Perhaps I could stay for a while," he said.

"And bring your friends, too. There are nine muses here to entertain them."

"Yeah! These guys have never had a muse before. But they'll try anything once."

"Let Erato teach them about love poetry and Polymnia sing them the divine hymns," Christabel said.

"Guess it beats losing their money at poker. But what's that sound?"

"It is Stanley playing the music of the spheres on his sitar."

"Not that guy. But he wants to get a proper guitar, like Elvis. No, I mean that bell ringing in the woods."

I'd just picked it up, too. It grew louder and seconds later a police car with blue flashing light and clanging bell appeared on the path.

It skidded to a halt at the edge of the glade.

Holdsworth jumped out of the front passenger seat while two uniformed plods scrambled out of the back.

We'd hardly taken that in before another cop car roared down the path. It pulled up behind the first and Ted Wilson leapt out.

A cloud passed briefly across the moon.

The muses screamed and scattered.

Christabel threw her head back and shouted something in Greek.

And Zach's head darted from side to side, like a hunted man. "Christ, this is a set-up," he yelled.

Shirley grabbed my arm and yanked me towards her.

She slapped my face. It stung. And hurt. Not just on the flesh. Shirley had never hit me before.

Shirl's eyes were dark with fury. "You promised, no cops," she screamed. "You promised. We're finished, big time journalist. Get that. It's the F word. Finished. Sums you up, useless as a dead dingo."

She slapped my face again and ran into the cottage.

Mayhem broke out in the glade.

Zach fled into the wood.

Jock and Toby tumbled out of the cottage's back door and took off in different directions.

Ted and Holdsworth shouted accusations at each other.

Christabel fell to her knees. Perhaps to pray. Perhaps to hide. Perhaps to search her memory about what to do in this situation.

The uniformed plods didn't know whether to arrest the muses or ask them to dance.

Shirley hustled out of the cottage. Her face was streaked with tears. Her body shook with emotion.

"Where's my Ma?" she yelled. "She's not here."

No, of course not. Zach would be too clever to hide her in the cottage. Especially when the boys were round for poker. Only he would know where she was hidden.

And he had fled into the woods.

I took off after him.

Chapter 19

Behind me the noise of the ruckus outside the cottage faded as I plunged into the woods.

So did the light from the muses' lanterns and the cop cars' headlamps. I smashed into the branch of a hazel tree as I blundered forward. The damned thing whiplashed back and stung me across the side of my face. It hurt - but not as much as Shirley's slap.

I realised I wouldn't find Zach by crashing about like a rutting boar in search of a mate. I stood still and listened. The wind whistled through the trees' canopy like an out-of-tune hornpipe. It was an eerie sound. The kind that would have a more suggestible soul than me looking nervously around for the ghost that came with the wailing.

I snuck a quick glance over my shoulder. But I couldn't see much. It was dark in the wood, but nowhere is ever completely black. I couldn't see much ahead of me.

I seemed to be standing on a rough track which had been trodden down over the centuries by the passage of feet. Perhaps Cromwell's Roundheads had marched this way. Perhaps the Conqueror's Normans. Maybe even a Roman legion. This was an old path. It had to lead somewhere. And Zach would need to find a way through the woods. I had nothing else to go on. I had to hope he'd fled this way.

I strained my ears to hear any feet pounding on ahead. But the whistling wind was like white noise deadening other sounds. In a Hollywood movie, this would be the point where our hero hears a twig snap so he knows where to sneak up on the villain. But I wasn't in a Hollywood movie. I was living a real-life nightmare. And there was no snapping twig.

I pushed on up the track more slowly than before. The side of my face was still sore from the sapling whiplash.

About a hundred yards further on, the track forked. The main track led off to the right, a narrower track to the left. Zach could have taken either of them. I had to choose one or the other. A fifty per cent chance of getting it right. Or wrong.

I needed Robert Frost here. But the poet had died two years earlier. He would have advised me to take the path "less travelled", just like he did in his verse. But then he wasn't chasing Zach.

I paced around in a circle wondering what the hell to do. I kicked at a fallen branch in frustration. For a brief moment the wind eased up and I heard running water off to my left. When Shirley and I had followed the muses, there'd been a brook chuckling alongside us. Perhaps this was the same one.

Christabel had said something about the brook feeding a well. If there was a well, perhaps it was used by another cottage. If there were another cottage, perhaps Zach held Barbara Goldsmith there. It wasn't a very convincing argument, but I didn't have a better one.

I took the path less travelled - the left fork - and followed the sound of the burbling brook. I hoped it would make all the difference, as it had for old Frosty.

After a few yards, I began to wonder whether I'd made the best choice. The track was much narrower than the other one. It was overgrown with brambles. They snagged my trousers. Figgis wasn't going to be pleased with an expense claim for a new pair of Marks & Spencer's finest.

I stumbled on in the darkness.

Low-hanging branches brushed my face.

I tripped over a tree root.

My hand was stung by a nettle.

I trod in something squelchy.

I hoped Zach was having worse trouble.

The track twisted sharply to the right and came out into a glade. Moonbeams bathed the place in a pale yellow light.

It wasn't the kind of glade you'd expect to see fairies prancing around. In fact, I was doing it a favour even to call it a glade. It was more of a clearing in the woods - and one that had become overgrown over the years. Broken branches littered the ground. Little clusters or toadstools grew in leaf mould. The new season's stinging nettles had sprouted.

A fetid stink hung over the place. As though the body of a dead badger festered in the undergrowth.

But I had taken the right path. (Thank you, Robert Frost.) The clearing held a tiny dilapidated cottage. Its thatch had long rotted. The glass in the windows had fallen out. The door swung unsteadily on its hinges. They added a high-pitched squeal to the threnody of the wind.

And there was a well.

Not, it's true, a well that looked like the one in a picture book I'd had as a kid. The one with the "Ding, dong, bell, pussy's in the well" nursery rhyme. Any pussy in this well would have turned to bones long ago. There wouldn't have been any Tommy Stout to pull her out.

The well had been built out of narrow red bricks which had crumbled with age. Some had fallen out. Lumps of mortar were strewn on the ground.

There was an iron winding arrangement over the well. It would have once held a bucket suspended from a rope. But the bucket had long gone and the iron was rusted.

To the far side of the well, there was a narrow building that reminded me of the outside privy we had at our house when I was a kid. It was built out of breezeblocks and looked more modern than the cottage. It had a sturdy wooden door which fitted tightly into its frame.

I stood on the edge of the clearing and listened.

The wind wailed in the trees.

The swinging door squealed.

The winding mechanism creaked.

I advanced slowly into the glade and walked towards the cottage.

The place looked deserted, but I had to check inside. I stepped up to the front door and pushed it gently. The hinges howled as the door lurched inwards.

I stepped over the threshold. It was darker inside the cottage. Little moonlight penetrated the tiny windows. But there was enough to see it had been long abandoned.

I moved forward.

And a hand reached out from behind the door and grabbed my neck.

It was a big hand with strong bony fingers.

The hand squeezed and I yelled in pain. I tried to struggle free but the hand squeezed tighter. I could feel the tendons in the fingers and thumb tightening around the back of my neck. I tried to kick backwards at my attacker but my foot flashed through air.

Then the hand pushed hard and I stumbled forward. I crashed into something hard - it was a table. I turned around as a dark shadow loomed over me. The faint moonlight glinted on something metal which hurtled towards me. I leapt to one side as the head of a woodsman's axe smashed into the table.

The dark figure wrestled with the axe's haft but the blade had sunk deep in the table and it was hard to free.

While he tugged at his weapon, I nipped forward and let fly with another kick. This time my left foot connected with his ankle. Just where I wanted - on the point where there's little flesh and the nerves are close to the skin.

The dark figure screamed in pain and I knew I'd found Zach. When the bruise blossomed, he'd walk with a limp for days.

Perhaps he'd need a walking stick. Or a wheelchair.

Right now he was hopping on his good leg and yelling like a banshee. Any louder and his old drug-dealing mates in New York would hear him.

I didn't wait to find out what Zach would do next. I nipped smartly out of the cottage door and ran towards the far end of the glade. By the time I'd taken a dozen steps, I knew I'd made a big mistake.

In a tight corner, always head in the direction of a known escape route.

I'd assumed the track led out of the glade on the other side to where it had come in. It didn't. Instead, I ran up against a thick patch of brambles.

I turned to retrace my steps, but Zach had hustled out of the cottage. He wasn't limping as much as I'd hoped. He didn't have a walking stick. But he did have his axe. He didn't look like a man planning to invite me to chop some firewood.

His head swivelled back and forward searching for me.

I ducked down behind the well, but he spotted me. He limped in my direction. The bruise must already be forming. I hoped it would be one of those bright red ones with a big bump.

I waited until Zach decided which way he was coming round the well. He moved to the right. I moved to the left. If I was going to save myself from Zach, the mad axeman, I'd have to get past him. If I could do that, I was confident I could outrun a limping man on the track back to Gingerbread Cottage.

He wouldn't want to pursue me now the cops were in residence.

We faced each other off on either side of the well.

I said: "Right now the cops are putting two and two together. After they've spent a bit of time making five, three and three-quarters, and the square root of nothing, they'll finally get to four. Then they'll come down the same track I did to arrest you."

I moved to the right.

Zach swerved to cut me off and I dodged left.

He said: "I had you down as a limey smartass right from the start. The cops haven't come to arrest me. Not before I've sunk this axe into your head. Not ever."

I feinted to the left and said: "You've got to catch me first."

Zach lumbered closer to the well. He said: "And you've got to get past me. There's no other way out."

He had a point. Getting past him would be a bit like swerving around a back to score a try at rugby. Except that a rugby back wasn't usually wielding an axe.

I said: "What have you done with Barbara Goldsmith?"

"Is that the Aussie broad?"

"My girlfriend's mother."

"She caused me big trouble right from the time we grabbed her."

"Where is she?"

"Somewhere you're not gonna find her, sucker."

I dodged left. Took a couple of steps. Zach moved to cut me off. But at the last minute I sold him the dummy. I skipped to the right and ran hard.

Zach turned, but he'd committed himself to cut off my left move. He turned around but the axe and the ankle slowed him down.

I pounded around the well. I was going to make it. And then my shoe hit a tree root. I took off and flew three feet. I crashed into the ground. The fall knocked the wind out of me.

I pushed myself up on my arms as Zach lumbered around the well. I was on my feet as he took the last step towards me. He swung the axe in a vicious arc. I ducked and felt the air ruffle my hair as the axe flashed over my head.

Zach had put so much energy into the blow, the weight of the axe carried him round in a circle. And the guy had worked up a sweat, too. I could see it glisten on his forehead.

Zach stumbled to regain his footing just as the axe flew from his sweat-slippery hands. It sailed five feet through the air and plunged into the well.

We were both so astonished we gaped while we waited for the splash as it hit the water. The distant sound came two seconds later.

"You won't get that back," I said.

"Don't need it to croak you," he said.

He lunged towards me. I skipped backwards but too late. Zach grabbed my arm in his powerful fist. I struggled but I couldn't free myself. His other hand grabbed at me and he lifted me off the ground. I tried to hit him, but he'd pinioned both my arms to my side.

He lifted me and stepped towards the well.

He said: "You can join the axe."

I said: "If you ever give up drug smuggling, you could become a circus strong man. Why spoil a promising career with murder?"

He said: "Quit your yowling. In two seconds, you'll be a pile of flesh and bones and I don't even need to bury the evidence."

I struggled hard, but he leaned forward on the brickwork around the well and held me over the gaping hole.

I glanced down into the blackness.

I said: "Don't I get any last words."

"Make them 'goodbye cruel world'."

"I was thinking something more upbeat."

"Like what?"

"Like those rotten bricks you're leaning on are about to give way and if you don't watch out you'll follow me down."

"Try another one, loser."

But then two bricks came loose and tumbled into the well. Zach slipped forward. He let go of my right arm to steady himself.

My arm shot up and my hand grabbed the crossbeam of the winding gear above the well. I prayed the rusted old iron would hold my weight.

More bricks gave way and Zach leant dangerously forward, His hold on my left arm slipped and I grabbed the crossbeam with both hands.

It was like clinging to a trapeze. Except that I had a two hundred feet drop into water (not forgetting the axe). The rust of the iron rasped my hand. The contraption creaked under my weight.

But Zach was in more trouble. He'd leaned forward too far to hold me over the well. Now the wall was collapsing under his weight and he couldn't regain his balance. He looked up at me. His eyes were filled with terror. But there was nothing I could do to help.

There was a deep rumble as a section of the wall came away and tumbled into the well. Zach fell forward so only his knees leant against the outside of the well. He grabbed at some bricks to steady himself but they came away in his hand. He slipped further towards the hole.

And then the rest of the wall gave way under his weight.

He screamed as he fell.

A long ululating wail of terror.

The scream chased him to the bottom of the well.

There was a splash followed by a crunch and then more pieces of wall collapsed into the well.

I realised that if more bricks fell the winding mechanism would come lose and slip into the well. I swung backwards like a trapeze artist. Put every effort I could into my legs as I swung forward and jumped.

I landed on the wet grass.

Behind me, the winding gear collapsed and followed the bricks down into the darkness.

I lay on the grass gulping in air. I was shaking - and not from the chill wind. I felt like I wanted to vomit. My stomach churned round and round like a washing machine in a laundromat. It was like I had the week's wash - shirts, socks and dirty knickers (*ugh*) - turning over in my belly.

I belched with the force of a foghorn. Out at sea, ships' captains would race to the bridge and put telescopes to their eyes.

I sat up and looked around. I'd landed inches from the edge of a ragged hole which marked where the well had once stood.

I staggered to my feet. I needed three efforts to do it.

I looked around trying to understand what had just happened. My mind couldn't take it all in.

But I was still alive.

And I still had a mission.

I had to find Shirley's mother.

I walked across the clearing towards the building I'd called the privy. The wooden door was secured on the outside by two sturdy bolts.

I shot the bolts and opened the door.

And looked into the face of a woman with a bouffant blonde hair-do. Strands of loose hair, some still with hairpins, hung around her face. She had a graze on her forehead and a bruise on her chin. Her mascara had run in streaks across her cheeks. She had smudged lipstick and angry eyes.

Her right arm circled towards me like an attack from a king cobra.

Her fist connected with my face. I jolted backwards.

And then everything went black.

Chapter 20

"Shirley never told me her mother was a female wrestler," I said.

Ted Wilson grinned. "Apparently she fights under the name of Battling Babs, the Bash 'em Beauty."

"She certainly laid me out for the count."

It was three hours after my encounter with the Battling Beauty in the woodland glade. Ted and I were in an interview room at Brighton Police Station.

I had a bruise the colour of a ripe tomato on the side of my face.

Owen Griffiths was sulking downstairs in one of the cells.

Christabel and the muses had been told by the cops not to leave Natterjack Grange as they'd be needed for questioning.

Stanley had broken another string on his sitar during the raid. He planned to sue Holdsworth for brutality.

Barbara Goldsmith was reunited with Shirley. Neither of them wanted to see me.

Ted said: "I feel I ought to charge you with something, but I can't think what."

I said: "That's rich coming from you. When I called you from Griffiths' room at Steyning Grammar School to tell you I was heading for Natterjack Grange, you swore blind you'd keep a low profile. That was important because I'd promised Shirley I wouldn't call the cops. You made me look like I broke my promise. Now Shirley thinks I'm a heel and she's dumped me."

Ted shook his head. "It's not what you think."

"What was I supposed to think?" I said.

"After I got your message, I planned to pick up a couple of uniformed plods and drive quietly to Natterjack Grange. We were going to sit out of sight somewhere until we were needed. You'd never have caught Zach yourself. But one of the plods blabbed and my boss got to hear about it."

"Detective Chief Superintendent Alec Tomkins?"

"The very same. He decided we couldn't intervene without the local cops being present. It was a territorial thing. As the Grange is in the West Sussex police division, and we're in Brighton, Tomkins insisted I inform Holdsworth out of courtesy."

"And Holdsworth roared in with all bells ringing. Just what was needed to warn Zach so he could make a run for it."

"Some officers make up in energy what they lack in brains," Ted said.

I said: "Energy, brains - Holdsworth has neither."

"Anyway, under the circumstances, the chief in West Sussex has asked me to take over the case," Ted said.

"The Spencer Hooke murder?"

"No, the drugs smuggling. We still have the Hooke case down as a hit-and-run."

I thumped my fist on the table so hard a coffee mug fell off and smashed on the floor. "You must know that's nonsense," I said.

Ted looked at the mug and said: "It's an offence to damage police property. Besides, I haven't seen any evidence to contradict the hit-and-run finding."

"If Zach did it, we'll never know now."

"From what I've heard of him, I don't think Zach would've confessed anyway," Ted said. "Now Griffiths might cough to killing Hooke. He strikes me as the timid type. And he had the motive - he was being blackmailed."

"And he lied to me about being at a chemistry society meeting. I found out it had been cancelled."

"What about Tom Hobson? If Hooke knew about his role in the smuggling, he'd be into him for some blackmail cash?"

"I've had an officer at Shoreham harbour looking for Hobson. He's vanished and so has his boat."

I said: "He'll turn up in a few months in Spain pretending to be Pedro the Fisherman."

Ted nodded: "Yes. Somewhere with no extradition treaty with Britain. We'll never get him."

Ted drummed on the desk with his pencil. "It's going to be difficult to get the drug charges to stick without a confession - especially as none of them were caught with drugs on them. Even Griffiths could walk if he gets a clever lawyer to explain away his late-night experiments. To get a conviction, we need to find the drugs."

"The latest consignment - the one Hobson picked up on Friday night - will have been passed down the distribution chain by now," I said. "But if you could find Mr Big who put up the finance, you'd be able to roll up the whole operation."

Ted nodded morosely. "Yes, and Zach was the last link in that chain. Now he's at the bottom of the well."

"And you have no idea who Zach reported to?" I asked.

Ted shook his head.

"Me neither. So Mr Big walks free as well." I said.

I ran my hands over my face to get the circulation going. It was late and I was tired. I had a story about the rescue of Barbara from a kidnapper. But I didn't even know what had happened in the hour after she'd flattened me.

I said: "How did you find me in the glade? Barbara laid me out cold."

"After she'd floored you, she heard the racket outside Gingerbread Cottage and came charging through the woods. Shirley was stomping around like an avenging fury, cursing you like you were the very Devil. But when she saw her Mum, she just flew into her arms. I ordered one of our cars to take them both back to Shirley's flat. We'll take full statements in the morning."

"And you explained to Shirley how Holdsworth came to charge in with all bells ringing?" I said. "The last thing she said to me was that we were finished."

"I told her everything," Ted said. "She's still mad that you broke your promise. She's threatening your manhood if she sees you. But I don't think she'll cut both of them off."

Ted grinned. "But I don't know which one she'll leave hanging there."

I didn't arrive back at my rooms in Regency Square until past two in the morning.

So late, it wasn't even necessary to sneak in to avoid the Widow. As soon as I opened the front door I could hear her snores echoing down the hall.

I flopped on my own bed and tried to sleep. But there was too much running through my mind. A couple of days ago, I was confident I could crack an unsolved murder - and roll up a drug gang as a bonus. But even Ted was now dubious about whether the drugs charges would stick. And he'd written off the murder charge - just like hopeless Holdsworth.

I couldn't get one thought out of my mind - that there was a connection between the murder and the drug ring. If only I could discover it, I'd have enough front-page stories to keep Figgis happy for weeks.

The thought ran round and round in my mind, like a show pony in a circus ring until…

My eyes opened and I focused on the bright light through my thin curtains. My nose twitched at the burnt cardboard smell of stewed coffee. Downstairs I could hear the Widow clattering about in the kitchen.

Reluctantly, I climbed out of bed and then remembered it was Sunday. I wasn't due at the paper, so I might as well climb back in and doze the morning away. But what good would that do?

I shuffled towards the bathroom like an old man with a double hernia.

A cold shower can revive even the most tired body. Or so I've been told. But you won't catch me risking any of that treatment. I might catch my death. So I spent five minutes under a steaming shower until the water started to run cold and I knew I'd emptied the Widow's hot tank.

Ten minutes later I made my way downstairs. I was debating whether to risk a piece of burnt toast in the Widow's kitchen or walk down the road to the local greasy spoon for the full English.

But I didn't get to make the choice.

As I stepped off the last tread, the Widow burst out of her kitchen. She hurtled down the hall waving something.

She said: "Look what I've got, Mr Crampton."

I said: "What is it - another letter about your lifetime ban from the Mothers' Union?"

The Widow skidded to a halt on the hall runner and said: "It's a Mother's Day card from my daughter. Today is Mother's Day."

"I thought you didn't have any children. That's why you've been thrown out of the Mothers' Union."

"I asked you to think of a way to get me back in and you ignored it."

"Not so, I've got plenty of excellent ideas."

"Such as?"

"You could say your daughter lost her memory, forgot she had a mother, and has only just recovered it and remembered that she's got you."

"Those harridans at the Union would never believe an obvious lie like that."

"Then tell them she was abducted as a child by gypsies and you only recognised her years later when she came to the door selling clothes pegs."

"Ridiculous. I never buy clothes pegs."

"Well, this one is a winner. Your daughter's had a sex change operation and he's now your son. You didn't like to mention it because he's sensitive about his wispy moustache."

"Now you're being disgusting," the Widow said. "Besides,

I've thought of a better idea. That's where this Mother's Day card comes into play. I've faked the card. But the old biddies at the Union won't know. I got Mr Patel at the newsagents to sign it so it's not my handwriting."

I took the card and looked at it.

"He's signed it Arundhati," I said.

"It's the unexpected detail in a lie that convinces people it's the truth," the Widow said.

"Like a woman who's never been further east than the Ganges Curry House in Kemp Town has an Indian daughter?" I said.

The Widow ignored that and ploughed on. "I'm going to pretend that I had a daughter who was taken from me to give to a wealthy woman who couldn't have children. She never knew who her real mother was until this week."

I gawped at the Widow like she'd just offered me a rent rebate.

Or offered to darn my socks.

Or said I could hold a sex orgy in my rooms.

"If you don't close your mouth, you'll catch flies, Mr Crampton," the Widow said.

"What?"

"Your mouth. It's hanging open."

I closed it and turned for the door.

"Aren't you going to congratulate me on finding my daughter?"

"I hope you'll be very happy together," I shouted as I opened the door and hurried into the street.

My mind felt like some ancient mechanical device that had just been oiled. It was clanking into action, but not all at once.

Since I'd first discovered Spencer Hooke's body on the Bostal road, I'd been convinced he'd been murdered.

There were plenty who'd had the motive to kill Hooke – but not the opportunity.

But now I knew who'd had both.

The trouble was I still didn't know how I could prove it.

I hoped to find the answer in church.

Chapter 21

The Reverend Simon Purslowe stood in front of the altar and made the sign of the cross.

He said: "May peace and goodwill be with you always."

Ted Wilson whispered in my ear: "He's got a hope."

Ted fidgeted like a man who knows something bad is going to happen.

We were sitting in a pew in the nave of St Andrew's church in Steyning. Ted on my left, Bernard Holdsworth on my right.

The Mother's Day service had just ended. The congregation had sung *All Things Bright and Beautiful* as though they meant it.

Holdsworth didn't look bright or beautiful. He had a beetled brow and a scowl on his face that could've cracked a stained glass window.

After I'd steamed out of the Widow's place an hour and a half earlier, I'd driven to the *Chronicle's* newsroom. I'd called Ted and explained my theory about Hooke's murder.

He'd listened and said: "Sounds incredible to me, but I suppose if I don't come to the church, you'll find some way to make me look bad in the paper."

"Would I do that?" I'd said. "But bring Holdsworth."

I rang off before he had time to ask why.

Then I'd called Purslowe. I told him two police officers would be attending his service. They wouldn't be bringing their mothers. But they would want to speak to certain members of his congregation after the service.

It wasn't news that had him ringing the church bells. But, then, he couldn't ring them anyway. One of the six bell-ringers was dead, one was in custody on drugs charges, and one had scarpered.

Three down, three to go.

I glanced at the front pew. Five of the people who'd each

played a key part in this mystery sat there.

Clothilde bowed her head and gave a little sniff. Her pince-nez hung from its lanyard around her neck. She was wearing a tweed suit and a brown cloche felt hat. She opened her handbag and took out a handkerchief. She dabbed her eyes discreetly and put the hankie back in her bag.

Georgina Staples, sitting next along, patted Clothilde's shoulder. She whispered something in her ear. Clothilde gave a wan smile and nodded. Georgina had caused a stir when she'd walked into the church. She was wearing a low-cut blouse and a mini-skirt which ended a couple of inches below the Book of Revelations.

Beyond Georgina, Lady Evangelina Fox and Charles Fox sat rigid and tense. Not like the loving pair I'd seen in the photograph of them at Natterjack Grange. In the photo, Fox had towered over the tiny Evangelina. But the anger in their faces seemed to diminish both of them. They looked like a pair who'd just had a ten-round argument. Fox's face could have been chiselled out of granite. He tried to say something to Evangelina but she shook her head dismissively. Fox adjusted his tie and brushed an imaginary fleck of dust from the lapel of his country tweed jacket.

Evangelina flashed Fox a contemptuous glance as he did it. She was wearing a smart lime green skirt and jacket. It looked like the kind of pricey clobber she'd have picked up at a West End dressmaker. I couldn't see into the pew but I was willing to bet she was wearing a pair of shoes with killer heels, just like she was in the photo. She fiddled with the rope of pearls around her neck. She raised her eyes to Heaven. But she wasn't going to get much help from that direction today.

At the far end of the pew, Christabel stared at the stained glass behind the altar with her dreamy eyes. She was wearing a green kaftan. She had rings on her fingers and fancy bangles around her wrists. She'd plaited her hair with multi-coloured ribbons.

The Reverend Purslowe stepped down from the pulpit and watched the last of the congregation struggle out of the church. The huge oak door slammed shut with a thud that sounded like the crack of doom.

Purslowe turned to the five and said: "I'm so sorry about this. Can we please keep this brief? Mrs Purslowe's got a leg of lamb in the oven for lunch and she becomes quite touchy if it's overdone."

Ted Wilson stood up and faced the group. Gave his beard a couple of nervous strokes.

He said: "I'm a police officer."

"Tell us something we don't know," Fox said irritably.

"Very well. We're here to talk about two subjects you won't normally find mentioned by the vicar from the pulpit."

"What subjects?" Evangelina said.

"Murder and drug smuggling," Ted said.

Everyone shot one another nervous looks. Georgina put her hand to her mouth. Christabel reached for Evangelina's hand. Clothilde looked down at the hymn books in the front of the pew.

Fox barked: "Fine way to end a church service, vicar."

Purslowe started to say something but Ted stopped him.

He said: "I know how news travels along a grapevine in a small village. So you'll all have heard about the incident at Natterjack Grange last night."

"You call it an incident," said Fox. "I'd call it a riot."

"Be quiet," Evangelina hissed.

Ted pointed at me and said: "As Mr Crampton was involved in the incident," - he stressed the word - "I'd like him to explain something to you."

I stood up and moved towards the pulpit. Resisted the temptation to climb into it. What I had to say might sound like a sermon. But it wouldn't have any of this bunch shouting hallelujah.

I said: "Last night I was nearly dropped down a well. I almost joined your former bell-ringer Spencer Hooke up at the Pearly Gates. A character called Zachariah - Zach for short - tried to kill me. He'd been living in an old woodsman's cottage on the Natterjack estate. But he was no woodsman. He was the fixer in a drug-smuggling ring."

The five shot one another more nervous looks.

"Happily, his fixing days are over. He was the one who ended up at the bottom of the well. But as the Duke of Wellington said after the Battle of Waterloo, it was a damned close-run thing. And an unnecessarily dangerous thing as well. We could have cornered and captured Zach alive if it hadn't been for the clumsy intervention of a police officer who roared up at the last moment with all bells ringing. Isn't that right Detective Inspector Holdsworth?"

Holdsworth glared at me. "You can't speak to a police officer like that. I'll sue you for slander."

I said: "Your case won't get far. Because it wasn't just a clumsy mistake to have the police car bell ringing, was it?"

"What are you insinuating?"

"You've been taking pay-offs from Zach to keep quiet about his drug smuggling operation."

Holdsworth jumped up and wagged an angry finger at me. "You don't have a shred of evidence to support that allegation."

"Last night while Zach was trying to throw me down the well, I warned him that police had arrived and would arrest him. He sneered at me and said something that didn't register with me at the time, but has now. He said, 'Those cops haven't come to arrest me.'"

I strode up to Holdsworth. Our faces were inches apart. I could smell whisky on his breath.

I said: "You roared up like the Keystone Cops in a circus parade to warn him to get out fast."

Holdsworth gave me a nuclear-powered hate glare and turned his back on me. He stomped to the other side of the church and leant on a pillar. His lips puckered into a petulant pout.

I said: "My suspicions about you started when you refused to treat Hooke's death seriously. You knew that if it became a murder case, an outside team of detectives would come in. They'd interview everyone in the area, including the residents of Natterjack Grange. Including Zach. The last thing he wanted was police attention. He paid you to treat the case as a less important hit-and-run."

"How would I know about any drug runners?" Holdsworth blustered.

"You gave the game away when I interviewed you: 'Hardly anything happens in Shoreham harbour that I don't get to hear about.' Those were your exact words, weren't they? And you did get to hear about the drug smuggling through the harbour. But you were paid by Zach to turn a blind eye. When the anti-corruption squad examine your bank accounts, I'm betting they'll find deposits you won't be able to explain away."

Holdsworth moved to a pew and sat down heavily. He folded his arms across his chest. The mute of malice pose.

Ted crossed the church and rested his hand on Holdsworth's shoulder.

He said softly: "It's over, Bernie."

Holdsworth looked up at Ted. His eyes had clouded. "I never meant it to get this far," he said.

Ted said: "I have officers waiting for you outside. It's better if you surrender yourself to them."

Holdsworth nodded. He stood up. His shoulders hunched and he looked like an old man. He walked slowly to the back of the church, opened the door, and stepped outside.

The place fell silent.

Then Fox said: "So, a bent copper. Is that why you kept us? We'll be on our way." He went to stand.

Purslowe said: "If that's all, perhaps we can get off to our lunches."

I said: "It's not over yet, vicar. That was a sideshow. Now we can turn to the main event."

"Will this take long?" Evangelina said. "I've got a goose roasting in the oven and I don't want it to burn."

I said: "Your goose will be well and truly cooked by the time you leave here."

"What do you mean by that?" she snapped.

"Let me explain," I said. "I knew about three players in the drugs chain - Hobson, Griffiths and Zach. But I didn't know who the money man behind the racket was. And now that Zach lies dead at the bottom of the well, I shall never be able to ask him. But the answer came to me this morning. When I was at Shoreham harbour on Friday evening, I heard Tom Hobson tell his associates: 'I've netted the money from the big fish on the way'. Who could the big fish be? I'd followed Hobson from the church where he'd attended a bell-ringing practice. He'd not stopped during his drive from Steyning to the harbour. So he had to have collected the money at the church."

"This is going nowhere," Fox said.

"It's coming right back to you, Mr Fox. When I saw you enter the church that evening you had a bag - a kind of satchel - looped over your right shoulder. I believe the money for the drugs deal was in that satchel. When you came out, you were empty-handed. I can just see you handing Hobson the satchel in a quiet corner before you both climbed up to the bell loft for the practice."

"A jury would laugh that evidence out of court," Fox said.

"They won't laugh at the evidence of the satchel. At the harbour, I'm certain Hobson transferred the money from the satchel to an oilskin which he hid in the bottom of a lobster pot. There were three other witnesses who saw him do it. One of those witnesses - Steve, who tried to kill me with a forklift truck - is handcuffed to a bed inside Southlands hospital and he'll confirm the money came from that satchel."

"Except that you don't have the satchel."

Ted stepped forward. "My men are searching the hut."

I said: "When they find the satchel, they'll discover your fingerprints all over it."

"I'm a respected banker," Fox said. "Why shouldn't I have money in a satchel?"

I said: "You're a broke banker. Skint. You've had a string of bad deals. You had to find a way to keep solvent. When your daughter Christabel introduced you to Zach, you spotted another wheeler-dealer. And, as it happened, Zach had been no stranger to the drug scene in New York, where Christabel met him. But I'm prepared to accept that Christabel didn't at first know about Zach's hard drugs trade."

Christabel looked down at her feet.

I turned back to Fox: "With Zach's Yankee contacts and your Brit ones, it wouldn't have taken the two of you long to cook up an international drugs operation. And where better to run it from than a remote cottage on an estate where the other residents were too spaced out to know what was going on?"

"No-one will ever believe that."

"Then perhaps they'll believe the evidence of the kidnap note that was left at my girlfriend's flat. It was the note telling us that Shirley's mother had been kidnapped. It had distinctive black and red capital letters. I think we'll find it was typed on a typewriter in the Brighton branch of your bank."

Fox gave me a flinty look. "Even if it were, doesn't mean to say I had anything to do with it."

He looked away from me and tried to take Evangelina's hand. She withdrew it. Made a point of looking away. Fox turned towards Christabel, but she edged away from him.

I said: "I would never have uncovered your drugs racket, Mr Fox, if Spencer Hooke hadn't been killed."

Fox flared: "I never killed Hooke."

"I accept that," I said: "At first I thought the drug dealing provided the motive for killing Hooke. As several of you had discovered to your cost, young Hooke was an enterprising student who had a great career ahead of him as a chemist - or a blackmailer. He'd discovered Owen Griffiths's role in the drug ring and had been bleeding money from him for several weeks. I suspected he may also have realised Hobson was involved and had him on a retainer. But it wasn't Hobson's van that mercilessly mowed down Hooke on that dark and stormy night. So whose?"

"Whatever happened to love thy neighbour?" wailed Purslowe. He slumped down in one of the pews.

"Can you help us on that point?" I asked Georgina. "After all, you were one of Hooke's blackmail victims."

"That had nothing to do with drugs," she said.

"But you had your motive for killing him. And you have a car."

"I stayed in the night Spencer died. I had a gentleman caller that evening."

"Who was?"

"I told you when you poked your nose into my shop it's none of your business."

Ted's voice echoed around the church: "But it may become mine."

Georgina looked at Ted, back at me. "It was Owen Griffiths," she said.

"What were you doing? Showing him your dolly mixtures?" I asked.

Georgina's eyes flashed. "No, we were screwing," she said.

Clothilde gasped. Christabel giggled. Evangelina sneered.

Fox shouted: "Tally ho!"

Ted Wilson stroked his beard.

Purslowe said: "Miss Staples, please remember where you

are."

She looked up, still angry. "Sorry, vicar."

I said: "Miss Staples, did you know Owen Griffiths was the chemist for a drugs racket?"

She shook her head.

But you both had good reason to wish Hooke dead.

"If wishes were horses, beggars might ride," she said.

"Did you drive your car over the Bostal the night Hooke was killed?"

"No. I've told you. I was with Owen."

"Then how do you explain the damaged number plate on your Ford Anglia?"

"That happened in Brighton earlier in the week. I tried to squeeze my car into an impossible parking slot in Ship Street. I dinged the car in front of me. I left a card under the car's windscreen wiper and the owner rang me the following day. He said the damage was light and I wasn't to worry about it. I can prove that. I have his name and number at the shop."

"What were you doing in Brighton, Miss Staples?" Ted asked.

"It was private business," she said angrily.

"Nothing is private in a murder enquiry," he said.

I moved over to Ted and whispered: "I'd leave it, if I were you. It won't be relevant."

"Don't tell me how to run police business," he snapped. "Now, Miss Staples, I must ask you again. What were you doing in Brighton?"

Georgina jumped to her feet. Hustled out of the pew. Stormed up to Ted. Her cheeks were flushed and her eyes blazed with fury.

"If you must know I was at a photographer's studio. Being shot in the nude." She pulled up her blouse. "People pay good money to photograph these tits."

The others looked at one another goggle-eyed.

Purslowe crossed himself, then put his hand over his eyes.

Fox said: "By gad, what's the going rate? Do you charge individually or do they come as a pair?"

Evangelina slapped his face. "You foul beast," she said.

"I wonder if she takes cheques," Fox said.

This was getting out of hand. I threw my hands in the air like John the Baptist and shouted: "This is not a carnival."

Everyone fell silent. Looked a bit sheepish.

Clothilde murmured: "Well, I never!"

Georgina pulled back her blouse. Bowed her head and walked over to her seat.

Ted said: "We know that Hooke was killed by a car. And it seems to me we've ruled out all the cars owned by members of the drugs ring and those associated with them."

"All except one," I said.

Ted's eyes crossed in a puzzled look.

"Which one?" he asked.

I strode over to the pew where Christabel was sitting.

I said: "I think you can help us, Christabel. The first time I visited you at Natterjack Grange I noticed that your Austin Cambridge was being painted in psychedelic livery - just like your hippie bus. That would be the ideal way to hide any scratch marks or damage. But a proper forensic examination would reveal what's under the flower-power painting."

Christabel's eyes darted anxiously from me to Ted Wilson. They flicked from Ted to Evangelina. Then to Clothilde. Christabel looked down at her hands. At the rings on her fingers and the bangles around her wrists.

She looked back at me. Not anxious now. She'd made up her mind about something.

She stood up. "Yes, I was driving my Austin Cambridge the night it hit Spencer Hooke," she said.

Evangelina's hand reached for Christabel's. Clothilde stirred anxiously in the pew. Georgina buried her head in her hands. Fox looked ahead like he was staring at the end of the world.

The air in the church became heavy with silence.

Then Evangelina stood up. She edged out of the pew and tottered on six-inch stilettos towards Ted. Her high-heels clacked like castanets on the church's flagstones.

She said: "There is no greater love than a daughter who wants to protect her mother - especially on Mother's Day. But Christabel was not driving the car that killed Spencer Hooke. I was."

Ted glanced at me. His eyes glazed with confusion.

He started to speak but before he could get more than a couple of words out, Clothilde stood up. She swayed slightly and gripped the pew in front of her.

She said: "It is time for the truth to be told. There are two noble women who wish to protect me for reasons I will never divulge. But I drove the car that killed Spencer Hooke."

Ted turned to me and said: "What on earth is going on? Which one really did it?"

I said: "You wait ages for a murderer to confess and then three come along together."

Chapter 22

Ted Wilson's shoulders slumped like a man who knows he's lost a battle.

He said: "Now let's get this clear. Which of you three ladies was driving the car that killed Spencer Hooke?"

"Me," Christabel said.

"Me," Evangelina said.

"Me," Clothilde said.

"You can't all have been driving it," he shouted.

"Inspector, please, remember where we are," Purslowe said. "Surely at this difficult time, we must remember the wise words of Augustine of Hippo who, when faced with a beggar who'd stolen a goat... Or was it Augustine of Goat and a stolen hippo... Oh dear, my mind has become a jumble."

I said: "Perhaps I can help sort out that jumble, vicar."

Ted said: "If you must." He sat down heavily in a pew.

I walked over to where the three would-be murderers stood in a huddle.

I said: "Christabel, Evangelina, Clothilde - you all had a motive for killing Spencer Hooke. But only one of you could have been driving the car."

They all started to speak, but I held up my hand.

I turned to Christabel. "Hooke was blackmailing you, wasn't he?"

Christabel ignored the question and sat down.

"I'll take that as a 'yes'," I said. "When I first visited you at Natterjack Grange, you made a strong point of telling me that you disapproved of illegal drugs. I wondered about that as you'd travelled with the Merry Pranksters who'd had a reputation for juicing themselves with exotic substances. But I decided to take your denial at face value. After all, you have a lot to lose - Natterjack Grange itself."

"I don't know what you're talking about," Christabel said.

"The night you showed Shirley and me into the library, the table where you wanted to put the tea tray was covered with papers. Ever helpful, I gathered up the papers to make way for the tea. I put the papers on a shelf, but I couldn't help noticing they included a fat envelope from the Sussex Coast Building Society and solicitors' letters about the debt outstanding on the estate."

Christabel's eyes flashed angrily. "Snooper," she said.

"I prefer the term investigative journalist," I said. "But let's not quibble over words. The brief glance I had of your papers showed that when you'd inherited the estate it was loaded with debt. You'd taken out a mortgage to clear those debts and try and put the place on a sounder financial footing. Good for you. But you knew that there are two points building societies insist on when they grant a mortgage. They want repayments made regularly and they won't allow you to use the place for anything illegal. If you do, they can call in the mortgage immediately."

"I was making the repayments," Christabel said.

"Yes, but you were also allowing the estate to be used for Zach's drug smuggling operation."

"He deceived me. When I met him in New York, I thought he shared the ideals of the Merry Pranksters. Instead, he used us as cover for drug running. I didn't realise he was doing it at the Grange until that odious Spencer Hooke told me."

"On that point, I believe you. Hooke had a way of ferreting out people's secrets. I suspect he picked up on Zach's trade during one of his visits to the Grange."

"He demanded I pay him a monthly allowance, as he called it. The building society payment was already more than I could afford."

"And so, when an opportunity came to kill Hooke, Merry Prankster Christabel joined the conspiracy."

"And drove the car," she said.

"Now that wasn't a merry prank. But who raised the possibility of killing Hooke?"

"I won't tell you."

"Then let me tell you. It was your mother, Lady Evangelina, wasn't it?"

Evangelina moved towards me and said: "I've already said I was responsible for killing Hooke. Leave Christabel out of it."

I said: "I'd like to leave you all out of it, but in your different ways you're all in it. And you all had a strong motive for killing Spencer Hooke."

"What kind of motive?" Evangelina snapped.

"The most common kind. Money."

"*Psshaw*! I'm a wealthy woman. As the only child of the late Earl and Countess of Herstmonceux, I've inherited their fortune."

"But that's not quite correct, is it?"

"Now you're being insolent."

"I'm sorry," I said. "It's an occupational hazard. But the fact remains. You didn't inherit the Earl and Countess's fortune outright. You receive the income from a trust fund. We have an exceptionally bright business reporter on the *Chronicle* - Susan Wheatcroft. She told me about the trust fund and the restrictive covenants in it."

Evangelina said: "The income from my trust fund would make your own salary look like the coppers in a pauper's begging bowl."

I grinned. "I'm glad you mentioned that, Lady Evangelina, as I'll be expecting a big salary rise after landing this story. But to get back to the trust fund, in order to receive its monthly stipend, you have to be the birth daughter of the Earl and Countess - one of the covenants Susan mentioned."

Lady Evangelina drew herself up to her full height (four feet, eleven inches) and said: "I hope you're not insinuating that I'm not the Earl's daughter."

"Not at all. The late Earl was your father."

I waited for Evangelina to reply. She said nothing. I suppose that was a pregnant pause. Appropriate under the circumstances.

I added: "But the Countess was not your mother."

I turned towards Clothilde. "Was she, Miss Tench-Hardie?"

Clothilde collapsed into a pew. She buried her head in her hands. Her retching sobs echoed off the church's stark stone walls.

Evangelina hurried to her side. Slid into the pew and embraced her. Clothilde reached into her handbag and took out her handkerchief. She wiped her eyes.

Fox sat ramrod straight in his place. He stared at his wife like a man who's just seen his world collapse.

He said: "Is this journalist Johnnie correct, Evie? You're not the full meat and potatoes?"

Evangelina turned angrily towards him. "Shut up, you pompous prig. The only thing you care about is my money. Well, now there isn't any. So take that to your bank and stuff it in the vault."

Clothilde wiped her eyes again and put the handkerchief back in her bag.

I walked over to her and asked: "When did Spencer Hooke tell you he'd discovered the truth?"

"Four weeks ago. It's been an agony for me and Evie ever since. How did you know?"

"Christabel told me that when she moved into Natterjack Grange, she sent boxes of family papers to the County Records Office at Chichester. You told me how you'd introduced Hooke to family research and told him about the Records Office. You mentioned he'd visited it during half-term, about four weeks ago. I'd also learnt that Hooke had told one of his partners-in-crime at the grammar school that he thought he'd hit the big time in blackmail after his visit to the office. I thought this might have something to do with the family papers Christabel had sent - especially as she didn't know what was in the boxes. I've been puzzling over this conundrum until this morning when my landlady said something which provided an obvious solution."

I turned to Clothilde: "How did you come to give birth to Evangelina?" I asked gently.

Clothilde had composed herself. She spoke with a clear voice. "My father was a tenant farmer. He farmed land owned by the Earl. It was a hard life and not a rewarding one. He'd had three years of poor crops. Disease had riddled his herd of cows. But none of this interested the Earl. He wanted the rent and my father couldn't afford to pay. He faced being evicted from his farm. That's when the Earl proposed an alternative. The Countess could not have children but desired one so much that she pined away. The two of them decided that they should adopt a child. But they couldn't go through the usual adoption process because that would make the matter public. There were legal issues in the deeds of the Earl's estate that meant an adopted child would have trouble with inheritance. And the Earl wanted the estate and his fortune to pass down his own line."

"And you were selected to bear the child?" I said.

Clothilde nodded. "I was nineteen. I was treated no better than a farmyard heifer. The experience has lived with me ever since. I can barely go to bed at night without smelling the brandy stench and sweat of the Earl grunting on top of me."

Christabel gasped. Purslowe crossed himself. Ted Wilson wrote something in his notebook.

Georgina said: "Disgusting. He sounds like a rutting goat."

Clothilde said: "I was sent away to a small seaside town in Somerset for the nine months of my pregnancy. I understood that the Countess had gone abroad so that the local people could not see that she hadn't carried the child she later claimed as her own. My Evangelina. She was taken from me fifteen minutes after her birth. I wasn't even allowed to choose her name. But

I've come to love it - for all of my life, but from afar."

"And you didn't speak out before, because the Earl paid you to keep silent," I said.

"He set up a trust fund - the rich always seem to hide their wealth in trusts - which has paid me every month since the night of the conception. But on the strict understanding that I keep the secret. The money is my only income. I had no choice."

"Until Hooke threatened to blow the deception wide open," I said.

"I felt betrayed after all I'd done for him. But I couldn't afford to pay what he demanded. He was going to tell Evangelina. But the news couldn't come from him. Last week, I visited her at home and gave her the news. As gently as I could."

"And so mother, daughter and granddaughter all had a motive to murder Spencer Hooke," I said. "But you couldn't all have been driving the car that hit him."

"I drove my Austin Cambridge," Christabel said.

"No, it was me," Evangelina said.

"You both know I was behind the wheel," Clothilde said.

Ted Wilson moved towards them. "Now look here," he said. "A car can't be driven by three people at once. If you don't tell me which of you really did it, I shall charge you all with wasting police time."

I said: "That's not much of a threat, Ted, when they're already confessing to murder."

"So unless two of them admit they're lying, we'll never know who did it?" he said.

"It's time to reveal that." I said.

Chapter 23

I said: "Spencer Hooke's killing involved three things.

"The first two were a car and a driver. But the third was the most important."

"And what was that, clever clogs?" Fox said.

"It was a plan," I said. "Three women discovered they had done foolish things - and now they needed a plan to save themselves."

I quoted some Oliver Goldsmith: "When lovely woman stoops to folly, And finds too late that men betray, What charm can soothe her melancholy, What art can wash her guilt away?"

I said: "I expect you know the answer to that question, Lady Evangelina."

She stared straight ahead as she quoted in a clear voice: "The only art her guilt to cover, To hide her shame from every eye, To give repentance to her lover, And wring his bosom - is to die."

A grim little smile twitched on her lips.

"Except, Lady Evangelina, the plan was that none of the lovely women would die. It would be the tormentor who'd exploited their folly."

"If you say so," she said.

"And that is how the plan was born. I can see the three of you sitting around the teacups dreaming up scheme after scheme - each more improbable than the last. You couldn't shoot Hooke. None of you had a gun or knew how to use one. You couldn't stab him. I expect none of you can stand the sight of blood. Besides blood is difficult to wash off those expensive clothes you wear, Lady Evangelina. As for poisoning, that would involve slipping some deadly substance into Hooke's tea. And I expect the most deadly thing you could lay your hands on was the home-made fig jam I saw in Clothilde's kitchen when I visited.

"And then the vicar provided you with the perfect answer."

Purslowe bristled: "I do hope you are not suggesting I was involved in this dreadful business, Mr Crampton."

"Your role was completely unwitting," I said. "You put up one of those new Royal Society for the Prevention of Accidents posters on the church noticeboard."

Purslowe asked: "Do you mean the one with the slogan 'Stop accidents on the road'? The one with the picture of that unfortunate woman sitting in a wheelchair."

"That is the poster that gave our three stoopers-to-folly the idea," I said. "Except they didn't plan to leave their victim in a wheelchair. They planned to leave him dead. They planned to run him down in a car while he was on his bicycle."

"Oh dear, I shall take the poster down immediately," Purslowe twittered.

"Bit late in the day for that, vicar," Ted said.

"But it wasn't too late in the day to plan a killing. Was it you who initiated the plan, Lady Evangelina?"

Evangelina tossed her head.

"I'll take that as a 'yes'. The poster gave you the idea, but you immediately realised the plot was fraught with danger."

"It all depended on catching Hooke on his bicycle," Ted said.

"Yes, the plotters couldn't spend their time sitting in a car hoping Hooke would cycle by. They needed to know where he would be cycling at a specific time. Even more, it would have to be somewhere they could run him down with a reasonable hope that no-one else would see what happened. Witnesses would have been fatal to the plan. And that's where you contributed your idea, wasn't it, Christabel?"

"If you know so much, you tell me," she said.

"When we spoke in the library at Natterjack Grange, you lied to me about whether Hooke had visited you."

Christabel went to protest, but I held up my hand.

"It's no use. I'm a crime reporter. I spend much of my life listening to lies. I know when I'm hearing one. And I'm willing to bet my Parker fountain pen to a penny that Hooke visited often because he was intrigued by your way-out lifestyle. But mainly because he fancied you."

"Think I'd make out with a square schoolboy like that? *Ugh.*"

"No, I don't think that. But I do think you typed the note which enticed Hooke to a meeting at the barn on the estate the night he died. The note was typed on a card with distinctive rounded corners. When I was in your library, I noticed there was a handsome wooden stationery holder on the desk holding some of those cards."

"So what? I've already admitted I was driving the car that killed Hooke. What's the point of all this?"

"The point is to get to the truth," I said. "And I haven't finished with your contribution yet."

"This is worse than a bad trip," Christabel said.

I said: "The other problem you faced was which car to use to run Hooke down."

"Yes, that gave us some problems," Evangelina said. "I could hardly use the Bentley - much too distinctive. But, of course, I did drive the car we finally chose."

"You rightly expected the car to take some damage as you knocked Hooke roughly off his cycle," I said. "And when Hooke was found, the police would look for a car with a damaged front or wing. So you couldn't send it to a local garage for repair. Local car body shops would be first on the cop's list. Right, Ted?"

Wilson nodded.

I said: "And this is where Christabel once again, came up with the answer. She volunteered her Austin Cambridge. It was a dowdy green colour. When I visited the Grange, the car had been partly painted in a flower power livery - bright primary colour images of flowers and birds and butterflies. It was the perfect way to disguise any damage."

"My car, my bum in the driving seat," Christabel said.

"But was it?" I said. "We now come to the night of the killing. And I think I can reconstruct what happened. It began with Clothilde and Evangelina driving to Natterjack Grange to collect the Austin Cambridge."

I turned towards Clothilde. "You drove your Morris Minor with Evangelina as a passenger."

"That's pure guesswork," Clothilde said.

"I don't guess. Sherlock Holmes said guessing was destructive to reasoning. I find it leads to libel suits. In any event, there was no need to guess. At one point on the driveway into Natterjack Grange, there is a hollow where a spring flows onto the track. The spring has spread a sandy mud over the road at that point. You can't avoid it as you drive through. The following day, I found the stuff had stuck round the wheel-arches of my MGB. I'd already seen it on the wheel-arches of your Morris Minor, Clothilde. I had a sneaky look after you'd generously fed me on tea and cake."

Clothilde frowned and gripped her handbag more tightly.

"Fine way to repay hospitality," she said.

"Better than killing the guest," I said.

"You're missing the point," Evangelina said. "Clothilde may have driven me to collect the Austin, but I drove the Austin up on to the Bostal."

"Yes, you did," I said.

Evangelina's eyes goggled. "How can you be so cocksure about that?"

"Because of what happened while you and Clothilde sat in the car in the lay-by waiting for Hooke to appear."

"You can't possibly know what was said in a private car by two people," Evangelina said.

"Not know, but infer," I said.

"What does that mean?"

"It means I draw on what I already know - and on one piece of vital evidence - to be able to reconstruct the main drift of your conversation."

"This I've got to hear," Ted murmured.

I gave him one of my cool looks and pressed on.

"To begin with, each of you knew a bit about the others' driving experience. Evangelina, you knew that Clothilde had a reputation as a driver who was a hazard on the road. The vicar had innocently mentioned Clothilde's erratic driving when I'd met him at the vicarage."

Clothilde shot Purslowe a fierce glance. "How could you do that – a man of the cloth?"

Purslowe's eyes travelled upwards. "I shall seek divine forgiveness."

I ignored him and said: "But that wasn't the end of the argument in the car. Because Clothilde knew Evangelina as a lady-of-the-manor more used to being driven around by a chauffeur than sitting behind the steering wheel herself. When I examined the lay-by, I noticed that a larch sapling had recently been snapped - probably by a car backing into it. Perhaps Evangelina had snapped it when she reversed into the lay-by. Anyway, there was certainly enough doubt about the driving prowess of both of you to question which should be at the wheel to commit the deed. After all, it had to be done right. You would only get one chance."

"It was me," Evangelina said.

"No, me," Clothilde said.

I looked at Christabel.

She shrugged. "You know it wasn't me now."

I turned back to Clothilde and Evangelina. "You'd stooped to fresh folly with a plan to kill Hooke. And there you were in the car, minutes before Hooke's appearance, arguing about who should do it."

"We weren't arguing," Clothilde said.

"We were discussing," Evangelina said. "In a civilised manner."

"Can murder ever be civilised?" I said. "I doubt it. But I am certain that you, Evangelina, agreed that Clothilde should be behind the wheel to deliver the fatal blow."

Evangelina bowed her head in acceptance. "Yes," she said quietly.

"And you, Clothilde, had a knock-out argument," I said. "You told Evangelina you only had a few months to live. If anything went wrong and the plot was discovered, you wouldn't be around to stand in the dock."

Clothilde opened her handbag and took out her handkerchief. She dabbed her eyes.

"It's true," she said.

"I know," I said. "I saw the bottle of pills for your heart trouble in your kitchen - along with the jars of fig jam. My own mother took them for her heart problem. Pills, that is, not jars of fig jam."

"None of that counts as evidence that would stand up in court," Ted said.

"You won't have to rely on it. There's something that clinches the case. When I was looking at the tracks of the Austin in the dried lay-by mud, I noticed there were some deep circular depressions around the car. It looked like someone had walked round the car with a thin garden dibble and made holes. In fact, they were made by the heels of Evangelina's stilettos. When she agreed to change places with Clothilde, she climbed out of the driver's door and walked around to the passenger's side to get back in. Meanwhile, Clothilde slid across the bench seat behind the wheel.

"And moments later Spencer Hooke appeared on his bicycle ride to death."

"Now this is what I call a Mother's Day present," Frank Figgis said.

He held up a proof of the *Chronicle's* front page and grinned at it like a kid who's just been given his first teddy bear. The page carried my exclusive about the murder of Spencer Hooke. The screamer headline read: THREE WOMEN FACE MURDER CONSPIRACY CHARGE.

Further down the page, another headline reader: BANKER ON DRUGS PEDDLING RAP.

It was the following morning and we were sitting in Figgis's office.

I said: "A great story, I agree. But a Mother's Day gift? Did you usually hand your own mother a conspiracy to murder?"

"Usually a box of Dairy Milk - when I remembered. When I didn't she'd give me a clip round the ear."

"Sturdy character building stuff," I said.

Figgis put the proof in his out-tray and lit up a Woodbine.

He said: "What I still can't figure out is why they all wanted to take the rap for the killing. It's usually the other way round, with the killer pointing the finger of suspicion somewhere else."

I said: "You've got to remember that when the three hatched this plot, they expected to get away with it. They thought they'd planned the perfect crime. And if Holdsworth's sloppy investigation had run its course, they would have. When they walked into St Andrew's church yesterday, they never imagined they'd walk out in handcuffs."

"I get that," Figgis said. "But why were the three all so keen to put their hand up to the dirty deed?"

"Until last week, the only person who knew the truth about Evangelina was Clothilde. For years she'd had to bottle up the knowledge that her own daughter loved another woman as her mother. She kept the secret because of the promises she'd made and the Earl's regular pay-off, which she relied on. When Hooke arrived with his blackmail demand, she was initially appalled and frightened. But I think it became a strange kind of relief to her. It gave her an excuse to tell the truth.

"And she had the courage to do it. But the truth came as an

emotional earthquake to Evangelina and Christabel. Suddenly, Evangelina realised the woman she'd worshipped was not her mother. And Christabel had been close to the Countess whom she believed to be her grandmother. Now both Evangelina and Christabel were faced with the fact that the central belief of their life - the love of their mother and grandmother – had been based on a lie. It's not too difficult to see how that cuts loose any kind of moral judgement."

"And leads to a murder plot," Figgis said.

"Yes, and to the desire to pay the penalty for it. When a cataclysmic event challenges everything you ever believed, it can lead you to both evil acts and good. And that morning they'd just listened to the Reverend Purslowe preach an emotional sermon about how Moses was abandoned by his real mother and found by the pharaoh's daughter among the bulrushes. Purslowe may be a twitterer in real life but it turns out he's passion on stilts in the pulpit."

"Hooke, the schoolboy blackmailer, didn't understand the forces he'd unleashed," Figgis said.

"He broke a cardinal law of blackmail," I said.

"Which is?"

"Never let your victims meet. When they think they're alone, they feel vulnerable. As soon as they know there are others in the same trouble, they take strength from one another. They scheme for a way out. Hooke was too greedy. He paid the ultimate price."

I stood up and headed for the door.

Figgis said: "I'm hearing newsroom gossip that your Aussie girlfriend has given you the big E."

I turned. "You've been a news editor long enough to know that not all rumours are true," I said.

But I wasn't sure whether Figgis was right or wrong.

The last time I'd seen Shirley was when I took off after Zach in the woods at Natterjack Grange. Holdsworth's cop car had raced up the track with its bell ringing. Shirley had screamed that I'd betrayed her.

Despite what Ted Wilson had told me, I didn't know whether she still felt the same way.

It was early evening before I reached her flat in Clarence Square.

I lifted the knocker on the front door and gave a tentative tap. I wasn't feeling confident about this. I felt like a travelling circus had just pitched camp in my stomach. And the trapeze artistes were practising their somersaults.

The door opened and Shirley stood backlit by the bulb from the hall lamp. She was wearing a pink sweater that fitted her like a second skin and blue jeans.

She'd had the impish grin on her face - the one that made her look like a schoolgirl who's just put a whoopee cushion on the teacher's chair.

The grin vanished when she saw me. She had a stern look in her eyes.

She said: "Are you alone or are the blue meanies about to race round the corner with all bells ringing."

I said: "I never meant the cops to arrive like a carnival parade at Natterjack Grange."

Shirley shrugged. "You'd better come in."

I smiled. "Thanks."

"For a few minutes," she added ominously.

She stepped aside to let me through the door. She smelt of that perfumed Camay soap she used in the shower.

We walked into Shirley's sitting room. She faced me with her arms folded.

"Well, let's hear your excuse," she said.

"It's an explanation, not an excuse. When I knew Zach was involved, I realised I wouldn't be able to tackle him alone. The plan was for Ted Wilson and a couple of uniformed plods to sit quietly in their car, hidden in the woods. You'd never have known they were there. But Ted was ordered to pass the information to Holdsworth - and you know the results."

Shirley relaxed a little. "Ted explained that to me while they were still trying to bring you round. But it doesn't alter the fact that you broke your promise."

"With the best intentions. Besides, all's well that ends well. Your Ma is safe. I was the one who ended up laid out on the ground."

Shirley grinned. "Yeah. I'd normally expect you to grovel, but I guess my Ma doled out your punishment. So I suppose I'll have to give you a free pass this time. Are you going to stay for supper?"

"Try and stop me." I sniffed the air. "Smells like you're cooking something delicious."

"I'm not doing the cooking tonight," Shirl said.

A shadow loomed in the kitchen doorway.

Barbara burst into the room. She had false eyelashes like bat's wings and smudged lipstick.

Her huge breasts wobbled over the top of her low-cut dress. They looked like a pair of barrage balloons that wanted to tug free of their moorings.

"Thanks for the bonzer words about my tucker," she said. "For a pom, you're not bad looking. I could eat you myself. No hard feelings about the fisticuffs, I hope."

She crossed the room and threw her arms around me. She plonked a lingering kiss on my lips. Her hand foraged down my back and squeezed my bum. She jiggled her breasts against me so it felt like I was snuggling up to a water bed.

I wriggled free.

I shot Shirley an imploring look.

"Will your Ma be staying long?" I asked.

Epilogue

Mothers' Day 1966.

"Come back to bed," Shirley said.

I sat on the edge of the bed and pulled on a sock.

"I can't," I said. "Figgis has insisted I come into the office today."

"You don't normally go on Sunday."

"This is special. Figgis wants me to write a retrospective on last year's Mother's Day murder."

"I remember. The one where that schoolkid got croaked by those mad women?"

"They weren't mad. They were scheming - as the court at Lewes Assizes found when it sentenced both of them for conspiracy to murder."

"Two? I thought there were three."

"Clothilde Tench-Hardie - the one who was driving the car - died before she came to trial. You can't try a dead woman."

"So the other two had to carry the can by themselves?"

"Afraid so. Life sentences for each. The trial judge said Christabel Fox should serve a minimum of twelve years and her mother Lady Evangelina fifteen."

Shirley sat up in bed and rubbed her eyes.

"They won't like that," she said. "Not a couple of right figjams like them."

I looked puzzled. "Figjams - is that some kind of Aussie word?"

"It's one of those words made up from the first letters of other words."

"An acronym."

Shirley nodded. "'Fuck I'm good - just ask me'. Means someone who thinks they're the bee's knees."

I grinned. "I suppose both Evangelina and Christabel were figjams in their own ways. Apparently, Christabel has taken up transcendental meditation in jail. She drives the prison warders crazy with her chanting. And Lady Evangelina has become the chatelaine of Holloway."

"That's the top women's prison in London, isn't it?"

"Yes. Her ladyship has started up a branch of the Women's Institute in the jail. She makes marmalade in the prison kitchen and has got inmates embroidering flowery designs on their prison gear."

"Makes a change from those arrows," Shirley said.

"She's even invited me to speak at their monthly meeting."

"Not that joke about the archbishop again?"

I frowned. "No, not that one. My subject is to be 'Great Prison Escapes'."

"Sounds like she's got a dinkum set-up."

"That kind always do. Her husband Charles Fox is in Pentonville. He was sent down for fourteen years for drug smuggling and bank fraud. Apparently, he's turned himself into the prison cigarette baron. None of the screws have yet worked out how he gets the fags in. My guess is that he has someone on the outside who chucks them over the wall during exercise periods."

"Didn't Fox have some little helpers, too?"

"Yes. Owen Griffiths is in Wandsworth nick. I gather he signed up for the prison educational service. He gives lectures on chemistry. The rumour is he runs a private class for safe breakers on cooking up explosives. Tom Hobson got away, sailed to Spain and sold his fishing boat. Now I hear he's drinking away the money. He'll run out and come back to Blighty eventually. Then he'll be arrested and serve his time."

"What about the guy who tried to kill you with the forklift truck?"

"Steve. They couldn't prove that. So he just got six months

for criminal damage - driving the truck into the harbour. And his mates Jock and Toby vanished. Nobody has seen them since. They'll have changed their names and be scraping a crust from a life of crime around some other harbour."

"Did that bent copper get away?" Shirley asked.

"No. Holdsworth was found guilty of corruption and jailed. But none of the other lags like a bent copper, so he spends his days in solitary confinement playing chess against himself."

"So they all lived unhappily ever after," Shirley said. "Sounds like you've got your story sewn up already. So it won't take you long to write."

"Have you got anything to do today?" I asked.

"Nah! I rang my mum at midnight last night. It was already Mother's Day in Australia - eight in the morning. She was just cooking her breakfast. Two steaks and the heart of her latest victim."

"So she's still in the wrestling ring."

"Yeah. Had a match two nights ago. Beat Esme Cracker, the Melbourne Mauler, in five rounds."

I reached for my other sock.

"Seems we both don't have much to do this morning," Shirley said.

"True," I said. "My story is for tomorrow's paper so I could write it this afternoon."

"So you gonna put that sock on? Or take the other one off?"

I looked at Shirley. She winked at me.

Twice.

I peeled off my sock and threw it into the corner of the bedroom.

Bonus chapter

Now read chapter 1 of *The Tango School Mystery*, Book 1 in the Deadline Murder Series

The Tango School Mystery

A Crampton of the Chronicle adventure

Peter Bartram

Deadline Murder Series Book 1

Chapter 1

My Australian girlfriend Shirley looked at her porterhouse steak and said: "That's a real beaut, Colin."

The lump of meat which overlapped Shirl's huge dinner plate was the same shape as South America - broad at the top, narrowing down to a tip. It was cooked so rare I half expected to see the thing twitch. It had a kind of fierce red which made it look as though it had been out in the sun too long rather than under a grill.

A rivulet of blood oozed from one side - roughly where Sao Paulo would be - and merged with a slice of grilled tomato. As though the steak had been served with a blood clot on the side.

I said: "Don't you Aussies believe in cooking your food?"

Shirley seized her knife and fork and made an incision in the steak close to Venezuela. "If I were back in Adelaide, I'd have slapped this on the barbie so quick it would barely have had time to brown its bum." She forked a lump of the meat into her mouth and chewed contentedly.

We were sitting at a corner table in Antoine's Sussex Grill in Brighton's Ship Street. The place had oak-panelled walls, a green carpet, and dusty chandeliers. It was like being in a baronial hall on the baron's night off. In this case, on everyone's night off. Shirl and I were the only diners.

But that suited me just fine after the day I'd had in the *Evening Chronicle*'s newsroom. Twenty minutes before the afternoon edition deadline, the Press Association ticker spewed out the news that the Prime Minister, Sir Alec Douglas-Home, had announced that the long-awaited 1964 general election would take place on the fifteenth of October. That meant a tasty little front-page splash I'd conjured up about a jewel heist in Lewes got bounced to an inside page.

And with politics dominating the news, my byline - Colin

Crampton, crime correspondent - wasn't going to appear on the front page much before polling day in just over three weeks' time.

Not that I'd have much time for proper journalism. Not with the special assignment my news editor Frank Figgis had handed me. But I wasn't going to trouble Shirley about that.

Not just yet.

Shirl wiped a dribble of blood from her chin with a napkin. She cut a slice off Ecuador and stuffed it into her mouth. She pointed at my own plate and said: "What's that? It looks like bits of a dead rat."

I said: "It's jugged hare."

"I'd rather eat a juicy steak than a mouthful of hair."

"It's not hair with an A I R. It's hare with an A R E," I said. "You must have heard the story about the creature that got beaten by the tortoise."

"Guess the bludger should have spent less time snoozing by the road. Then he wouldn't have ended up in the pot with all those vegetables."

I reached for the bottle of Burgundy we'd ordered and refilled our glasses.

Shirley hoisted her glass and had a generous slurp.

"Still, this is ace tucker. I'll hand you that," she said.

I cut some of the hare's tender stewed flesh from a leg bone.

"It should be," I said. "This place is owned by a bloke who used to be head waiter at the Ritz hotel in London before the war. Made a name for himself by cooking crêpe Suzette at the table for Winston Churchill."

Shirl made a long cut in her steak somewhere near the Atacama Desert.

"I bet the old boy's never eaten here, though," she said.

"Not likely to now. He's retiring from Parliament at this election. But he may have eaten near here when he was a kid."

"How come?" Shirley asked.

"He was at a school in Hove for two years. Sent there by his mum and dad after they'd discovered he'd been savagely beaten by a sadistic headmaster at his previous school. Never happened to him here, though. The Hove school was run by two maiden ladies - they were sisters. I think someone told me their name was Thompson. According to the stories, Winston loved it here. I suppose anywhere would seem good after your bum had been whipped until the blood ran down your thighs. Anyway, he later went on to Harrow, the posh public school, so I guess the Misses Thompson must have done him some good."

"Guess so," Shirley said.

"Anyway, speaking of blood, I don't remember seeing that blob before." I pointed at Shirley's steak. A little red lake had formed in the Amazonian rain forest.

Shirl brushed it to one side with her knife. "Probably released from inside as the meat cools," she said.

Plop.

A fresh drop of blood landed in the Argentinian Pampas.

"But that wasn't," I said.

"Jeez," Shirley said. "I've never seen that before."

We looked at each other for a couple of seconds. Together, our necks swivelled back. Our gaze travelled up to the ceiling.

A round crimson patch, like a carnation in bloom, flowered on the plaster. Our eyes widened and our jaws dropped. We watched blood ooze through the ceiling. It formed into the shape of a teardrop. For a moment it swayed gently from side to side. Then it detached itself, slowly as though reluctant to leave its resting place.

It fell like a solitary raindrop. A scarlet raindrop.

Plop.

It landed on the tablecloth and splattered like a gunshot wound.

"Antoine's not going to be thrilled by the laundry bill," Shirl said.

I switched my attention back to her. "It may be a laundry bill down here, but what's the damage upstairs?"

Shirley dropped her knife and her hand flew to her mouth. "I must be as dumb as a box of rocks. What's up there?"

"It's an apartment over the restaurant. Nothing to do with Antoine. I don't know who lives there."

"And I guess he hasn't just dropped a raw steak on the floor. Not for that amount of blood."

"No. I'm going up there to find out what's happened."

I pushed my chair back from the table and stood up.

I looked at Shirley. Her eyes had glazed with concern.

"What a way to end the day," she said. "It couldn't be worse."

"Not worse?" I said. "I'm not so sure. Not after what happened earlier today at the *Chronicle*."

To continue reading *The Tango School Mystery* go to:
http://getbook.at/tango-school-mystery

Read more Crampton of the Chronicle stories at
https://www.colincrampton.com

Read more Crampton of the Chronicle stories at:

www.colincrampton.com

Author's note and acknowledgements

There is an old saying that life imitates art. In the case of The Mother's Day Mystery there is some truth to that - and an extraordinary coincidence. Shortly after I'd finished writing the first draft of the book I read a news story in a British newspaper about a "very intelligent" schoolboy who'd been jailed for four-and-a-half years. He'd committed a string of crimes including trying to blackmail his headmaster. What made the coincidence even more remarkable was that the schoolboy in question was described by the trial judge as "possibly the most able chemist the college has produced in recent years".

I mention this to emphasise that the crimes of Spencer Hooke are not based on those of the jailed schoolboy. But the coincidence is a sharp reminder that sometimes - perhaps more often than we realise - the inventions of fiction find echoes in the world of reality.

Steyning Grammar School is very firmly in the world of reality. At least, it certainly was when I was studying for my A levels there in 1965, the year in which The Mother's Day Mystery is set. In those days, it was an old-fashioned grammar school, which did have a chemistry lab but without a drugs testing chemistry master. These days it continues successfully as a comprehensive school, which it became in 1968. I should make it clear that Steyning Grammar School was not the alma mater of the real-life blackmailing schoolboy.

As always, I must thank all those people without whom a

Crampton of the Chronicle book could not appear. First among these is Barney Skinner who formatted the book for publication and designed not one but two wonderful covers. Followers of the Crampton books voted to choose the cover they liked best. Barney is also the webmaster behind the popular Colin Crampton website. If you've never visited the site, you'll find a wealth of background material about the books and some short stories to read.

I must also send a big thankyou to the members of the Crampton of the Chronicle Advanced Team who read the draft manuscript and made many helpful suggestions and corrections. In alphabetical order those who helped included: Nancy Ashby, Jaquie Fallon, Sue Gascoyne, Andrew Grand, Jenny Jones, Mark Rewhorn and Christopher Roden. Needless to say, any errors that remain are mine and mine alone.

I also want to thank you, the reader, for reading this book. An author without readers is like a town without people. So a huge thankyou to everyone who enjoys reading the Crampton of the Chronicle books.

I'd like to finish with a final plea. In these days of internet sales, online reviews are very important for an author. So if you have a few moments to add a short review on Amazon or Goodreads, I would very much appreciate that. Thank you.

Peter Bartram, November 2018

About the author

Peter Bartram brings years of experience as a journalist to his Crampton of the Chronicle crime mystery series. His novels are fast-paced and humorous - the action is matched by the laughs. The books feature a host of colourful characters as befits stories set in Brighton, one of Britain's most trend-setting towns.

Peter began his career as a reporter on a local weekly newspaper before working as a newspaper and magazine editor in London and finally becoming freelance. He has done most things in journalism from door-stepping for quotes to writing serious editorials. He's pursued stories in locations as diverse as 700-feet down a coal mine and Buckingham Palace. Peter wrote 21 non-fiction books, including five ghost-written, in areas such as biography, current affairs and how-to titles, before turning to crime – and penning the Crampton of the Chronicle series. There are now 10 books in the series.

Follow Peter Bartram on Facebook at:
www.facebook.com/peterbartramauthor

Follow Peter Bartram on Twitter at:
@PeterFBartram

More great books from Peter Bartram…

HEADLINE MURDER

When the owner of a miniature golf course goes missing, ace crime reporter Colin Crampton uncovers the dark secrets of a 22-year-old murder.

STOP PRESS MURDER

The murder of a night watchman and the theft of a saucy film of a nude woman bathing set Colin off on a madcap investigation with a stunning surprise ending.

FRONT PAGE MURDER

Archie Flowerdew is sentenced to hang for killing rival artist Percy Despart. Archie's niece Tammy believes he's innocent and convinces Colin to take up the case. Trouble is, the more Colin investigates, the more it looks like Archie is guilty.

THE TANGO SCHOOL MYSTERY

Colin Crampton and girlfriend Shirley Goldsmith are tucking into their meal when Shirley discovers more blood on her rare steak than she'd expected. The pair are drawn into investigating a sinister conspiracy which seems to centre on a tango school.

THE MORNING, NOON & NIGHT TRILOGY

Three books in one.

The adventure starts in *Murder in the Morning Edition*… when crime reporter Colin Crampton and feisty girlfriend Shirley Goldsmith witness an audacious train robbery

The mystery deepens in *Murder in the Afternoon Extra*… as the body count climbs and Colin finds himself hunted by a ruthless killer.

The climax explodes in *Murder in the Night Final*… when Colin and Shirley uncover the stunning secret behind the robbery and the murders.

Read all three books in The Morning, Noon & Night Omnibus Edition or listen to them on the audiobook available from Audible, Amazon and iTunes.

Printed in Great Britain
by Amazon